9/09

THE CRY OF THE DOVE

THE CRY OF THE DOVE

Fadia Faqir

Black Cat
New York

Printed in the United States of America

FIRST EDITION

ISBN-10: 0-8021-7040-4
ISBN-13: 978-0-8021-7040-8

Black Cat
a paperback original imprint of Grove/Atlantic, Inc.
841 Broadway
New York, NY 10003

Distributed by Publishers Group West

Printed with the cooperation of Doubleday
a division of Transworld Publishers
61-63 Uxbridge Rd, London W5 55A
a division of the Random House Group Ltd.

www.groveatlantic.com

07 08 09 10 11 12   10 9 8 7 6 5 4 3 2 1

Ramesh, Gul, and Harry, absent,
present friends, this one is for you.

THE CRY OF THE DOVE

Where the River Meets the Sea

THE WHITE SHEEP DOTTED THE GREEN HILLS LIKE TEASED wool and the lights of the solitary mill floated on the calm surface of the river Exe. It was a new day, but the dewy greenness of the hills, the whiteness of the sheep, the grey- ness of the skies carried me to my distant past, to a small mud village tucked away between the deserted hills, to Hima, to silver-green olive groves gleaming in the morning light. I used to be a shepherdess, who under a barefaced sun guided her goats to the scarce green patches with her reed pipe. The village of Hima at this time of year would be teeming with camels, horses, cows, dogs, cats, butterflies and honeybees. Horses raced, their hoofs releasing clouds of dust on the plain. It was springtime, and the season of engagements had already begun. Wedding celebrations would be held just after the harvest. I was one of the girls of the village who were ripe and ready to be plucked. 'Mother, I saw the moon at night,' I prayed for my black and brown goats, 'up there in the sky. Forgive me, Allah, for I have sinned. The heat of passion had made me bend.'

I stuck a liner to my pants, pulled them up my shaved

and oiled legs and realized that I was free at last. Gone were the days when I used to chase the hens around in wide pantaloons and loose flowery dresses in the bright colours of my village: red to be noticed, black for anger, green for spring and bright orange for the hot sun. If this small glass bottle were full of snake venom I would drink it in one go. I dabbed some perfume behind my ears and on my wrists, took a deep breath, tossed my no longer braided and veiled hair on my shoulders, pulled my tummy in, straightened my posture and walked out of Swan Cottage, which was the name Liz had chosen for her semi-detached house. I filled my chest with the clean morning air, inflating my ribs until my back muscles were taut and raw. I could see shreds of blue sky between the luminous white clouds that stretched out in different shapes: the mane of a horse, a small foot, a tiny, wrinkled hand like a tender vine leaf that has just burst open.

The cathedral in the distance looked dark and small. The feeble English sun was trying hard to melt away the clouds. I walked past the student residences, past the large white houses with neat gardens and barking dogs, past HM Prison. I looked at the high walls, the coiled barbed wire, the small barred windows, and realized that this time I was on the wrong side of the black iron gate despite my dark deeds and my shameful past. I was free, walking on the pavement like an innocent person. My face was black as if covered with soot, my hands were black and I had smeared the foreheads of my family with tar. A thick, dark, sticky liquid dripped from the iron railing I was holding all the way to the walkway. I shook my head trying to chase away the foul smell and looked towards the Exe.

Some seagulls were flapping their wings, encircling their prey then diving into the water for the final kill. My number was up a long time ago, but for some reason I was living on borrowed time.

My nose followed the perfume of flowers in bloom, but the smell of the honeysuckle travelling down the hill was suddenly overpowered by the smell of grease, which was the first indication that Peter's Plaice, the fish-and-chip shop on the corner of the Clock Tower, was not too far. I sniffed the air. A group of young students stood there shouting, 'Time is running out for education.'

'Time is running out,' I repeated.

A few years ago, I had tasted my first fish and chips, but my mountainous Arab stomach could not digest the fat, which floated in my tummy for days. Salma resisted, but Sally must adapt. I kept looking up *adapt* in the *Oxford English Dictionary*: *Adapt: fit, adjust, change.* Apparently in England the police stop you in the street and check your papers and sense of belonging regularly. An immigration officer might decide to use my ability to digest fish as a test for my loyalty to the Queen. I chewed on the parts that were still frozen and said to the young man who bought them for me, with tears in my eyes, '*Yumma!* It delicious!'

'Yummy!' he said rebuking me.

In Hima my mother used to rebuke me all the time. Salma, did you feed the cows? Did you clean the barn? Why didn't you milk the goats? *Yumma*, I did. Every God-given morning I stuck the end of my embroidered peasant dress in my wide orange pantaloons and ran to the fields. I held the golden stems of wheat in one hand and the sickle with the other and hit as hard as I could. All that holding of dry maize and wheat chipped my hands and grime lined my fingernails. Rough, dirty hands, I had. That was before I ran to freedom. Now I stood shaking my head and rubbing the big fake yellow stone on my ring with my smooth hands, which were always covered with cocoa butter, and sighed. Gone were the days when I was a farmer, a shepherdess, a peasant girl. I am now a seamstress, an assistant tailor in a shop in Exeter, which a few years ago was voted the most beautiful city in Britain. Now Salma the dark black iris of Hima must try to turn into a Sally, an English rose, white, confident, with an elegant English accent, and a pony.

Liz, Elizabeth, Queen Elizabeth I, Her Highness, my land-lady was still asleep. The smell of cheap wine clung to everything: the sofa, the armchairs, the kitchen table and chairs, the curtains and the musty carpets. When I first met Liz she looked tall in her navy jumper, blue shirt, cream riding breeches and flat, black leather boots. Her long, straight grey hair was gathered neatly in a ponytail and the puffiness of her eyes was concealed with compact powder. She stood erect as if inspecting her guards. I was looking for a room to rent. After walking all the way to Cowley I was able to find King Edward Street. I knocked gently on the door of Swan Cottage. When she opened the door I was wet and trembling in my thin shirt and fleece. It was my first attempt to get out of the hostel into the outside world. I tried to say good morning, but I could not control my quivering chin. I stood there thin and dark, shifting my weight from one foot to another, gazing at the tip of my shoes until I was finally able to say, 'The sun shining,' although it was pouring with rain. She asked me to come in.

*

When I got back Liz was snoring so I sneaked into the
bathroom, shut and bolted the door. The sound of a gate
being shut, footsteps, and walking on cold paving stones
looking and looking for her. The tub was full so I added
few drops of bath oil to the hot water. The smell of sage
filled the small bathroom and reminded me of the long
afternoons in Hima, when we used to drink sage tea and
spin and weave. Instead of walking up the mountains
looking for sage bushes, picking the soft green leaves,
washing them then drying them, there they were: cut,
squeezed and stored into little dark blue bottles for ma
lady's convenience. With a lubricated razor, I shaved my
legs and underarms carefully. Before your wedding night
they spread a paste of boiled sugar and lemon between
your legs and yank away the hair. My grandmother Shahla
said, 'When they finished with me I was covered with
bruises, but as smooth and hairless as a nine-year-old girl.
Your grandfather preferred it clean. I looked so pure and
innocent, he said.' The painful and sticky sugaring
belonged to the past, together with marriage, my black
Bedouin madraqa robe, and silver money hats, all shelved
there at the end of the horizon, overseas. Foam on the
legs, then shave – puff – no hair. Nice and easy and washes
away instantly like love in this new country, like love in
the old country.

I got out of the bath and cleaned the tub with hot
water, making sure that every black hair was sliding down
the drain. Liz did not like to see any black hair around the
house, but my hair was falling everywhere: in the sink,
bath, washbasin, on the carpet, on bed linen, on the back
of the armchair, which I used to sit in when Liz was out

5

of the house. 'You have been sitting in my chair. Look! Your dark hair is everywhere.' A thin olive-skinned fractured reflection, with big brown eyes, a crooked nose and long dark thick frizzy hair, looked back at me in the broken mirror. If I did not know me I would have said that I was Salma, whole and healthy. 'I called you Salma because you are healthy, pure and clean. Your name means the woman with the soft hands and feet, so may you live in luxury for the rest of your life. Salma, my little chick, my heart, may God keep you safe and sound wherever you go, darling!' If I did not know me I would have said that I was Salma, but my back was bent and my head was held low. I wrapped my trembling body with the warm towel and sniffed the air.

'Your breasts are like melons, cover them up!' my father haj Ibrahim said.

'Your tuft of wool is red,' my mother said, 'you are impulsive.'

My brother Mahmoud kept an eye on me while brushing his horse; I started hunching my back to hide my breasts, which were the first thing Hamdan had noticed about me. When I first met him I was walking along the stream looking for bugloss which my mother brewed and drank to ease her backache. I touched the clear water with my fingers, then I saw Hamdan: a reflection of a dark face, white teeth and dark curly hair covered with a chequered red-and-white headdress. I fell in love instantly when I saw the reflection of his shoulders in the water. When I started watering the vegetable beds three times a day and fondling the horse my mother shouted, 'Salma, you stupid child, are you in love?' I fixed the white scarf on my head, pulled my loose pantaloons up and nodded.

The film star, in her short tight skirt and long black leather boots which went up her thighs, was still holding her Prince Charming under the glass display of the bus stop by the White Hare, where they played hard rock music for skinheads all the time. Love in this country came wrapped in chocolate boxes, in bottles of champagne, in free drinks. It came in pubs, buses and discos, even on British Rail with the wings of its ever-flying red eagle. Savage love, like the one I used to have for Hamdan, was now a prisoner of silver screens. It rarely happened in real life. You saw it in old black-and-white films shown on Sunday afternoons, and you heard it in the trembling voices: 'Oh! Don't go. Please don't leave me.' The flickering screen, the sighs, the white handkerchief, the sobs, 'I love you the length of the sea and sky, the height of the Sheikh Mountain and the width of the Sahara.'

My black Bedouin madraqa, embroidered with threads so colourful they would make your eyes water, was tucked away, like my past, in the suitcase on top of the wardrobe. The Indian corner shop sold ethnic clothes, fabrics, jewellery and rugs. The red elephant above the main door carried a howdah on its back. Through the show window two Indian goddesses made of carved wood with hands all over the place were always looking at the passers-by. The embroidered silk was so colourful, bright and uplifting it took you all the way to the Taj Mahal. The shop was full of English women in their flowery dresses and missionary sandals, fingering the cascading Indian fabrics. 'When in India, sitting under frilled parasols, they used to watch their men in white playing cricket on the lawn, while Indian waiters ran around serving cold sherbet.' My Pakistani friend Parvin blew her fringe off her face and added, 'What is left of the Empire are those little islands of nostalgia.'

One afternoon while I was still in the backpackers' hostel lying in an ex-army bed I heard the forceful knock of the porter on the door. I looked around me: the curtains were drawn and my shoes, trousers, shirt and underwear were scattered on the dirty floor. I was a hedgehog hiding in dark tunnels exhaling and inhaling the stale air.

Using his master key, the porter opened the door and let in a short, thin, dark young woman. I covered my body and half of my face with the grey sheets.

When she looked at me she could only see the slit of my eyes and a white veil so she turned to him. 'Where does she come from?'

'Somewhere in the Middle East. Fucking A-rabic! She rode a camel all the way from Arabia to this dump in Exeter,' he said and laughed.

'I am not going to share the room with an Arab,' she spat.

I pretended that I was asleep and that I could not hear a word.

'This is the only decent hostel in Exeter. It's the only empty bed we have, Miss P-a-r-a-f-f-i-n,' he said carefully.

'Parvin,' she screamed.

'Yes, miss,' he said.

'She is also covered with sores. It could be contagious!'

'It is not serious. It's the only bed we have, miss.'

'All right! All right!' She put her rucksack on the floor

and sat on it, looked around then said, 'What a dump!'

I looked at her straight hair and long fringe and turned in my bed. The smell of hurt and broken promises filled the brightly lit room.

She was emerald, turquoise encased in silver, Indian silk cascading down from rolls, a pearl in her bed, pomegranate, fresh coffee beans ground in an ornate sandalwood pestle and mortar, honey and spicy ghee wrapped in freshly baked bread, pure perfume sealed in blue jars, rough diamonds, a dew-covered plain in the vast flat open green valley, a sea teal at the edges and azure in the centre, my grandmother's Ottoman gold coins strung together by a black cord, my mother's wedding silver money hat, a full moon hidden behind translucent clouds.

That evening I had a shower, covered my scabs with cream, washed my dirty clothes and cleaned the room, while Parvin was lying in bed watching me. I tried to make the room look cheerful, but with two ex-army beds, a chest of drawers, an old wardrobe and a dirty grey carpet it was impossible. When I pushed the window open Parvin turned around and went to sleep. I switched on the bed-side lamp and began inspecting local papers for jobs. *A sales girl required. Presentable with good command of English* . . . I looked up 'presentable' and 'command' in the dictionary. I was neither presentable nor able to speak English well. Nothing that would suit a woman like me with no looks, no education, no experience and no letters of recommendation. I was also ill, very ill. I took my reed pipe out and began blowing until the soft hoarse sound filled the room, the city, and travelled overseas all the way to my mother's ears. Parvin looked up then went back to sleep.

I found myself standing in front of the shop that sells baby clothes, something I am not allowed to do under any circumstances. The doctor said, 'You have to cut your ties with the past, you are here now so try to get on with it.' I pulled my foot back, put the other foot behind it and made myself walk away, but not before I had a glimpse of a white satin and chiffon dress. A line of pearls was stitched carefully above each frill. It looked like a luminous white cloud, like dawn; the pearls shone like tears of joy. It was a promise of a reunion, a return. That white dress was home.

Liz was confused when I moved in with her. Was I a lodger, a confidante or a servant? Her state of mind altered according to the amount of alcohol she had consumed. She regulated my access to the kitchen to half an hour in the morning and an hour in the evening and she would get upset if I washed the wooden cutlery and crockery. 'I have coated them with olive oil and I would like it to stay to protect the wood, thank you very much. Look what you've done!' What she did not know was that as soon as I arrived in her dirty house I wanted to boil some water, put it in a bucket, add some washing-up liquid and walk around scrubbing clean every glass, every piece of china, every utensil. I also wanted to wash the floor, the walls, the ceiling and above all the toilet seat, which had some dry excrement stuck to the wood. I was a goddamn Muslim and had to be pure and clean. My bum was not supposed to have any contact with urine, which was *najas*: impure, so I either pulled the toilet seat up and squatted, but made sure not to have any contact with the toilet, which was a great balancing act, or washed my lower part in the tub with freezing water because hot water was only available between seven and eight in the morning on weekdays. So most days I would walk to work, my private parts frozen, looking for the warm mist of human breath.

Sadiq, the owner of Omar Khayyam off-licence across the road, was dark, thin and tall, with supple fingers. Before he started talking he would jerk his chin sideways as if looking for words, then say, 'Excellent also.' He prayed five times a day. Whenever I walked past his shop his mat would be spread on the floor and he would be standing, hands on tummy, eyes closed, muttering verses from the Qur'an. My father haj Ibrahim did not pray regularly. The mat was out whenever a goat was stolen or we were having a long spell of drought. One evening while I was sitting in his lap, stroking his beard, he told me that last winter they had no rain whatsoever, not a single drop, so they asked all the men of the village to gather together in a field to do the Rain Prayer. They all knelt in unison before their maker and pleaded with Him to send in the rain. Before they finished the skies opened and the rain pelted down. That afternoon, cold and soaking wet, they marched through the village repeating, 'There is no God but Allah, and no prophet but Muhammad.' When he finished talking he looked at me with his dark eyes, ran his flaky hand over my head then kissed my forehead. 'You are lucky to be born Muslim,' he said, 'because your final abode is paradise. You will sit there in a cloud of perfume drinking milk and honey.'

He smelt of Musk Gazelle, which he used to keep in a

hairy leather pod. 'Praise be to Allah,' I said and settled in his lap to soak up his warmth and feel his ribs rising and falling against me.

A cloud of perfume. The chemists promised that their dye would permanently cover grey hair, their body lotions would turn skin to smooth silk and their facial creams would iron out any wrinkles. Englishwomen were promised they would look 'ten years younger'. I always went to the most expensive counter and tried eye-shadows, eye-liners, creams and perfumes on my face and hands. 'Do you have a sample of this perfume?' I was pointing at an expensive perfume called Beautiful. The heavily made-up sales girl fluttered her eyelashes, which were caked with mascara, and looked suspiciously at me. She'd made up her mind. I was not the type of woman who would buy her new exclusive summer range. 'No, we don't do samples for this perfume,' she said dismissively. The sample-size bottles shone on the glass shelf under the spotlights like crystal. I looked down at my worn-out walking shoes and bit my tongue. You know, if I were her I would have thrown me out of the shop, a woman like me, trash. My tribe had raided her country seeking cheap booty. I would have got me arrested if I were her.

Noura was holding a small dark bottle full of green liquid which looked like poison under the cold moonlight. She pulled the cork, tilted the bottle and let one drop fall on the back of my hand. The cold sticky liquid spread on my skin and then was absorbed. It had a strong smell, as if I were sitting in a big farm where the orange, lemon,

almond, apple and pomegranate trees had flowered at the
same time. I sniffed the back of my hand. She was weaving
her long shiny black hair into a braid, her large luminous
brown eyes fixed on the iron bars of the small high
window. 'We were given this free by the old man who
runs the brothel, to massage our customers with. Satisfied
customers used to call our barn "the house of perfume";
dissatisfied ones used to call it "the house of poison".' She
bit her generous outward-tilting lower lip, rubbed her
pointed nose, ran her forefingers on her perfect arched
eyebrows and said, 'I used to like the density of it, the fact
that it might suffocate you, it might kill you at any
moment.' She held my hand, sniffed the perfume and said,
'All I want now is to be able to forgive.'

My dearest friend, Noura,

*Forgive me for writing to you all these letters. You
probably cry when you see another letter from me. But do
you receive my letters? Is the address complete? I stand in
this new country alone wondering about the final
destination of migrating birds. Wondering about us, why
are we here and what is it all about? What is it, Noura?
A heart made slightly larger than the ribcage or too small
to handle life? A mother who allowed you to swim in the
spring? A tuft of wool dyed crimson rather than green, the
colour of the village? Why am I still alive and what
brought me here?*

With love and gratitude,
Salma

I grabbed the tester bottle and sprayed myself abundantly
under the mascaraed disapproving look of the sales girl. In

a cloud of perfume I walked back to St Paul's, the place for the 'upworldly riff-raff', and sat down on one of the white chairs of the pavement café. The Algerian waiter, who pretended to be French, came running and asked me, 'What you like drink, madam?'

'Some water y'ayshak: may your life be long?'

He smiled, pretending not to understand the Arabic, and disappeared. After all, he was supposed to be Pierre, whose grandfather had served in the French army. Parvin told me that North Africans were known for forging army documents to gain entry into fortress Europe.

'What is your address?' the immigration officer had asked.

I did not understand him so I kept pulling the end of my headscarf.

'Where will you live?'

'Heengland, think,' I said.

'Where in England?' he asked patiently.

'The river meet sea,' which was the way Little Sister Asher had described Southampton to me.

'Oh! For God's sake!' he said.

'Yes, for God sake!'

Exeter was famous for its cream tea. When you saw a pot of tea, scones, some jam and clotted cream on a table then the person eating them was bound to be a local. Tourists and foreigners could not handle the richness of the cream so they ordered espresso or cappuccino instead. Cream tea I could not stomach; cream tea I did not deserve. If you had crossed lands and seas looking for answers, looking for a daughter, looking for God you end up drinking bitter coffee out of a small cup. It was my shopping day, I reminded myself. It was the most enjoyable day of the week, when I would picture myself in Parisian make-up, expensive hairstyles and a glamorous dress drinking mineral water and reading *Marie Claire* in a seaside café. It took me ages to twist my tongue and pronounce 'Marie Claire' with a faint French accent. My broad Bedouin Arabic had to be hidden over there at the end of the horizon. I used to say to Hamdan, 'Your love in my heart is kicking and shoving like a captured mule.' He used to hug me and say, 'Love me!' meaning squeeze me tighter, pull me closer.

I sat, back straight, tummy flat and sipped my sugarless coffee to the very end. Here things were different. You measured everything in tiny spoons. If you fancied somebody, you never mentioned mules, you just whispered over coffee or fizzy mineral water with thin slices of lemon, 'Would you like a cup of coffee?'

I offered coffee to everyone: immigration officers, policemen, the milkman, the postman, sales girls. My tent was open and coffee with cardamom was being brewed all day, its aroma calling friends and neighbours. One morning I opened the door for the postman to collect a parcel for Liz. Instead of Jack, a young man with short dark hair, big blue eyes and sticking-out ears stood there. It was frosty that morning so after I signed my name, Sally Asher this time, I asked him whether he wanted a hot cup of coffee.

'Are you sure?' he asked.

'Yes, must be cold out there,' I said.

He said that he would come back for it at six o'clock in the evening. I wiped the coffee table clean and bought some English tea biscuits and put them on a plate. He arrived at six on the dot, but I did not recognize him. His dark hair was swept back with gel, his shirt was bright and clean, his mouth smiling, and he held my hand a bit longer than he should. I asked him to come in and directed him to the sitting room and brought the coffee and biscuits on a tray. He had a sip of his coffee and then said, 'Why are you sitting there? Come sit next to me on the sofa!'

'I am fine,' I said and smiled. He was my first guest.

He got up, stood in front of me, placed his fingers under my chin and tilted my face up towards him.

I jumped up and said, 'No.'

'What do you mean "no"? You asked me to come.'

'No, sorry,' I said, hugging myself.

'What do you mean sorry?'

My lips were trembling when I said, 'More biscuits?'

He pulled his shirt down, pushed his hair back, rubbed his nose then walked out of the room. He opened the front door while shouting something that sounded like 'Coke tea man,' then left, slamming the door behind him. Maybe I should have served him Coke. Liz would be home soon so I got up and with trembling fingers I began chasing biscuit crumbs and stray dark hairs.

Hamdan and I had been playing hide and seek for weeks now. His mother complained to my mother over morning coffee that her young son seemed to be revolving around himself like a well-mule. My mother sipped her coffee and said, 'Brew him some camomile.' I was lying on the grass under the fig tree, my hair spread like a halo around my head, blowing my heart's desires into my reed pipe when Hamdan walked into my view. I stopped and looked at the praying expression on his face. Sunlight flickered through the leaves, the smell of jasmine filled the evening air, and I could hear the barking of shepherds' dogs coming home. I closed my eyes, bit my lower lip and held my breath. He ran his fingers through my hair, tightened his fist and walked away to come back later and claim what was his already, releasing me and imprisoning me for the rest of my life.

'AMERICAN MOTHER PAYS GUNMAN TO KIDNAP HER DAUGHTER'. I put the newspaper down and had another glance at the dark Italian sitting alone sipping his espresso. Hamdan, but instead of the wide white robe, he was wearing a white T-shirt with a sophisticated pattern and blue jeans. He smiled to me and I smiled back. Italy is fine, I thought, while trying to decode the latest poll in the paper. Conservatives behind. Labour five per cent lead. I tried to understand the politics of this country.

'You cannot go on being an ignorant Bedouin,' Parvin said, 'you have to learn the rules of the game, damn it.'

But I kept my head down, hopes up and supported victors: that was what my immigrant *A–Z* guide advised. My knowledge of British politics began and ended with *Spitting Image*, where I couldn't tell which dummy was who in real life. It was a rare occasion when I was watching television with Liz.

'Was that the shadow Chancellor?' I asked Liz.

'No, the Prime Minister. The Chancellor does not spit,' she answered and looked at the television screen, not wanting to be interrupted.

'Who are these puppets?' I asked.

'Foreigners! Aliens like you,' she said and smiled.

'Like me?' I asked.

'Yes, illegal immigrants,' she said.

'I no illegal,' I said, suddenly losing my English.

'Yes, you are. You must be,' she said.

'Would you like a cuppa?' I asked, imitating my friend Gwen and trying to change the subject.

'No, thank you,' she said, sounding more annoyed now. She did not like Gwen and her Welsh influence on me. 'A cuppa? Honestly!' she said, shaking her head.

Liz was right, I was scum.

Whenever I used to climb Rim, the highest mountain in Hima, with my goats, Hamdan would be following me discreetly, leaping behind rocks and shrubs. His shoulders wide, his brown cloak fluttering in the air, his white-and-red-chequered headdress hiding some of his curly thick dark hair, he would be running trying to catch up with me. One day it was so hot the haze of the heat descended on our valley. Playing my pipe I was guiding the goats to the Long Well. I filled the trough with cold water and instantly my goats began drinking. I pricked up my ears listening for the neighs of Mahmoud's horse. Not a whisper. I dropped the rubber bucket in the well again and heard it hitting the cold water, splitting it open then sinking deep. I screamed with excitement knowing that the brown eyes of Hamdan were watching me, his ears tuned to my cries. Behind the bushes Hamdan had gone quiet when I poured the contents of the bucket over my head. While washing my body, I sang one of my grandma Shahla's old songs. '*Hala hala biik ya walla, hey ya halili ya wala*: welcome, welcome, oh boy! Hey! My love! Oh boy! Welcome my soulmate! Welcome my husband-to-be.' When her husband took on a second wife my

FADIA FAQIR

grandmother died of heartbreak. A few months later my grandfather died too.

It was getting dark and the pavement café was about to shut down for the day; no encounters after five. At five o'clock the English normally rush back home to their cats and dogs and empty castles. I could see them in their small kitchens sticking the frozen chicken nuggets in the oven and frying frozen potato chips. In the early evening the city belonged to us, the homeless, drug addicts, alcoholics and immigrants, to those who were either without a family or were trying to blot out their history. In this space between five and seven we would spread and conquer like moss that grows between the cracks in the pavement. I sipped the dregs and put the small espresso cup in the saucer.

'You know, Salma, we are like shingles. Invisible, snake-like. It slides around your body and suddenly erupts on your skin and then sting, sting,' Parvin said and laughed.

I was lying on the ground when Hamdan walked through the vines and stood still above me. I was not hungry, but all the same I picked some grapes and began stuffing them in my mouth. When I looked up, his silhouette was squatting right in front of me. I held my breasts with both hands. An intake of breath was followed by a brisk kiss on my lips. The cool dusk air was whirling in my wide pantaloons, reminding me of the code of honour in our village. No. 'Have you gone mad? Do not be impulsive!' I could hear my mother shout in my ears. No. 'They will shoot you between the eyes.' Yes. No. No. No. I pushed him away. 'You will be full of regret later, oh beautiful,' he said, pulled a hair from his dark moustache and walked away. When his back disappeared between the vines I began shaking. The sun had set and it was getting cold. I wrapped my mother's shawl around me and walked back home.

The rooftops and glass windows of the red-brick buildings picked up the glow of the setting sun and sent it back golden and fading. I walked to the cathedral close, where among the pigeons and hymns the dark-haired man might feel comfortable to approach me. He might be Arab. A congregation of priests crossed the lawn and entered the cathedral. They looked bizarre in their long black robes and white collars. I could hear the doors of the dorms being shut. The turquoise silver necklace Sister Françoise had given me was in the Chinese satin box.

Pointing at me, the dark-haired man said, 'Hi?'

I looked behind my back to see if I was being watched. If my brother Mahmoud sees me talking to strange men he will tie each leg to a different horse and then get them to run in different directions. He was nowhere to be seen. I stuck my feet firmly on the ground to stop them from walking away and smiled. Here in this new country, only men spoke to me.

The Sisters would be bolting the heavy gates of the convent and the sound would echo in the hollow space inside. I would be running around barefoot on the cold cobbled floor looking for her.

'I am David. Call me Dave.'

'Sally,' I answered, using my English name and enjoying the sound of a human voice.

'Will you have a cup of coffee with me?' he said in a strong Devon accent.

'Yes,' I answered folding my newspaper and with it my hopes of meeting an Arab here, who would report me to the police or kill me instantly.

We walked down the road towards a shop that sells ethnic artefacts and doubles up as a café. A man with a 'Can't Pay Won't Pay' placard was shouting abuse at passers-by. David shielded me with his left arm and guided me through the doors. He insisted on paying, so I treated myself to a glass of fresh orange juice and a bottle of sparkling water. David ordered cream tea in a café that tries hard to sell itself as a trendy jazz club.

'Do you live in Exeter?' he said.

'Yes,' I said while looking at the handsome young waiter.

'I work in a health club,' he said.

'Oh! How interesting!' I said, trying to imitate the accent of the Queen. Liz, my landlady, would be proud of me.

'Where do you come from?' he asked.

If I told him that I was a Muslim Bedouin Arab woman from the desert on the run he would spit out his tea. 'I am originally Spanish,' I lied.

'I have visited Spain many times. Where in Spain?'

'Granada,' I said. At school we were taught so much about the glories of Muslim Spain and the Moors in Granada.

Watching darkness descend layer upon layer through the French window suddenly I got really tired. I could not carry this through. It had to be the look on David's face, full of hope and fascination. Salma ate the grapes, angered

the tribe and paid a heavy price. I was too fragile for close-
ness, my skin was still tender and bruised. If I were him I
wouldn't give me a second glance. The stupid plants were
getting larger and larger, turning the café into a green-
house. I could hear the clinking of cutlery downstairs and
the thudding of chairs being stacked up on tables. The
waitresses were getting impatient. I could not carry this
through. I was not the granddaughter of my grandmother
Shahla, who was made of a different metal altogether, who
was shameless and fearless.

Shahla, my grandmother, used to weave her long thin
white hair into braids and say, 'Follow your heart always,
daughter of mine.' Her marriage was a love match. She
belonged to the ferocious Udayy tribe and he belonged to
the Fursan tribe, which was constantly at war with hers.
He saw her by the spring one morning filling her clay jar
with water and he felt a tremor run down his spine to the
small of his back. 'Good morning, young gazelle,' he
shouted from the distance, afraid to cross to Shahla's tribe's
territory. From the way he had arranged his kufiyya tilting
to the right and covering his right eye she realized that he
belonged to the Fursan tribe. He began waiting for her
early in the morning when the wheat sheaves sparkled
with dew under the morning sun. Shahla looked at his
wide shoulders, his dark thick moustache, his long strong
dark hair woven into two braids and decided that she had
to go to the well every morning to make sure that their
horses and camels would never go thirsty. It was really
early one morning when his silhouette shouted at her,
'Tonight I will come to kidnap you. Prepare yourself!' She
shielded her eyes and looked at his outline in the distance.

He stood tall, dark and awesome, blocking the sunlight. Their *bait al-sha'ar* was four tents made of thin goats' hair so she chose to sleep in the guests' tent in order not to disturb her mother when he arrived. Her mother's mattress was positioned across the entrance to the tent as if she were a guard, so Shahla pretended that she was cleaning the brazier in the guests' tent until she could hear her mother snoring. She sat fully dressed waiting for him and when she was too tired to keep her eyes open she heard the sound of the galloping hoofs and the whining of his horse so she ran out to meet him. That masked man with a rifle swinging on his shoulder stretched his arm to her and she grabbed it and was swung in the air then placed firmly on the saddle in front of him. She looked back at their *bait al-sha'ar* with the flaps wrapped tightly around their tents, their horses tied to the pole, their camels' front legs tied together, the goats asleep behind their dwelling. Shahla sucked at her last tooth when she said, '*Tzz*' that was the last glimpse I ever had of my dwelling and tribe.'

What would Shahla have done in this dwelling? Would she have dinner with David and allow him to 'ride her until her brass hand and ankle bracelets get jumbled up'? Would she stretch her arm to a total stranger and ride away with him in the dark? Would faith outweigh doubt? And what about the past, that dark shadow stalking you?

Holding my shopping bags firmly, I headed towards the main door. He followed me and said, 'Will you have dinner with me?'

'Thank you so much, but I don't think so,' I said.

'Why not?'

'I am busy. I must go, Dave.'

I lowered my head and walked through the shop under the dry palm trees. Among the Indian peacocks, Buddhas, Mexican parrots and quilts and Chinese tables a new sound was being formed inside my head: 'No', which my immigrant *A–Z* had always warned me against. A brass unicorn leaping into the air trying to reach the sky caught my eye.

I said to David quickly, 'No. I am sorry.' And before he could answer I rushed out through the African door to the cold street sniffing the air for the aroma of home. The smell summoned me and I obliged as if in a trance. The smell of rich food being fried was mine.

I sniffed the smell of familiarity, freedom and home and listened.

'*Balak*: is that girl MI5?' the old man said.

'What's wrong with you? Agents don't go around dressed like Arab tramps. They wear big hats like Philsy, innit? White, blond, with a cigar in their mouth,' said the young man.

'You mean Philby, you idiot. And these days agents look like anything, look like Jesus Christ himself. How do I know?' said the old man in a North African accent.

'You are paranoid and all. At night when the leaves sway you think an American satellite is taking shots of you,' said the young man.

'Whoever she is I am not pleased about her hanging about like that,' the old man said and threw some new falafel rissoles in the bubbling frying oil. The cold air carried the aroma of rich fried food all the way to my heart. The sizzling sound of frying, the ladle fishing out, falafel being crushed in warm pitta bread and the pungent smell of chickpeas, parsley and coriander propped me up. Wrapped up tight in my Bedouin mother's black shawl in the middle of Exeter I flew over lands, rivers and seas to dry bleak mountains, a handful of goats and ripe olives weighing down silver-green boughs. I soared high above my homeland.

'She is harmless, Dad. She sits quietly sniffing the cold air,' the young man said.

I could not see the front of the kebab van, but I heard some commotion and a door sliding then the sound of feet. Before I knew it the old man was standing right there in front of me where the white mist meets the blue sky. He was tall, spindly, with large eyes whitening with age, grey stubble, thinning hair covered by a white crochet skull cap, wide embroidered black trousers tight around the ankles, brown leather pointed mules, and 'Bon Jovi No Pain No Gain' printed in large red letters on the front of his black T-shirt.

I was face to face with my past and present.

'I seek refuge in Allah,' he said.

I tightened my mother's black shawl around my head and said nothing.

'You come eavesdrop on us. Are you spy or something?' he said.

In the old country of the Levant I would have stood up, held his right hand, kissed it, called him *jiddu* and introduced myself, 'Welcome! Welcome! I am Salma Ibrahim El-Musa,' but I am in the new country now, a fugitive with a record, so I remained seated on the wooden bench pretending not to understand.

He hesitated, then said, 'I don't want you sniff around here. Shoo shoo,' waving me away.

25

I wished I could kiss the green protruding veins on the back of his ageing flaky hand, his forehead and his prickly grey beard, but I got up instead and rolled away through the mist of the evening until I disappeared, a rootless wind-blown desert weed.

Vines and Fig Trees

IN DARKNESS OR AT DAWN KEEP YOUR PETALS TIGHT SHUT and legs closed! But like a reckless flower opening up to the sun I received Hamdan. 'Salma, you're a woman now . . . you are mine, my slave girl.'

'Yes, yes, yes,' I used to say. There were no tissues, rubber or spermicide, just the fertile smell of freshly ploughed land. I washed my pantaloons in the stream and walked back home dazed. From then on I lay under the fig tree waiting for him most nights.

'My whore is still here!' he would say and take me quickly.

'More,' I would whisper.

When Hamdan stopped revolving in orbits and I stopped kissing the horse, the goats and the trees, my mother and his mother grew suspicious. 'You little slut, what have you done?' My mother yanked my hair.

'Mother, please.'

'You smeared our name with tar. Your brother will shoot you between the eyes.'

'Mother!'

My petals were plucked out one by one. She yanked, bit, belted until I turned black and blue and sank blissfully into darkness.

Walking alone under electric poles, whose shadows were getting longer and longer, I hugged my shopping bag. No, it was not easy living here in England as an 'alien', which was how the immigration officer had described me. I once wrote on the walls of a public toilet: 'A dark alien has passed through the skies of Exeter.' Every morning I was reminded of my alienness. Every morning, while mist was still enveloping us, Jack, the postman, would wave to me and call, 'Hello, girl!' I would get upset. I wanted to be 'chuck' like Bev next door. Despite correcting him several times, 'Salma, Jack. Salma, please,' he would forget the next day and call me 'girl' again. But Jack never had anything to remind him because I never received any letters with my Arab name, Salma Ibrahim El-Musa, printed on them. 'Salma with tender hands and feet. Salma as fragrant as white jasmine flowers and as pure as honey in its glass jars.' But sometimes I wanted Jack to shout abuse at me the way the skinheads did at the White Hare. 'Hey, alien! You, freak! Why don't you go back to the jungle? Go climb some coconut trees! Fuck off! Go home!' I did not deserve to be here, I did not deserve to be alive. I let her down.

I walked up South Street with its estate agents who could not wait to get their hands into your pocket. How far was I from becoming a first-time buyer? Two thousand miles? Thirty years? A lifetime? Oh! What would I give to have a house in Branscombe, where Minister Mahoney, the Irish Quaker, my saviour, now lived! A cottage with gas central heating, three bedrooms, a garden, a poodle, a microwave oven, a few sheep and goats, and a cow to milk every morning. Grass is not scarce there, so taking the sheep to the meadows should be easy, you see. I would spend my time farming, growing sheep and playing the pipe. A good English gentleman doctor would cure me of all my ailments. Happy and healthy I would be, living with my children. My brother would stop looking for me, thinking I was dead. My husband would be working overseas to provide for us. We would tell each other stories and laugh: the older mother and her beautiful children.

The sun shone on Minister Mahoney's house in Branscombe. Shelves decked with old books, the worn-out sofa, the old radio in the corner and the Bible with his reading glasses on top of its leather jacket. Miss Asher had asked him to take care of me because 'I have to go back to the region to try to save more innocent lives.'

'Salma is most welcome to stay for a few months,' he said slowly so I could understand. 'I will be going back to the Middle East myself in the new year though.'

When I finished washing up after breakfast Minister Mahoney would ask me to sit down in the dining room and my 'informal education' would begin, two hours of English, maths and science. Then he would prepare lunch and I would clear up. He went for long walks in the afternoon and I spent the time inspecting his late mother's display cabinet, his library and the photos over the mantelpiece. I inspected the photos looking for Minister Mahoney's young face. I dusted his mother's gold-rimmed and hand-painted china collection, repeating: 'Dinner plate, dessert plate, soup plate, dessert bowls, cake plate, cream and sugar set, teapot, teacup, coffee cup, saucer,' which he had taught me.

'She was attached to this Haviland set,' he said as soon as he walked through the door of the dining room.

I did not expect him back so early so I sat down, suddenly disorientated. 'Mother love her money hat,' I said.

'Does she?' he said. He took off his raincoat and tucked his shirt into his trousers.

I looked at his thin white arms, his wide back, his spindly legs and said, 'I not worthy of love.'

'Of course you are,' he said and sat down facing me.

'I did shameful things,' I said.

'We have all done things we regret,' he said. 'It's part of being human.'

'I left her behind. Deserve to die, not live, me,' I said and began crying. 'I also old, no home, no money, no job.'

He rubbed his tired blue eyes and said, 'Nothing stays the same, child. Respect, love, pain, illness: nothing stays the same. It comes and then goes. You can even earn back respect. As for your family, one day you might decide to go back, things might change.'

'Things might change? I might go back?' I asked while tucking strands of hair that had slipped out back under my white veil.

'Yes, one day you should,' he said.

'Things might change,' I said and began shaking.

He hesitated, ran his thin fingers over his grey hair, then hugged my trembling body and rocked me gently, repeating, 'Shush, *yakfi*: enough, shush,' until I stopped crying.

★

30

I crossed the road and walked down a side street in order not to be spotted by my boss Max, who might be working this Saturday. 'I do more when you're not all here chatterin' and twitterin'.' He was always leering through the nicotine-covered window at the passers-by. 'Look! Look at her hair! She must have had a controlled explosion in the kitchen,' he would say and laugh. A laugh so menacing you would lower your eyes and run the sewing machine on the hem twice. 'What did you say your name is, Salamaa? Oh dear! Oh dear!' Parvin said that rumour had it that Max was a supporter of the British National Party, which wanted to kill Jews, Arabs and Muslims. Whenever he looked at me with his penetrating eyes, a shiver would run through my body. Talking to one of his customers I once overheard him say, 'Sally is in one of her moods. Arabs are obsessed with sadness.'

Someone told me that that pub on the corner was quite nice, with live music and all. I preferred the White Hare where I was about to get beaten by a drunken skinhead. He wanted to dance with me and I couldn't say no. He looked thin and tall in his black leather jacket and trousers, his spiky hair was dyed bright red just like a rooster. 'Touch it! Shake it! *Break it!*' the young men repeated with the band then raised their right arm in a salute. His breath smelt of cheap beer when he held my hand, pulled me towards him until I could feel the cold metal spikes and studs against my body then he pushed me away from him and when I was far enough he swung me round. I was so obliging, like Liz's cloth doll. The singing became more frenzied and the smell of beer and stale breath filled the air. When he finally let go of me I was so sad to be still alive. I deserved to be mocked, beaten, even killed. I abandoned her, let them take her away.

I tightened my grip on the shopping bag and walked on. Students were flocking out of college. What was it like to be a student? What did they teach them here in England? Was it possible to walk out of my skin, my past, my name? Was it possible to open a new page, start afresh with those young awkward Goths? So I could sit with them behind desks listening to what the bright teacher had to say, then in the break I would eat my sugar and butter sandwich and drink dark bitter tea. I would spit in my sandwich to stop my classmates from snatching them out of my hand and eating my lunch. So when I was fifteen instead of going to prison, I would be going to the Arts Centre to see a French film holding the hand of a nice, shy boy. I could picture myself in a see-through black skirt, black T-shirt with 'Death' printed on the front in red letters, black make-up and black Dr Martens shoes. I could even dye my hair purple.

It was really cold the first time I went to school. The season of reaping was over and the sky was full of dense clouds threatening rain. I could smell the log fires in braziers and smoked wheat. My mother combed my hair and wove it into two braids then I pulled the black embroidered dress, which used to belong to my mother, over my head, put my spicy ghee butter and sugar sandwich into my cloth bag, together with my notebook and pencil, and rushed to school. Barefoot I walked by the olive groves then up and down the arid hill until I was able to see the two mud classrooms, which were built by the men and women of the village, in the distance. The walls were not straight, the windows neither triangles nor rectangles, the doors padded into shape by hand. Miss Nailah, 'the woman with the sealed lips', was waiting for us by the door. '*Yala!* Move it! You are late,' she used to say.

Holding my notebook and pencil, I walked in. Sitting on the broken chair, I tried to concentrate on the blackboard.

Miss Nailah said, 'H for Head. S for?'

'Salma,' I whispered.

'What?' she said, waving her stick.

I cleared my voice and said, 'Salma, miss.'

In her sharp voice she said, 'Good. Do you know how to write your name?'

'No, miss.'

'To the blackboard!'

I stood by the blackboard shaking, my bladder full and my pantaloons about to slip down.

She held the chalk and wrote 'S-A-L-M-A'.

I held the chalk, aware of ten pairs of eyes looking at me, and started drawing the letters 'Salma'.

'How old are you?'

'I am six, miss.'

Miss Nailah said, 'Well done!'

I ran back home to show my father what I wrote: 'Salma', 'head', 'donkey' and 'man'. He was so pleased that he asked my mother to brew me some tea with extra sugar 'for this clever girl'.

Wherever I went I saw churches in the distance: old, decaying and dark houses of God. Whenever I entered the cathedral or a church I would feel cold as if they had their

own hidden air-cooling system circulating the smell of
mould clinging to the old stones. They were always dark,
hushed and lonely places. If you did not force people to
go to church why would they? There had to be a strong
imam or priest shaking his stick, invoking God and
promising sorrow 'tailormade for each heart' if you didn't
worship Him. The cathedral was deserted except for
priests, who rushed about in their black robes and white
collars, a few old ladies with neat grey hair and two mad-
men standing next to the glass donations box. You would
find the odd alcoholic or homeless person sleeping on
prayer cushions spread on the long wooden benches.
Religion was as weak as the tea in this country. What was
left of it was, 'Is this your maiden or Christian name?'
which the immigration officer had asked me and I did not
know how to answer.
    'Muslim no Christian.'
    'Name? *Nome*? *Izmak*?' he said.
    '*Ismi? Ismi?* Saally Ashiir.'
    'Christ!' he said.

The mosque's blue dome and minaret, where the imam
stood to call for prayer, could be seen at the top of the arid
hill. The call for worshipping God and obedience came
five times a day. '*Allahu akbar!* Allah is greatest. Get up and
pray!' Old men woke up at sunrise, did their ablutions
and walked with reluctant, half-asleep young men to the
mosque. The imam stood there on his high platform
urging them to go in and ask Allah for his forgiveness.
    'We cannot sell our olives before getting a fatwa from
the imam,' my father used to say. I looked at my father
with my ten-year-old eyes and realized that he was weaker

than the imam. His thin tall dark body spoke of years of horseriding, ploughing and reaping. His wandering eyes spoke of days of looking at the sky, waiting for clouds to be blown in, waiting for the rain to come and save his crops. Why was that tall strong man weaker than the imam? Why should he consult him before selling the boxes of olives rotting in the storeroom?

A rainbow was floating in the river Exe promising rain. My father, haj Ibrahim, would have been thrilled to see it, its colourful stripes promising sacks of wheat in the storeroom, a trip to the city to sell crops, a new lamb's-wool cloak. Some in Hima would have seen in it a promise of making enough money to take on a second wife. 'I praise thee and thank thee, Allah,' they would have said. Right next to the railway dump it appeared as it was: a deceptive reflection of light on water. I wiped the sweat off my forehead and tied my hair back with a rubber band. I should watch a video about two male gangsters hiding in a convent pretending to be devout nuns. I was also a sinner pretending to be a Muslim, but was really an infidel, who would never be allowed to enter the mosque. Then I remembered that Liz forbade me from using the video player in the sitting room because I tampered with the timer and because my dark hair fell everywhere.

My landlady would be sipping her cheap wine and waiting for me to come home to give me advice on something or other. I put the shopping on the pavement and unlocked the door. Sure enough the sour smell of wine wafted to my nose. She was at it again. 'Hello,' I sang.

'Is that you, Salma?' she said.

'Who else, Liz?'

And then I knew what was coming, a question about the weather. 'It remained dry today?'

'It rained a little, but now it is dry.' I looked at her straight grey hair, her misty eyes, the fine web of red veins on her cheeks and nose, the slightly drunken recline on the sofa and said to cheer her up, 'There is a huge rainbow arched over the fields, the hills, and reflected in the river.'

Another sip from the dirty glass was followed with a hesitant, 'Maybe I should have a look?'

'Yes, yes. Do you want coompany?'

'Cumpany,' she said in an immaculate English accent.

'Cumpany,' I repeated after her, tightening my jaw muscles.

'Mother,' I screamed, spitting the sour lemon out of my mouth. The midwife was sticking sharp iron bars inside me. She scraped and scraped looking for the growing flesh. The fluid of tears did not put out the fire.

'Please,' I cried. Please she cried. 'I . . . I . . .' and before I could finish the sentence, my mother's inflated face disappeared into darkness.

When I woke up my mother said, 'Nothing. It is still clinging to your womb like a real bastard.'

My madraqa was soaked with blood, my dirty hair was stuck to my head and my face was burning with tears. With both hands I began beating my head and crying, 'What shall I do?'

'If your father or brother find out they will kill you.'

I knotted the white veil around my head, stood up and ran up the arid hill, down the arid hill to the school. Miss Nailah used to sleep in one of the rooms. I knocked on the iron door calling, 'Miss Nailah! Miss Nailah!'

'In the name of Allah, who is it?'

'They will kill me, shoot me between the eyes.'

'Who? What? Why?' she asked while unbolting the door.

I rushed in then stood in the middle of the room. Beating my chest with my right hand I cried, 'I place myself in Allah's protection and yours, Miss Nailah.'

'What is it?'

'I am pregnant.'

She went pale. 'You poor, wretched you.' She straightened her long hair, put on her veil, tightened the knot under her chin, swallowed hard then sat on the edge of the bed.

I stood there, in the middle of the almost empty room, trembling.

She finally said with difficulty, 'First of all you must hold your tongue. Don't tell a soul.'

'Do you want company, Liz?' I asked again.

'No. I'd rather finish this first.' She raised her stained glass of wine.

I tilted carefully the bottle of washing-up liquid, which I kept hidden behind the cereal box in the cupboard that Liz had allocated to me, until one tiny green drop fell on the yellow sponge. I must be careful when washing my mug. If Liz caught a whiff of the lemon scent we would have a row. I would lose my tongue completely and go silent and she would pour her Radio 4 English over my head. 'The cutlery and crockery are old. You must not wash them with chemicals. What is it with you people? Washing and cleaning all the time. No wonder you have sores all over you.' She would speak to me as if I were her servant in India, where she used to live, not her tenant who pays her forty pounds a week plus bills.

The kettle was boiling so I switched it off, poured some hot water in the mug and dropped a teabag in it, then stirred. Streaks of brown colour whirled in the water instantly. I was convinced that what I was making was not tea because I could not see the tea leaves and because the water turned brown instantly. Every afternoon in Hima I used to put some tea leaves in the metal pot then fill it with water, add some dry sage or cardamom pods and seven large spoons of sugar then place it on the open camp fire we kept under the fig tree. When it boiled, I would pick it up then put it back again to boil it one more time until the aroma of the tea and cardamom reached my mother's nose. I fished the wet round teabag out and threw it into the bin, then tried to open the milk carton. I pulled and pushed the wings, but it refused to open. I couldn't even open a damn carton! I was angry with myself for being so foreign so I stabbed the carton with a knife spilling the milk all over the worktop. In Hima, whenever you needed milk you would take a bowl and put it under-neath a cow then pull its teats until your hands were sprayed with fresh warm milk. I wiped up the milk with the multi-purpose cloth, which Liz used for wiping all surfaces including the floor. The cloth was impure so I washed my hands with soap and water, had a sip of the now cold tea and rushed up the stairs to my room.

I was not allowed to put my mug on the two antique chests of drawers, which squatted in the corner like shepherd dogs. So I put it on the cheap side table next to my bed, which squeaked whenever I sat or slept on it. I put my television, which I bought from a junk shop for twenty pounds, on the small antique table Liz had provided. Looking through the open made-to-measure curtains from my window I could see the railway line and the glow of the setting sun. The cream and navy curtains were the only promise in the room of a better future, a future of owning a house and furnishing it with new made-to-measure pieces. A few books and many glossy magazines rested on the DIY shelf. I emptied my shopping bag on the bed. I had got carried away this time. I bought instant hair colour, facial scrub, breath freshener, shampoo, E45 cream, Big Dum the toilet cleaner, which was on the top of Liz's list of prohibited items, and a jar of Nescafé. The rattle of coffee beans urged the lady to take action, go borrow some sugar from her dark, handsome neighbour, who had just moved in.

If I were not waiting for him out there among the vines Hamdan would make a shrill sound as if he were calling his dogs back to the barn. Whenever I heard his whistle I would sneak through the metal bars then jump down to meet him. Barefoot I would walk by the wall, by tree trunks, behind rocks, afraid to disturb the dog. When I arrived in the vineyard I would lie down quietly looking at the distant stars and listening for footsteps. I recognized his light ones, the paws of a hyena meeting the ground then leaping hastily again. He would grab my ankle, suppressing his cackle. Under the indigo sky and among the dark shadows of trees we would embrace.

He would tug at my hair and say, 'You are my courtesan, my slave.'

'Yes, master,' I would say.

He would push and push and I would lie still, biting my

lip in order not to let a cry escape. Panting I would rest my head on his chest and he would run his fingers through my hair and sing me love songs: 'Your love took hold of my insides, my soul.'

'My love for you is kicking and shoving like a mule,' I would say and he would laugh and hug me.

For few fleeting moments I felt that Hamdan loved me, cherished me. I would never recapture that feeling ever again.

'Lighten up! Groom yourself! Sell yourself!' Parvin said to me. 'You are now in a capitalist society that is not your own.'

She was right. Most hair colour was designed for blondes, and a dark woman like me, who had gone prematurely grey, found it hard to match the original colour of her hair. Yesterday a man was talking on the radio about 'institutional racism'. He must have been referring to the blondness of it all. A healthy blonde advertised the toothpaste, hairdryer and light yoghurt. Whenever I looked at the ornate mirror, which Liz had brought all the way from India, I saw a face dripping like honey wax, a face no longer young. My hair was dark, my hands were dark and I was capable of committing dark deeds, I thought, while looking at the well-lit first-class carriage of the London train. There, on the blue chairs, my future husband would be sitting in his grey suit and pink shirt reading the *Financial Times*. A sensitive, generous, rich white Englishman, who was dying to meet an exotic woman like me with dark eyes, skin, hair and deeds. I would rub my olive skin against him, and – puff – like magic, I would turn white. Just like that, without using a skin-bleaching cream for years I would become whiter and fairer. Just like that I would disappear.

'You have to leave this place immediately,' said my teacher Miss Nailah.

'Why?' I panicked.

'If you don't you will get killed.' She ran her tongue on her dry lips.

I pressed my wet face with my hands. 'Where shall I go? What will happen to my goats?'

'Never mind your goats. It's your neck we are trying to save here.' Miss Nailah blew out her kerosene lamp, put it on the floor, then held my wrist tightly. 'The best thing to do is to hand you over to the police and pray that they will keep you in protective custody for ever.'

Putting my shopping items on the bathroom windowsill I saw the colourful reflections of the old mill's lights on the water. The fractured lights were floating on the water of the river in different directions. I recognized that breeze. She was out there looking for a resting place, for a foothold, for rescue. She was out there tired and whimpering. She was calling me. I pressed my ears with my hands. A shiver ran through me as if I had caught a sudden chill and my ugly dark nipples, which were one and a half centimetres long, the size of my little finger up to the first joint, stood erect. I must not stay in tonight. I should go to warm pubs and brightly lit restaurants full of sparkling reflections of candlelight in wine glasses, where I would get embraced by warm human breath, by the murmurs and laughter and by the promise of finding degrading treatment.

In Swan Cottage I lay in bed watching the plaster peel off then tumble down to the floor. The room was as damp as the prison cell where I had spent five months. 'Solitary confinement,' I had repeated after the warden. The police officer told me that I was to be put in a cell for my own protection. My tribe had decided to kill me, they had spilt my blood among them and all the young men were sniffing the earth. 'We are trying to save your life,' said the warden. Her name was Naima. I used to count the scratches on the walls, add one every day. One thing: I was happy to be pregnant. What would I have done if I had my periods? Would I have sat on the tin bucket for six days?

When I went to the Turk's Head pub I clipped a red flower in my hair to look exotic like the girl in the advertisement for the Seychelles Islands. She had long smooth black hair, even olive skin, narrow black eyes and large breasts with invisible nipples. She stood on the beach with a coconut in her hand shaking her straw skirt to tribal music. 'Our golden crop, ya ya ya. Reap and put on top, ya ya ya.' The summer songs signalled the beginning of the engagement season, when all the girls of Hima started turning in their beds, looking through the iron bars of windows for signs of morning light. The bridegroom's mother would come tomorrow to propose, carrying gold necklaces, emeralds, rubies, silk brocade, linen damask, Hebron glass and Attar pure perfume in ornate glass bottles. They would finally stand in the cool shadow of a man.

Dear Noura,
    I am happy, so happy. I got married to an English gentleman from a very good family, and we are expecting

a daughter. We saw the scan. He is also so rich. His mansion is old and big. It is lined with beautiful books, colourful books from all over the world. The westerners read so much, not like us. They are also nice and humble, not like us. Imagine — the policemen stop the traffic to let ducks cross the road! We are horrible to our animals except my goats, I used to spoil them rotten. How is my mother? I do hope she is taking good care of herself. I still remember her rough hands running over my face, blessing it. I still remember the freshly baked bread, honey and spiced ghee butter sandwiches. She was half blind with grief when I left so I bought her some spectacles. They are expensive, I know, but my gentleman husband gave me the money and advised me to buy the bifocals.

Missing you,
Salma

She was crying for me. I held my heart tight and opened the freezer and got some frozen fishfingers out, then stuck five under the grill together with two slices of bread. The fishfingers were almost burnt when I pulled them out, but I would eat them all the same. I had a sip of my flat Diet Coke and started chewing at the cod, whose heart was still uncooked. Leaning on the windowsill, I made out a shadow of a round pearly light hiding behind translucent clouds. I opened the window and stretched those arms covered with dry scabs towards the distant sky. The cold breeze carried her muffled cries all the way to this godforsaken island. If I stuck cotton wool in my ears I might not hear anything: the rustling of leaves; the shunting of trains; Elizabeth drunk and knocking about in the sitting room; Hamdan's whispers; the whimpers and thud thud of my heart.

★

I was sitting on top of a pile of wheat, scoffing my butter sandwich, when Hamdan suddenly emerged out of a dust cloud and sat next to me. He walked towards me in his white robe like a panther without making much effort. His eyes were fixed on my dark thin ankles, which he pulled almost every night from under the vines. 'How is my sparrow?' he said and fixed his white-and-red-chequered headdress.

I swallowed hard then said, 'I am fine.'

'You look tired. Am I exhausting you with my needs?' he whispered.

I threw away the sandwich to the birds and said, 'I am pregnant.'

On the filthy floor of the prison room a bundle of flesh pushed its way out. I shouted, I cried, I begged, then delivered a swollen bundle of flesh, red like beetroot. Alcoholic women, prostitutes and killers of husbands watched while I, the sinner, gave birth on the floor of the Islah prison. Madam Lamaa fixed her pink scarf, wiped her face with both hands and hugged Noura, whose tears were running down her face when she said something that I could not understand. 'Some day you will . . . One day you will . . .'

Sage Tea

I SLIPPED OUT OF MY RED UNDERWEAR, WHICH I BOUGHT in the sales, and stood naked on the dirty carpet. 'You have improved recently,' I said to my reflection then immersed myself in the water. Just to lie in the hot water inhaling all the scents of soap and bath oils was enough. Enveloped in a cloud of steam and perfume, I felt warm and safe for a few minutes, broken promises, betrayal, shame and death were pushed away to the back of my mind. I stood up, wrapped myself with the towel and began scrubbing my face. My fingers went round the big crooked nose, the narrow forehead, the wide mouth and high cheeks. I scrubbed and scrubbed to get to the clogged pores and push them open. Suddenly the aroma of freshly ground coffee, the smell of ripe olives and the scent of white orange blossom filled the bathroom. I was sitting under the fig tree with my mother drinking mint tea. My mother put her glass down and ran her rough hands over my face, muttering incantations. Every Friday afternoon the whole village gathered around the only radio, outside the house of the sheikh, to listen to the Egyptian diva Faiza Ahmad sing:

45

'Don't say we were and it was.

I wish all of this had never happened.

I wish I'd never met you, I wish I never knew you.'

I splashed my face with cold water. The mirror looked blurred as if floating in the salty sea.

I lined my lips with a red pen, trying to make them look smaller and fuller. I sprayed myself with deodorant. Up and down my body went the cold scent. I chose the tightest and shortest skirt in the wardrobe and squeezed myself into it, slipped my legs into sheer transparent black tights then wore my shiny black high-heeled shoes. I fixed my wired bra and pulled the straps up to give my breasts a younger, fuller shape. The black crochet beaded blouse was tight enough to enhance the breasts without showing the ageing stomach. I stood erect in front of the mirror and pulled my stomach in. Those were the few precious moments of the evening when I forgot my past. Those moments when I looked at my reflection as if looking at a stranger were the best. My mind would be busy finding a new name and history for myself. 'Tonight I am going to be a movie star!'

If I kept stitching and fasting, if I kept silent, I would slip slowly out of my body like a snake shedding her old skin. I might stop being Salma and become someone else, who never had a bite of the forbidden apple. Time might pass quickly so I would slide gently from prison to grave. No pain, resistance or even boredom. I stitched my mother's letter together with the lock of hair inside a leather pocket and turned them into an amulet, which I wore around my neck like a necklace. The pale handwriting of Miss Nailah, who wrote the letter for my mother, was engraved in my head.

This is what Allah willed for you. I called you Salma because I had high hopes for you. I wanted you to be able to decode writing, to get married to one of the sons of the sheikh of the tribe, to eat almonds and honey for the rest of your life. I wanted you to have a better life than mine. But your tuft of wool has always been different from the other girls of the tribe. You dyed it scarlet. You liked attention. They told me that you have stopped eating and drinking in prison. I cannot visit you because your father haj Ibrahim and your brother Mahmoud forbade me to come. They said they would shoot me too. When I look at your black goats looking lost without you and getting thinner and thinner, I say to myself may Allah bring a merciful end.

Wrapping my mother's black shawl around my shoulders I tiptoed out of the house. Liz was having a chat with Sadiq, 'the Pakistani chap in the off-licence', her supplier of cheap wine. 'Madam, this is excellent, a good vintage also. Just try it, madam. Excellent also.' She would crack some jokes and laugh until her eyes were full of tears. This was her best self, when she was a little tipsy and her spirits were high. Her hand on his elbow, she would say, 'Sadiq, you should be ashamed of yourself, flirting with an old English woman like me.'

He would jerk his chin sideways as if looking for words, then say, 'Madam, you're not old also.'

Her laughter was so loud, affected, somewhere between a chuckle and a sob. Then she would break into another language. '*Kaise no tum?*'

'This is not Urdu, madam, this is Hindi,' he would say indignantly.

'*Theek hai!*' she would say and shrug her shoulders.

Sitting behind the old Singer sewing machine, I pressed on the pedal and rolled the needle over polyester, cotton, satin. Whatever the prison's wardens gave me I would sew: sleeves, trousers, collars, the hem of the warden Naima's skirt, the pocket of her uniform jacket, which was torn off by one of the inmates. I tightened my white scarf around my head and started stitching it back to the jacket. The room was stuffy and smelt of machine oil and urine. All you could see were bent, covered heads and all you could hear was the rhythmic shunting of the old sewing machines. 'Just keep those fingers moving,' I said to myself, 'and you will be all right.' I wanted to mend my life. I used to fit collars carefully and stitch them by hand first, then run the machine over them. What was written on the forehead, what was ordained, must be seen by the eyes. 'Isn't she a good seamstress?' the inmates used to say while looking at the carefully made garments. They didn't know that they were looking at my wasted life. 'I always thought that you are not white like jasmine or pure like honey in its glass jars. You are a slut!'

Walking along the road I was able to hear the shunting of trains, the sound of metal hitting metal. Slam. Slam. 'It was a bit chilly,' I heard myself say in 'Elizabethan' English. My landlady was haunting me. If not careful I would turn into an Elizabeth, an English rose, a Sleeping Beauty without a prince. A huge brightly lit board was the first thing I noticed about the railway station. They took down the advertisement for Tetley's tea with the Sleeping Beauty and the seven dwarfs and replaced it with a sleek image of a red Chevrolet convertible. A new company called Fax Home had taken over the rundown building next to the railway line. They sandblasted the outside, installed double glazing, brought in photocopying and faxing machines, and offered their services for a reasonable price. I could see the machine in the dimly lit office faxing away messages to missing persons. Mrs Smith of Post Office Counters smiled whenever she saw me rushing through the door, but it was a weary smile. She must be thinking to herself, 'Here she comes again, that dark woman!' Whenever I gave her another bundle of letters she used to put on her reading glasses and inspect the addresses. 'To Whom it May Concern', or 'To Noura, Islah Prison, Levant', she would read out, then lower her reading glasses and look up at me with her penetrating grey eyes. 'This does not seem right.' But later she stopped checking the address. She would shrug her shoulders and say, 'Oh! You must have so many friends out there!'

'Oh! Yes!' I would say in a cheerful tone. I had friends: my teacher Miss Nailah, my dearest friend Noura, Madam Lamaa, Officer Salim, Sister Khairiyya, Sister Françoise, Minister Mahoney, Gwen and Parvin.

'Who made this white dress? I want to meet her,' shouted a woman in a Lebanese accent at Officer Salim, the prison governor. 'My name is Khairiyya and I want to see her.' She was my first visitor ever. I stood up, straightened my flowery dress and put on my plastic shoes. I was guided by the prison guard through the maze of corridors to the governor's office. A beam of sunshine lit the grey desk. I blinked and tried to make out the people in the room. A small dark lady in a high-collared grey dress was holding the white dress I made years ago. Officer Salim said, 'Sit down, Salma.'

I swallowed and sat down on a chair next to the woman.

The officer was balding and tall, but had a kind expression on his face. 'Did you make this white dress?'

I spent hours making that baby-girl dress. I spent hours trying to imagine what a white water lily would look like floating in clear water on a luminous jolly night: Layla. I tried to make the shape of the dress similar to that of a lily. I was willing the life of whoever wore it to be happier and whiter than mine. The zigzagged hem, the flowery collar, the small rose-like pockets, the tiny puffed sleeves, the satin belt and the glistening pearls stitched around the collar.

I nodded my head . . .

The large steel hangar where the post was sorted was brightly lit. They sorted and delivered thousands of letters, but mine never came. What would it take to receive their letters or, even better, hear their voices? If I lay in the middle of the street like a sleeping policeman, then got run over by a big red Royal Mail van, would they notice me? Whenever I was about to have an attack I would look at the barred window and recite my mother's letter several times until my heart stopped beating and the sweat on my forehead dried up. I could read between the lines that my mother was advising me to start eating again, but could not say it openly, afraid of the men of the family. 'Why don't you wear my bra,' Noura said, 'it might ease

50

the pain.' I shook my head. I would press on my sore nipples gently to relieve my breasts of the unused milk, then change the pads. The dried-up milk felt like pebbles inside my raw breasts. My nipples became darker and longer with all that futile pulling and squeezing, with all that grief.

The night was cold and dry but the Exe ran wild over the rocks that blocked its way down to the sea. It sounded like an ululation followed by a scream. The Turk's Head car park was full of cars with misty windscreens: smart cars, expensive cars, the kind of cars that I would like to be driven in. Over time the two floors of the pub were divided across age lines. The old went up the winding stairs to the ground floor and the young stayed downstairs in the cellars. Through the misty windows I saw the colourful disco lights and heard the hoarse voice of the singer. Tens of young English men and women were jerking their heads and swaying their hips to the music. Some were drinking, some were nuzzled against each other, some were kissing, and others were dancing alone. The sign on the door announced 'A private birthday party'.

'I want to help you get out of the country,' said Khairiyya then crossed herself.

'Please introduce yourself to Salma,' said Officer Salim.

'I am a civil nun from Lebanon. I have saved many young women like you. I prayed for all of you for years, but now I only travel between prisons and smuggle out women. I cannot bear the thought of an innocent soul getting killed. Here it is. Driving around in the dark is my fate,' she said hurriedly.

'Salma, you are in protective custody, which means you are here not because you have done something, but for your own protection. If I release you and you stay in this country you will get killed in front of the prison gates. If you leave the country you will be out of harm's way,' said Officer Salim and pressed his fingers on his shiny desk.

'They will shoot me,' were my first words in weeks. I had lost my tongue and remained silent for days. The inmates called me 'the pipe-mute'.

'Look, I will make sure that they won't. We will be extremely careful and release you at night. By releasing you I will not be breaking the law. As far as the state is concerned you are innocent.'

Khairiyya ran her fingers round her collar and said, 'The Lord knows that I am here to help. I'll pick you up at midnight and drive you to Lebanon.'

'What about? What about my . . . my family?'

'My child,' said Officer Salim, 'your teacher delivered that letter six years ago and we have not heard from your family since.'

I would be in prison: the next day at two o'clock, when the visiting bell was sounded – they stopped ringing it since no one visited the women prisoners of Islah – the warden would shout on the loudspeaker, 'A visitor for Salma Ibrahim El-Musa.' I would straighten my clean clothes which I had washed especially for the occasion, put on my plastic shoes and walk proudly to the barbed-wire fence. There they would be: my father haj Ibrahim, my brother Mahmoud and my mother hajjeh Amina crying and holding a brown sack of oranges. We would stick our hands to the wire and push and push until our palms touched. My mother's hands would be as rough as ever, and endangering my lips I would kiss them through the barbed wire.

I walked through the wide doors into an island of warmth, smoke and noise. The singer's hoarse voice reverberated through the wooden floor. The first glimpse of those who were sitting on the red stools told me who was out hunting tonight. I chose a stool at the far side of the bar to avoid unwanted attention. The owner, who sat on a comfortable chair in the far corner, kept an eye on the numerous waitresses. The girl working behind the bar looked homely in her wide skirt and big blouse; she had a clear, open, unmade-up face that emitted honesty. 'Good evening.'

'Hello.'

'What would you like?'

'Half a pint of apple juice.' The colour of apple juice looked like beer so whoever approached me would think that I was open-minded, not an inflexible Muslim immigrant.

Right behind me I was aware of a group of men in their thirties discussing something. I drank some 'beer' then turned round. One of them had long ponytailed hair, pleasantly ageing face and a loose smoky-blue shirt. Sixties generation. He pointed at me and asked the man standing next to him something. The two heads met in consultation. I turned to my drink. He was about to smile to me. The pub was full of people congregating in groups. They were talking to each other, but wanting to be noticed. Almost everyone was on the lookout for better options, a better choice than the one leaning on his shoulder and laughing herself silly. Looking at my honey-coloured drink I thought that everything was silly, including buying apple juice and pretending that it was alcohol.

Khairiyya fixed a date for my release. Salim smiled and waved his hands in the air in agreement. I asked for some water. Escorted to my prison room by a guard, I started thinking about the coming Tuesday, when at midnight I should be packed and ready to go. 'Go where?' I asked the stained walls. 'Where?' Although there wasn't much to pack, I rehearsed the packing tens of times in my head. The most important possession I had was already packed and hanging around my neck like an amulet: my mother's letter and her lock of hair. I sighed and was jerked back to the present by the sight of tomato juice being poured into a glass. The redness of it startled me.

'What?' said the ex-hippy, who was now standing next to me and leaning against the bar.

I shook my head and said, 'Nothing.' I tried to cheer myself up by summoning a television advertisement. The chocolate ad reminded me of Hamdan. The coffee ad was better, where the couple were about to get together. I took a deep breath and smiled, flashing my teeth as if advertising toothpaste.

Winking at his friends, he asked, 'Can I buy you a drink?'

His face had seen better days, and his dark hair was going grey at the temples, but he looked clean and smelt of washing powder. I liked his thin fingers and the oval-shaped fingernails. Tucking a loose strand of hair behind my ear, I said, 'Tomato juice, please.'

'Virgin?' he asked.

'Yes, please.'

He smiled and with a shaky voice ordered the drinks in a south-western accent.

'Where do you come from?'

I foresaw with dread the next few minutes. How many times had I been asked this question since I came to Britain? After years of working in his shop, Max, my boss, still asked, 'Where did you say? Shaaam? Hiiimaa?'

'Guess?'

The list, as usual, included every country on earth except my own. 'Nicaragua? France? Portugal? Greece? Surely Russia?'

'No. There is a big chunk right in the middle.'

'Turkey?'

'No, the Levant.'

He was toying with his pint; he did not know where to put it, aware of his friends looking at him. Faithful to the script he said, 'Why did you leave your country?'

My belongings, which I was frenziedly packing, were: a reed pipe, cloth sanitary towels, a brown comb with a few of the teeth missing, a Qur'an, a black madraqa, my mother's shawl, a spoon, a toothbrush which I was taught how to use in prison, a plastic cup, a grey towel, the lipstick that Madam Lamaa had given me, the two mother-of-pearl combs and bottle of perfume that Noura had given me as a present. I put the amulet – my mother's letter and the soft shiny lock of hair – on top of the pile and tied the bundle tight.

'Why did I leave? I wanted to explore, I suppose.'

He sipped some beer, not knowing whether to call it a

55

night or to continue chatting up this foreign woman. 'Have you been living here long?'

'Yes,' I said, pulling my skirt down.

'Do you like it here?'

'Yes. It's fine.'

'Do you have a family back home?'

'Yes. I have a family.' A mother, a father, a brother and . . . and some friends.

'Do you miss them?'

'Yes.' He was trying hard to engage me into conversation. I never swallow bait. I take a long time to savour it, chew it, then spit it out before the hook tears right through my tongue. I had a sip of the cold tart blood in my glass then asked, 'What about you?'

'I live in Exeter. I have my own health-food shop.'

'Where do you come from originally?'

'I was born in Lincoln, but my family have been living in Lyme Regis for years. My father was a fisherman.'

Someone opened the door to leave and a sudden gush of cold air hit me. I knew that air. I sat there on the stool shivering and trying to stop my hand from pulling my skirt down. I put both hands underneath me and pressed hard while listening to the faint sound of running water, the clinking of glasses and the distant barking of dogs.

A hesitant knock on the prison's door told me that it was twelve o'clock: time to leave. The inmates were asleep. I looked at their faces, at the cold floor, the stained wall, the bunk beds, which were brought in a few months ago to replace the rubber mattresses, then I turned round, ready to walk out. If Noura had still been there, it would have been difficult to say goodbye. Holding the bundle that

contained all my possessions, I walked quietly behind
Naima. My eyes were following the floor of the corridor
I must have mopped hundreds of times. The walls were
covered with marks counting days. Tonight I added to the
maze of my scratches a final one with a dot underneath.
'What is this?' 'It is an exclamation mark,' we repeated after
Miss Nailah. To my surprise Naima hugged me and her
usually angry face was covered with tears.

I composed myself and said, 'Thank you and goodbye.'

Officer Salim hurried me through the gate saying, 'May
God guard you and protect you.'

I whispered a thank you and jumped into the waiting
car next to Khairiyya who took off instantly. The prison
building disappeared in seconds. I could just make out the
dark figures of Salim and Naima waving goodbye.

Khairiyya was concentrating on her driving. 'We don't
want you to get shot by your brother.'

Looking at the dark winding road and the distant stars,
which I had not seen for eight years, I whispered, 'No.'

'Please call me Jim,' said the ponytailed English man.

'Jim, would you like a drink?'

'I'll get it.'

'No, I will.'

'All right, double Scotch, please.'

Only nine o'clock and he was going for the double
Scotch, I thought, and dug deep into my purse.

'Shall we sit by the fire?'

'Yes.'

We made our way towards the fireplace where you
could hear the hissing sound of gas in pipes. You saw the
glowing logs, the bright, flickering flames and you realized

that, like the rainbow I had seen this morning, it was fake, a trick of the eye. I sat on the leather sofa and sighed. It was much better for my tired back. Looking at Jim's grey eyes I wondered how many women he had slept with. The couple in the Nescafé ad, after days of borrowing coffee, smiling over dinner tables, near misses, still had not kissed.

'What do you do for a living?' he asked, stretching his legs and showing his sensible shoes.

'I am assistant tailor,' I said.

'Oh!'

He must be thinking how boring. 'I also do part-time degree in English.' That put some warmth in his eyes. 'I taken an elective in Sociology and I to write a paper about the homeless. I don't know how get references on that. In the cathedral close the homeless scavenging for food. I still ten days to write it.'

'Your tutor could help you.'

Dr John Robson, my tutor, was distant, was busy; his eyes were always focused on something other than my face.

'Talk to the homeless.'

'About homelessness?' I asked. Imagine me: dark, immigrant, with minimum wage, asking the tramps, 'Why do you sleep rough?'

'Yes.' Jim smiled and sipped the last drop of his whisky.

Unintentionally I pulled my skirt down, then blushed because of the wrong direction of my hands.

The night we drove out of my country was very cold, a cold that penetrated the spine and froze the breath. I was wearing my flowery dress, my pantaloons and plastic shoes. When I started rubbing my hands together,

FADIA FAQIR

Khairiyya, who was concentrating on the road, said, 'Wrap up with the shawl!' I wrapped my shoulders with my mother's black shawl and looked through the window at the distant lights. We drove by whole villages that were made up of just a few lights in the distance. My country was a string of tens of lights followed by darkness. The smell of wood burning in braziers filled the night air. My mother would be spinning under the kerosene lamp in her mud house; my father would be looking at the sky antici- pating rain; and she . . . and . . . ? I was being smuggled out of the country. I held my cloth bundle tight. Whatever I did from then on, wherever I went from then on, I must not think about them.

I began warming up to this ageing man with grey eyes. We were both pulling our tummies in, holding on to our youth. 'Why do you come on your own to the pub?' he asked while running his thin finger around the lip of his glass.

'I don't have any friends,' I answered. I was lying. I had Gwen and Parvin.

'You must have been living here for years. How come you don't have friends?'

'I spend most of my time the shop working,' I said then with both hands I tucked my frizzy hair behind my ears.

He smiled.

I smiled back.

In the reflections of the whisky glass on the table I saw the actress's shadow turning round on the quay, smiling to the lieutenant in defiance of the whole village. I watched the film with Parvin in one of our rare meetings. In the fake flames Jim looked kind and welcoming like a

59

hostel with basic amenities; a hostel full of other people's belongings and warm breath. A roof above your head; a man's cool shadow.

He put his glass on the mat and said, 'Do you have a car?'

'No.'

'Can I give you a lift?'

I hesitated. Through the flames of the fireplace I saw her smiling at me, then my mother stretched her arms to me, Miss Asher slapped me, Minister Mahoney blessed me, then Elizabeth shouted at me, then mist trickled down the cold window panes. 'Yes,' I said.

I wrapped my shoulders with my mother's black shawl and walked through a congregation of his friends. They cheered. He smiled and said, 'Ignore them!'

Khairiyya looked unreal in her grey dress and white collar; her silver glasses, which were tied to a leather cord, were hanging around her neck like a necklace. She drove as if a jinni was pulling her with his almighty force. We drove on in complete silence. Layer after layer darkness began to lift. Noura would be in the House of Perfume, entertaining customers; the other inmates would be looking at the barred window and dreaming of seeing the sky; and she would be crying and crying for me. At the end of the horizon I could make out green-brownish hills, some sheep grazing and a vast plain covered with dew. The smell of cut grass and open fires filled the air. It was my first sunrise in eight years. The morning light lit up the mountains and the plains. I wondered what my black goats would be doing now. I turned my face towards the side window and saw the glittering lush green plain, which spread to the end of the horizon.

'The Beqaa Valley,' said Khairiyya.

Dew sparkled in the morning sun. I was free. With the end of my veil I wiped my wet face.

'I love the sound of running water,' I said while getting into Jim's old car.

Jim smiled and said, 'So there is something you like after all.'

'Yes, the sound water, sage-flavoured tea and chocolate cream cakes.'

He laughed and said, 'What a mixture!'

I noticed the waxy glow of his skin, his thin lips, his small ears.

'Sage tea? Yes. Do you drink a lot of herbal tea in your country?'

'Yes, camomile and sage and mint and thyme.'

'And do you grow these herbs?' he asked then took my hand.

My goats would be climbing the mountain, and I would be busy gathering herbs for my mother. I used to rebuke the goats if they ate the herb bushes. 'Yes, we do. Camomile, sage and thyme grow everywhere.'

'I import them from Greece, dry and beautifully packed, to sell in my shop.'

His trousers had a generous, comfortable cut; his shoes were sensible. He parked his car opposite Sadiq's off-licence then looked at me about to say goodnight.

'Thank you,' I said in a trembling voice and grabbed the handle ready to get out.

'Your hair is amazing,' he said and touched it.

The warmth of his fingers ran down my hair all the way to the side of my face. I tightened my grip on the handle. The street looked cold and unreal in the dim orange glow of the street lights. My heart was thumping, my hands sweaty and my chin was quivering when I finally said, 'Would you like cup of tea with sage?'

He ran his fingers through his hair, then down his ponytail, hesitated then switched off the lights of his car and said, 'Yes.'

It was not meant to be, but it happened. I inherited all Elizabeth's letters and diary. I forgot to give them to her niece so I became the holder of her Indian secrets.

My grandfather and my parents were invited to the Begum's wedding procession. It was siesta time and the reading room was dark and pleasantly cool. A hushed silence enveloped us apart from the buzzing of the odd fly. I climbed the wooden ladder and picked out one of my grandfather's forbidden books, which were normally kept on the top shelf. I put the book on the desk and it split open to this page:

'One day, while Shahriyar was out hunting, Shahzaman stayed in the palace feeling very depressed about his dead wife. He looked out at the garden and saw his brother's wife enter the garden with twenty slave girls, ten white and ten black. They undressed and turned out to be ten men and ten women, who proceeded to have sex together, while another slave, Mas'ud, jumped down from a tree when the Queen called out, "Come, Master." He pushed her against the tree, smothered her with embraces and kisses, then mounted her. The negroes and the slave

girls followed suit, revelling together till the approach of
night. Then they all got dressed as slave girls, except for
Mas'ud who jumped back over the wall and was gone.'
  Suddenly I felt thirsty and walked as if in a daze to
the kitchen looking for Hita.

Jim and I tiptoed through the hall and climbed the stairs
quietly. I put the kettle on and asked him to sit down. He
sat on one of the chairs near the window. The orange light
of the railway, suffused through the net curtain, made him
look like an alien. I took off my shoes and my shawl and
sat on the floor leaning against the cold radiator, hugging
my knees.

  'Are you cold?' he asked and squatted opposite me.

  I saw my father's face then my mother's then Hamdan
then Shahla then the Ailiyya convent in Lebanon then
Minister Mahoney's house. The men of the tribe spilt my
blood. My mother beat me up. The prison walls were
filthy and smelt of urine and tears. I knew that air. She was
out there crying for me.

  'Oh! Dear! Let me warm up your hands,' he said and
started rubbing my fingers. The water was boiling, filling
the room with steam; then the kettle switched itself off.
He placed his cold lips on mine. I had nowhere to go. This
country was the only home I had. I shut my eyes, shut out
the urgent love-making of Hamdan, and received his kiss.
He was gentle, rubbing me with his thin fingers as if I
were a jewel; as if I were fragile. Hamdan knew that I was
strong, that I could take it, so he roughed me up then
mounted me with his hand pressed hard against my lips.

  'Shall I make the tea?'

  'Yes,' he said and retreated to the chair.

63

I placed the two steaming cups on the table. The sage leaves, which were floating on the surface, got soaked and sank to the very bottom.

He sniffed the tea, then took a sip. 'It has a wild, strange aroma.'

I could hear the snoring of Liz downstairs. 'The landlady,' I said.

He put the mug on the table, pulled me up, held my head firmly between his hands and kissed me.

The vivid greenness of the Beqaa Valley; its brightness, openness, splendour brought tears to my eyes. My mind was kissing everything: the spacious blue sky, the green plains, the large trees, even the donkeys and other cars. I was free. Khairiyya stopped the car opposite a small makeshift shop. 'Stay in the car,' she said and rushed to the shop and bought two boiled eggs, two loaves of thin pitta bread and a cup of sweet tea. As soon as she handed them to me I began eating. Khairiyya smiled and said, 'In the name of the Father, the Son and the Holy Spirit, amen,' and began eating. In prison it was always lentils and crusts of dry bread. Other women prisoners asked me to play my pipe and they sang:

> 'Morning or evening: lentils.
> Summer or winter: lentils.
> Hot or cold: LENTILS.'

In the morning I gave Jim a cup of coffee and a bowl of muesli and said, 'B&B,' and smiled. Jim was a gentleman; he had his condoms ready; he hugged me between acts and looked me in the eye when he said, 'Why all this sadness, I wonder?' While chewing the muesli in bed, and among dirty tissues, ruffled sheets and scattered clothes, we said goodbye. He kissed me hurriedly on the forehead and walked out. I could hear him rushing down the stairs, slamming the door behind him, starting his car, and racing out of the street. I continued eating my breakfast. No yanking of hair, crying or rending of garments. You say goodbye tight-lipped. You keep your cool if you want to see him again. You never ask, 'Can I have your phone number?' or 'Was it good?' or 'Will I ever see you again?' You stay in bed next to him all night pretending to be content, asleep and all you wanted to do was to jump up and wash your body with soap and water including your insides, do your ablutions then pray for forgiveness. No, you just chew at your cold breakfast looking at the bright stripes of light between the curtains and the windowsill tight-lipped. You would smile because it was supposed to be the morning after the beautiful night before.

Lilac or Jasmine

FRANÇOISE, THE YOUNG FRENCH NUN, PUT THE BREAK-
fast tray on the side table and said in broken Lebanese
Arabic, 'Good morning.'

I opened my eyes and realized that I was no longer in
prison. The painted window of the convent reflected a
rainbow of light on the bed. It was my first experience of
a comfortable bed. In my village we slept on mattresses
spread on the floor. In prison I slept first on a
mattress, then on a hard metal bed.

'Good morning.' I smiled.

Last night we arrived late. Khairiyya looked pale when
she held the brass knocker and hit it against the base. A
ruffled old woman opened the gate and let us in. Holding
my bundle close to my chest I followed them dutifully
through the candlelit corridors. When the old nun opened
the door and said, 'Your bedroom,' my chin started
quivering. My bedroom was a spacious, well-lit room,
with a huge bed in the middle covered with clean white
sheets, pillows and blankets.

'Don't be silly!' Khairiyya snapped.

I held the tears back. 'Thank you.'

They closed the old wood door and said, 'Goodnight.'

I opened the window and saw the moon in the middle of the sky above the deep valley. A handful of lights twinkled in the darkness. The sea was a silver sheet spread at the feet of the steep cliff. I opened the door and ran barefoot up and down the cobbled corridor, but could not find a soul. The candles were put out and the corridor was cold and dark. I went back to my room and looked through the window again at the sea, where waves broke into each other leaving streaks of foam behind. Where was I? How far was I from my mother? How far was I from her?

I tiptoed downstairs to the kitchen in order not to be spotted by Liz. I could not face an interrogation this morning. The carpeted stairs were cold under my bare feet. I hugged myself. I always rushed out of bed in my T-shirt and then remembered the coldness of it all. I made myself a cup of coffee. The house was quiet. I went to the sitting room, hoping to find Liz's comfortable armchair empty, but there she was, in her dark-blue jumper and baggy Indian trousers, sitting on her chair, sipping her tea and watching *Tom and Jerry* on TV. 'Good morning.'

'Good morning, Sal.'

I didn't like being called 'Sal', which sounded like a man's name in my native language. I sat down on one of the straw chairs, drinking my coffee quickly.

'Did you have a good time yesterday?'

Tom was chasing Jerry around the house. 'Yes, thank you.'

'Who was it?'

Jerry was trying to tie Tom's tail to an electric iron. 'A guy who has a health shop.'

'Does he have a name?' she asked, running her fingers over the buttons of the remote control.

To my shame I could not remember his family name.

'Yes.' Before Jerry was electrocuted Liz switched channels. 'A cold day in the south with some scattered showers in the afternoon.'

I held my warm mug close to my chest, unable to locate myself, centre myself.

'I stained my family's name with mud,' I told Françoise, the Little Sister in Ailiyya convent. She was folding towels and pieces of cloth carefully.

'But no, my child, we all make mistakes,' she said and rubbed her left eye. She was young, with a beautiful, open face. I thought that all foreign women were blonde, but Françoise, although French, had dark hair and eyes.

'Françoise,' I said and smiled, knowing that my tongue couldn't twist itself around her name.

She smiled back.

'Where are we? How far are we from my country?'

Her Arabic was watered down, sounded foreign, but she rushed into it breathlessly. 'We are north of Beirut, on the coast of the Mediterranean. Your county is further south, almost south-east. A number of hours' drive.'

'So we are not very far.'

'No, but far enough.'

I wiped my mouth, put the breakfast tray on the wide stone windowsill and said, 'I shall go back one day.'

She looked through the window and said, 'Look, the sun is shining. I will take you for a walk around the farm to show you our vineyard. I brought you some sensible shoes and some clothes. Go on, have a bath.'

She was emerald, turquoise encased in silver, Indian silk cascading down from rolls, fresh coffee beans ground in an ornate sandalwood pestle and mortar, honey and spicy ghee wrapped in freshly baked bread, Françoise, a white pearl glistening in her brown and white costume, a balm for your wounds.

I went to the bathroom of the convent and was surprised to see a high toilet and a bath. In prison we were allowed to have a shower once every two weeks except for births and deaths. We used a low toilet, a mere hole in the ground, then washed ourselves with water from a plastic ewer. Using the shower was much easier than pulling cold water out of the well, then pouring buckets of it over your head. The smell of olive oil filled the old bathroom. I took off my clothes and for the first time in my life I looked at the reflection of my body in the long mirror fixed to the wall. A horse with a long horn and a thick tail was engraved on the corner of the mirror. I looked thin and dark, and had long bushy hair. My face was just two big, dark eyes, a crooked nose and a large mouth. I lowered myself into the hot water then lay down in the tub, making sure that the whole of my body was covered with soap and water. Morning light was freely bouncing off the walls, the floor and the water. I could hear the sparrows twittering away their welcome to the morning.

With the end of my sleeve I wiped the mist off the sitting-room window. 'Yes, it's a bright day.'

Liz continued asking about 'this chap' I brought home last night with me.

I wanted to be nice to Liz, but couldn't. I could not tell her which party he voted for. 'You don't ask people about politics when you first meet them. It's private.'

'Oh! Stupid girl! Of course you do. You don't want to end up with a Marxist,' she spat out.

I didn't know what she was talking about so I changed the subject. 'Liz, the weather is glorious today. Why don't you go for a walk?' I knew that Liz liked the word 'glorious'.

She ran her fingers through her grey hair and said, 'I should. Shouldn't I?'

The flowers on the mantelpiece had withered days ago. I should get Liz some daffodils. The room could do with more sunshine. I went upstairs to my room, snatched my towel and rushed to the bathroom.

I rubbed my hair with the hard cube of soap until I had a rich lather. The Little Sisters of the convent made it themselves. I filled the jug with water and washed away the dirt. Light brown water whirled down the drain. I scrubbed my body with a thick loofah until my skin turned red, poured clean water over my head until all the dirt of prison rushed down. With a white towel, I dried my hair and body. Its softness and warmth reminded me of my mother's rough hands. She held my body firmly between her legs, massaged my head with olive oil, combed my hair, wove it into two braids, then patted me on the shoulder and said, 'Put on your madraqa and run to school! I don't want you to be illiterate like me.' Miss Nailah taught me how to decode Arabic letters and how to put them together to form words. 'Head, heads. Repeat after me!' I memorized one word then another until I became literate. In prison after I started talking and reading old newspapers to the inmates I used to change the few news items to make them laugh. 'An honourable donkey got married to a chaste monkey and they gave birth to a prison warden.' 'A flower has withered: with a heart full of sorrow we announce the death of our cat Mishmish.' The changed news used to get a round of applause. Then I began learning another language. 'If only you could hear me, Mother, reading Englisi.' I could see my mother's lips meet in a Bedouin smack, '*Tzu*'! Illiterate: you are not any more. In trouble: you are. Speaking different tongues does not lessen the burden of the heart.'

Circles of light were still filling the bathroom of the convent like little rainbows. I put on pants and a bra, which I had never worn before. I put on the pair of blue jeans and the T-shirt Françoise had given me, tied my hair into a ponytail, tied my white veil around my head, and walked out of the bathroom: a new, clean and awkward woman, conscious of the tight elastic around her hips and breasts. The bright sun welcomed me when I walked out of the main gate. Shielding my eyes, I looked down. The green-blue sea spread at the feet of the high brown mountains. I could smell the fertile soil and the salty sea. I breathed in as much fresh air as possible, then walked behind Françoise, in the sturdy walking shoes she had lent me. The vineyard expanded to the end of the horizon. Tens of young, western nuns in brown and white were either digging the soil or watering the plants. They were all humming a foreign tune and working in unison.

'They shouldn't be watering the vine trees,' I said.

'Why?' Françoise asked.

'Because vine trees don't need much water. If you want a sweet crop then you shouldn't water them much.'

Her dark eyes were smiling when she said, 'Of course, you used to be a farmer.'

'And a shepherdess,' I said.

The pots of African violets and wandering Jews were my only contact with farming now. They stood like a question mark on the windowsill of Swan Cottage. I cleaned them, fertilized them and over-watered them. When you lived in this street a garden was out of the question. You were besieged by the railway and the garages. At least I had a good view of the river and the hills; a good view of other people's gardens. There was a house in New North Road with a big, beautiful garden. At night, when there were no people around, I would stand on the pavement and stick my head through the hedge to have a look at their seasonal flower beds. They changed the design every three months. You would be passing by and you would smell honeysuckle, lilac, heather or jasmine depending on the season.

I woke up early in the morning, washed and changed, had group breakfast with the nuns, then went for a long walk, down the valley, then up the mountain. My only companions were the amulet hanging around my neck and my reed pipe. I would watch how the sea woke up when touched by the morning light, its colours changing from grey, to coral, to gold, then to turquoise like my grandmother's necklace, which was a string of beads encased by silver. The sun would fight the darkness of the sea. The sunlight would win the day, filling the air with light. The dark-blue sea, exhausted, grew mossy green around the edges. That was the time to join the nuns in the vineyard. I walked towards them, playing their French hymn on my pipe. 'Oh! My saviour! Oh! My beloved!' they chanted together. I rolled up my sleeves and the ends of my trousers, kicked off my shoes and barefoot began working in the farm. 'Look at her,' Françoise said, 'she weeds like a whirlwind.'

The sky was blue, with a few patches of cloud. I snatched my handbag then rushed out of the house, slamming the door behind me. I wanted Liz to know that I had left Swan Cottage. My friend Gwen, who usually expected me Sunday mornings, lived in number eighteen. The door bore a brass plate with the inscription 'Docendo Discimus', which was given to Gwen by her colleagues on her retirement. She had explained that it was Latin and it meant 'We learn by teaching'.

As soon as I moved in with Elizabeth I began walking by the river every Sunday. Once I was crossing the street and saw an old lady bending down to pick up her walking stick, so I picked it up and gave it to her. 'Thank you,' she said and tidied up her coiffed hair.

'It's nothing,' I said and smiled.

'Do you live around here?' she asked.

'Yes, number fifteen,' I said.

'Are you walking to the river?'

'Yes,' I said.

'Do you mind if I join you?' she said and smiled.

That afternoon we did not stop talking. We talked about

the colour of the rainbow arched above the river, Gwen's dog that was so old and ill it had to be put down, my boss Max and absent friends.

As soon as I knocked on the door I was able to hear the shuffling of her feet and the fumbling with chain and key. 'Good morning, beautiful,' I said and kissed Gwen on the cheek.

She smiled, pushed her glasses up her nose, and hugged me. 'Come in, Salma. Right on time for tea and biscuits.'

I sat on the kitchen chair and watched Gwen, over-weight and aproned, making tea. She used to be the headmistress of a comprehensive in Leeds, which she described as an ugly, beautiful, paradoxical and industrial city, and decided to retire in Devon. She bought this semi-detached house, dumped all her belongings in a hired van and drove down the motorway.

'Gwen, why don't you sit down? I'll make the tea.'

'No, I will become dependent on you. Can't have that,' she said in her sing-song Welsh accent.

Flushed and exhausted she put the tray on the kitchen table. When she wiped her glasses with the apron and sighed, I knew that I could start talking. 'I brought you some French strawberry jam and a George Eliot book.'

'Oh! How kind of you. But you shouldn't bring me presents. Not with your salary.'

'Look, the jam is a present but the book is not. You asked me to buy you *Daniel Deronda*, remember?'

She smiled then produced a five-pound note from the pocket of her apron. The kitchen was cold and dark with just one window overlooking the railway. We sat there sipping our tea and chewing our coconut biscuits. Her son Michael was always the centre of our conversation on

Sunday. Michael has done this, Michael has done that.
'He's sent me a postcard, look. Tour Eiffel, but upside
down and wearing trainers. He's got a new girlfriend,' she
said, tidying her short grey hair with her trembling hand.

'Really? Is she nice?'

'She must be. They've gone to Paris together.'

He had gone to France, but coming to Exeter was too
costly for him. To stop myself from saying something that
might upset her I blurted, 'He must be happy.'

'Yes, Salma, he must be,' she said and tucked the ends of
her short grey hair behind her ears.

*When I got pregnant with you, Layla darling, my mother
begged me to leave the village before my brother found
out. 'He will shoot you between the eyes with his English
rifle. You must go, daughter, before you get killed.' She ran
her rough fingers over my face, murmured verses of the
Qur'an, kissed me then pushed me away from her. Miss
Nailah held my hand and pulled me away. Hand in hand
we walked to the police station.*

*Now I live in Great Britain. I have a job, a car, a
husband and a large house. I am rich, so rich I could pay
for your university education. One day you will see me
right in front of you. I am sure that my heart would
recognize you, would single you out even if you were
among hundreds of children.*

We worked in the vineyard for hours then the whistle of
Mother Superior told us that it was time for lunch. We
gathered in the middle of the vineyard around a built-in
wooden table laden with food. I would wash the mud off
my hands, get a plate and join the queue. We ate freshly

baked bread, mountain tomato, green peppers and goats' cheese with thyme and olive oil. I ate quickly with my hands, pushing the slices of tomatoes into my mouth. The nuns would laugh at me. 'Nobody is chasing you with a stick in his hand, eat slowly,' Françoise said.

'*Shwayy, shwayy?*' I pretended not to understand her Arabic.

She would smile.

'South-east of here, you said?'

'Yes.' She began collecting the empty plates and putting them on the table.

When the seagulls soared overhead we knew that it was time to go back to work and leave them the leftovers.

'Take me to the sitting room?' Gwen asked feebly. I held her hand and helped her legs, stiff with arthritis, up the step between the kitchen and the sitting room. When she finally settled in her chair, I gave her the book which would keep her busy for a few days. 'Look what I have knitted for your Layla.' She spread a small white baby jacket on her blanketed knees. I looked speechless at the intricate pattern of flowers and stars. It must have taken her months to weave it with one needle. 'But she must be sixteen by now. But, of course, how silly of me!'

Holding her ageing hands I looked for the familiar in her blue eyes, trembling lips and lavender scent. Running my fingers on her green protruding veins my fluttering heart settled and I was able to hold back my tears.

'There was, there was not, in the oldest of times, a young girl called Jubayyna. They called her that because she was

76

as white as goats' cheese. She had dark hair, tomato-red cheeks and big eyes. She used to play in the yard with the hens, goats and camels. They all loved Jubayyna. One day when she was chasing a dog the evil giant snatched her, flung her on his back and took her prisoner in his far-off castle. One of her camels followed her, and stood in the valley surrounding the high castle singing:

> "Your camel, Jubayyna,
> Once he shouts, once he cries,
> To cut the chains, he tries."

'The camel shouted and screamed. Jubayyna cried and cried until her tears flooded the valley surrounding the castle.' Then my mother suddenly stopped talking.

'Mother, what happens next?' I gasped.

'Her camel might save her,' she said, hugged me, kissed me then covered me with the white sheepskin rug.

After I did the washing-up and tidied the kitchen I kissed Gwen on the cheek as always and left. I walked up the side street and continued walking on the main road, ignoring the footpath made especially for pedestrians. What if I got run over by a lorry? Would anyone anywhere shed a tear? My hands were trembling when I filled in my donor card. Give any part of my body to anyone who needs it after my death. Get in touch with . . . My family did not know my whereabouts and I did not know the whereabouts of my daughter. I scanned the list of people I knew in this country: Parvin, Miss Asher, Liz, Minister Mahoney, my boss Max. 'In case of emergency contact Gwen Clayton, 18 King Edward Street,' I wrote. If I died, Gwen wouldn't be able to cope and would ask her son Michael to help her, so my death might bring them closer.

Miss Asher, one of the Little Sisters, the English one, who spoke holding her mouth tight, sat on the bedside trying to convince me in her broken Arabic why I should go with her to Britain and leave the Little Sisters Ailiyya convent in Lebanon. I was happy there.

They had got me a sewing machine and I spent my mornings working in the vineyard, and my afternoons making pillowcases, robes, underwear, petticoats, belts, lamp covers and collars. I copied anything they brought from France. I sewed and sewed, then at sunset, I took my pipe and walked to my favourite spot at the very top of the mountain where I blew happy tunes watching the sun sink into the water and listening to the jingling of cow bells and the bleating of sheep. The kerosene lamps were lit one by one in the valley. It reminded me of my village Hima, my mother and my teacher Miss Nailah. She no doubt would swim out of the castle to safety and then her patient camel would carry her home.

Looking at the wooden bowl full of grapes sitting firmly on the wide windowsill, I said to the English lady, 'No, I am not going anywhere, miss, I am happy here.' Arianne, the Mother Superior, tried to talk to me about Jesus, who died to save all humanity. I asked her not to talk to me about God. She stopped, but remained kind and understanding. They stripped me of everything: my dignity, my heart, my flesh and blood. My mother's face was lit up with love when she told me the story of Jubayyna. She kept telling me that I was better than everyone else until I believed her, then I fell, and fell.

Even the camel knew the meaning of friendship and ties.

Whenever I walked to town up New North Road, I passed by the big old white house next to the tennis club, my favourite because of its spacious garden. I stuck my head through the hedge to have a look at the neat flower beds. A big apple tree stood in the middle, its trunk covered with ivy. The white lace curtains of the old small windows fluttered in the breeze. Suddenly, I realized that the black shadow near the gate was a Rottweiler so I offered it my head. It began jumping up and barking so I closed my eyes hoping that it would wrench my flesh strip by strip, that it would gouge my eyes out with its black paws, that it would paralyse me with one bite of its scissor jaws. 'Stop it, Raider!' a woman shouted from the upper-floor window and I missed the chance of ending it all.

One morning a tired and serious-looking Françoise came to see me. It was still early, and I was lying in bed, trying to decide whether the shriek I heard was that of a seagull or a raven. If it were a raven some kind of parting was about to take place.

'I must talk to you, Salma.'

I sat up then smiled a good morning to her.

She was gazing at her feet when she said, 'Khairiyya sent me a letter this morning saying that your family has found out that you have escaped from prison. Your brother Mahmoud is looking for you.'

Mahmoud? When I was young he used to buy me Turkish delights, but a few years later he started yanking my hair with his thin brown fingers. Mother used to watch him in distress. I sat up.

'Sister Asher, who is one of us, wants you to go with her to Britain.'

I covered my arms with the white sheets.

'You will be safer there.'

I wanted to cover my head with the quilt and just lie still in the darkness.

She rubbed her left eye and said, 'We cannot take any chances. A policeman has visited Khairiyya recently and asked her about the whereabouts of all the girls we managed to smuggle out. You must go with Miss Asher to England.'

'*Hinglaand? Fayn hinglaand?*'

'It is far enough,' said Françoise and rubbed her left eye. If the left eye fluttered then parting was upon us. She placed her long wooden rosary around her neck then pulled the tassel down.

'*La ma widi hinglaand,*' I said and hugged her.

'I know you don't want to go, but you'll learn to like it, *habibti,*' she said.

The grey concrete building of Exeter Public Library looked like army barracks, but its glass windows gleamed in the warm light of the sun. When I opened the door I was met with a hushed polite silence so I cleared my voice and said to the middle-aged librarian, 'I would like to join the library,' but my 'o's came out all wrong. I was afraid of being turned down. She looked for a form. A leaflet warning against AIDS, 'Positive women: call us . . .' was pinned to the noticeboard. I waited for the librarian, who was rummaging through the drawers, to find an excuse to deny me membership. You are an alien, we have no national insurance number for you; you cannot get in. 'But

I am not an indefinite-leave-to-remain holder, I am not a temporary-visa holder like them Albanians, I am a British subject,' I repeated like a mantra, 'I am a British citizen.' I swore allegiance to the Queen and her descendants. Flushed and embarrassed, she produced a form for me to fill in. I was so grateful to be given membership, to be treated like them, that I dropped the form and the pen on her shiny black shoes.

I was wrapped in a blanket and sitting on the floor when Miss Asher, the English Little Sister, said, 'I changed your name to Sally Asher and got you a temporary document.' I stuck my head out from the covers and saw a middle-aged woman with silver-framed glasses, leather sandals and buttoned-up grey shirt. The expression on her face was similar to that of the Jesus crucified on the wall of the big hall. 'A lawyer in Beirut has done the papers of adoption for me. The visa section did not like the idea of adopting someone in her twenties. I had a long chat with the ambassador, who is a secular fundamentalist, and told him that you had lost all members of your family in South Lebanon and all your documents, and that you are suffering from a severe psychological disorder. Jesus will take care of her and we will give her a family,' she crossed herself and added, 'I will show her the way of the Lord and teach her English.'

Françoise was translating what her English Little Sister was saying. Holding my reed pipe tight I listened to her in silence.

'Here is your temporary Lebanese passport and your travel documents. At three o'clock we will take a boat to Cyprus.'

I looked at the white nightdress with flowery pockets I was making for Françoise and the big bowl of grapes and repeated like a parrot, 'But I am happy here.'

Françoise rubbed her left eye, held my hands tight and said, 'Child, you must understand that your life is in danger. You must leave.' She stuck her hand in the pocket of her brown robe and produced a shred of blue sky. 'This turquoise necklace belongs to my distant past in the back streets of Paris. I want you to have it.'

I fingered the cold blue beads set in a silver pendant and imagined what Paris would look like. 'Thank you so much,' I said and stuck the necklace in my cloth bundle.

I sat on one of the chairs and placed a large illustrated book on the table. The library was quiet before the lunchtime rush. An old Greek woman, wearing a black dress with a wide skirt, her head tied with a black scarf, was patiently sweeping the yard of her old white cottage. *Hidden Greece* was the title of the book. One of these days I would go there, play my pipe for the sheep, chase the hens, run after the dog and ride the horse. The white-washed walls of the cloister kept the heat of the sun away. I closed the big black book and looked at the bowing heads of readers in the library. They would smile to each other, greet each other, but never say what people of Hima used to say to strangers: 'By Allah, you must have lunch with us. I won't take no for an answer.'

Arianne, the Mother Superior, held a special prayer for me. I hugged them tightly, kissed Françoise, whose tears were trickling down her face, and walked down the hill with Miss Asher. I was told that Mahmoud, my brother, would be there at any moment, his dagger tied to his belt and his rifle loaded. I'd better hurry, I was urged. I could hear their French hymns and see the flickering of their candles even when walking towards the sea. The seagulls were soaring above us like white clouds. A taxi was waiting for us; before getting into the passenger seat, I looked up and waved to the convent with its painted glass windows and crucified Jesus.

Miss Asher tugged at my sleeve. 'Let's go.'

'Lits goo,' I repeated. Those were my first words in English.

Peaches and Snakes

THE BACKPACKERS' HOSTEL WAS TOTALLY QUIET. ITS residents had finally gone to sleep. While watching the flickering reflection of the orange street lights on the dirty curtains I heard Parvin's muffled sighs coming from her ex-army bed. She must be crying. I put the kettle on and made her a cup of tea. 'Miss, tea?'

She looked at me with her red swollen eyes and said, 'I don't want your tea.'

I held back the hot mug.

She began crying and repeating, 'Sorry. Yes. Thank you. Sorry.'

'Drink,' I said and she held the mug and drank some tea.

'Too sweet,' she said.

'Only four spoons,' I said.

After she drank the tea to the last drop, she sat up and asked, 'Where do you come from?'

'Over the sea,' I answered.

'Are you Arab?'

'Yes, Bedouin me.'

'Wow! A fucking Bedouin Arab!'

'I fucking no allow,' I said.

She smiled.

She put the mug down, pulled herself up, put the pillows behind her head and sighed. She said that she did not know how she ended up in this dump. Her father wanted her to get married to an ignorant bastard from Pakistan. She tried to dissuade him, pleaded with her mother, but no, she either went ahead with it or he would disown her in the papers. 'Parvin is not my daughter.' She ran away and ended up in a refuge run by Pakistani women, not far from Leicester, where she used to live, but the women advised her to move down south because some of their girls were kidnapped.

' "Kidnapped" what means?' I asked.

'They took them away by force. They push them into a car and take them away,' she said.

I smacked my Bedouin lips in disbelief. The only English words that came to mind at that moment were, 'Trouble your heart.'

Although her hazel eyes were glistening with tears she smiled and asked, 'Trouble my heart?'

'Not. Not,' I said.

She pressed her head with her hands and began crying.

'What's your name?' I asked.

'My wretched name is Parvin,' she said and wiped the tears with the back of her left hand.

'Many names I. Salma and Sal and Sally,' I said.

Parvin began crying again. I sat next to her on the bed and stuck my hands between my knees. She was thin and short, with shiny straight black hair and large hazel eyes, which she kept hidden behind her lowered thick curled lashes. She had a small nose and full lips that remained

partly open showing a chipped front tooth. She was wearing a white shalwar kameez, which emphasized the
darkness of her skin and her angular shape.

'Parvin, stop crying please. Your tears gold,' which was
what my mother used to say whenever I cried.

She ignored me.

I got up and sat on the ex-army bed. What brought me
here? What brought her here? Who was watching over
her?

In the twilight the small port looked haunted, with boats
covered with nets and dirty pieces of cloth. An old
Lebanese fisherman spat in the water then began swearing
when he saw us approaching. We were late. I threw my
bundle on board then stepped on the side to get in. When
I pressed with my foot on the bottom of the boat it began
swaying. I held Miss Asher's firm hand. When we were
both seated on a wooden bench inside a small cabin, the
old fisherman wiped his hands on the wide black
pantaloons and pulled a string. The engine began purring
and suddenly the whole boat began shaking. 'Yala!' he
shouted and the boat sped through the water. I held Miss
Asher's hand to steady myself. When I was able to look
back through the small door I couldn't see any lit
windows although it was dark and the convent looked like
a big dark eagle, wings spread, beak open, perched on the
top of the mountain.

My skirt, top, underwear and dirty tissues were scattered
all over my bedroom floor. What was Jim's family
name? All of that fumbling in the dark so that you would
forget who you were for a few minutes. The bed was

ruffled and the mattress cover was stained. The room was stuffy and smelt of sweat and sage. I pushed the window open and sat down on the bed. The small leather bag containing my mother's letter folded around the lock of her hair looked like an amulet hanging on the side of the Indian mirror. My tribal protection had been removed, my blood was spilt and my arms had broken out with red sores. A shiver ran through me as if I had caught a sudden chill. A cold evening breeze rushed through the window. I put on a fleece and began stripping the bed and the pillows. I put all the dirty linen and clothes in the washing machine in the bathroom and turned the knob right up to ninety degrees for ultra white. I sat down on the toilet seat watching the clothes being tossed around in the soapy water, spun, then tossed around again. Finally the whirring and vibration of the machine spinning the laundry dry shook the old wooden floor. I wished that I could put me among the washing so I would come out at the other end 'squeaky clean', without dry stains or dark deeds. Without the approval of the elders, without papers, without a marriage contract I went ahead and slept with a stranger. They should cut me into pieces and leave each at the top of a different hill for birds of prey. 'Salma,' called Liz from the landing, 'I need the toilet. You have been in there for an hour and a half.'

The rhythmic sound of the pestles of Hima grinding roasted coffee beans was an early sign of weddings in the offing. It was Aisha's turn this year. A dark farmer from the valley had come to take her away in his cart. Her dowry was a piece of fertile land by the river. I was not sure whether I should go to the wedding, but my mother said if I didn't old tongues would start wagging. On Friday I went to the women's tent, greeted everyone, then sat on the ground with the other women of the tribe. It was so hot sweat trickled down my nose. I was young, pregnant and unmarried. The horse race filled the village with clouds of dust and shouts of victory or defeat. Aisha went to the tent with her husband. The men held hands and began bowing and singing in unison, '*Dhiyya, dhiyya, dhiyya*,' until their voices were just a hoarse drawing and releasing of breath. A young boy handed them a white handkerchief so they stopped singing and dancing and began shooting in the air celebrating Aisha's honour, her purity, her good fortune. Suddenly among the cries of joy and ululations we heard Sabha's mother shout, 'Sabha was shot. Oh, my brother! Sabha was shot.' Sabha was my school mate. Some whispers in the dark turned into a rumour and then turned into a bullet in the head. I swallowed hard. An old woman in black squatting next to me and sucking on her long pipe whispered, 'Good riddance! We've cleansed our shame with her blood!'

Listen for the galloping of horses, for the clank of daggers being pulled out of scabbards, for flat-faced owls hooting in the dark, for bats clapping their wings, for light foot-steps, for the abaya robe fluttering in the wind, for the swishing sound of his sharp dagger cutting the air. Sniff the air for the sweat of assassins. Listen to his arm grabbing your neck and pulling it right back, to his dagger slashing through flesh and breaking through bones to reach the heart. Listen to your warm red blood bubbling out and drip dripping on the dry sand. Listen to your body convulsing on the ground. An ululation. A scream. Rending of black madraqas. Rhythmic banging of chests. A last gasp.

Miss Asher sat under the kerosene lamp reading her Gospel loudly in English. Ali, the fisherman, was singing in Arabic about faraway lands and solitary stars. His hoarse voice ebbed and flowed with the waves. I sat huddled to the cold wood, looking through the round window for signs of Cyprus. The mist and the waves told me that I was moving further and further away from my country, my mother and above all from her. My mother's black shawl was wrapped tight around my shoulder, but I could still feel the cold. Whenever I was beaten by Mahmoud, my brother, Mother used to stroke my head to calm me down. 'It's all right, child. It's all right, princess.' She would undo my braids, rub my head with olive oil, run her fingers through my hair, stroke my face with her rough fingers, fondle my ears, massage my hands. 'You are so tender and healthy, Salma. I want to bite you so much.'

While stitching hems, folding collars and ironing dark-blue suits in Lord's Tailors, under the watchful eyes of my boss, Max, I dreamt of whiteness. Sitting in a cloud of steam and starch, I dreamt of happiness. To sit in a department store coffee shop, buttering my scones, sipping my tepid tea and looking at the colourful dresses and shoes on display as if I belonged. While ironing I read the labels on dresses and shirts: Dream Weekend, Evening Lights, Country Breeze. Sitting in a cloud of steam, I dreamt of weekends in country mansions, tea with the Queen and whiteness. What if I woke up one morning a nippleless blonde bombshell, like the ones that splayed their legs in the *Sunday Sport*, which was the only newspaper Sadiq, the off-licence owner, would read. What if I turned white like milk, like seagulls, like rushing clouds. Puff, my sinful past would disappear, a surgeon would slice away part of my mind and my ugly nipples! I would turn white just like Tracy, who worked and talked non-stop while holding the pins and needles in her mouth. No more unwanted black hair; no more 'What did you say your name is?'

It did not take long to get from the Ailiyya convent to Cyprus. It was dark when we arrived and the shore was deserted except for a few men shouting in Greek. Ali, the fisherman who sang sad songs all the way to Cyprus, was tying the small boat to the harbour. Sister Françoise had told me that Cyprus was a beautiful island, with good food and cheerful people who played the bouzouki and drank ouzo. 'Your pipe and the bouzouki are similar, they produce sad tunes.' I tightened the knot of my veil and jumped out of the boat, happy to be able to stand on solid ground again. Despite the chilly breeze the sand was warm. We were met by a woman who looked like Miss Asher. I took off my shoes and walked behind them barefoot. 'Bedouin style,' Miss Asher said to the other woman. We walked on the shore until we reached a rundown building. 'Sun Holiday Flats,' said the woman who looked like Miss Asher. New identical blocks of flats were built around a courtyard which had a vine trellis in the middle. Like Hima the air smelt of broken promises, spilt honey and heartbreak. I was about to burst into tears when I heard the sleepy voice of the landlord, 'Khello, khello. Do you have good journey?'

'Yes, thank you,' answered Miss Asher abruptly. She was tired.

The street lamps outside the hostel were switched off, but I was still wide awake inspecting the sores on my arms and legs. Parvin was tossing and turning. I crossed over and covered her with the blanket, which had slid down to the floor earlier. The curtains were shut, but the distant and intermittent sound of traffic filled the room. I heard someone screaming in the adjacent bedroom as if having muscle spasms or giving birth. The wind blew against the curtain inflating it. Two brown feet in leather sandals stuck out from underneath the curtain. Blood was running down my thighs. I held the pillow tight. When the horse broke his leg and lay on the ground gasping with pain my father pulled out his gun and shot it. It was his favourite horse, the horse that had grown with him since he was a boy, the horse that took him to the nearest town once a month. He loved that horse yet he shot him. I looked up at the dark figure behind the curtain and said, '*Yala tukhni w khalisni*. It will be my deliverance.'

Parvin turned her head then squinted her eyes and said, 'Who are you talking to?'

'Someone in the room after me,' I said.

She got up, looked under the beds, behind the wardrobe, and outside the door.

'Behind the curtains,' I said.

She pulled the curtain open and there was nothing, no Mahmoud, no sandals and no rifle. 'He must jump the window,' I said.

'How on earth would he slide through a five-inches-wide slit? He must be an acrobat, a cat,' she rebuked me.

'Cannot you see how ill I am?' I pleaded, stretching my arms for her to see the sores.

She sat down, pushed her fringe back and said, 'Salma, you are not ill.'

'I am, I am,' I said and began crying.

She stretched her hand to touch me.

'Stay away. Might infect you,' I said.

'Allah is the maker and breaker. Sometimes you get broken, sometimes you are made whole.' While Miss Asher was on her knees, praying to the dark wood cross on the bed, I opened the door to the balcony and stepped outside to do my own praying. I could hear two Greek people talking to each other. The dark sea was covered with white foam as if the waves were fighting themselves. I breathed in the air which carried the smell of ripe olives and white orange blossoms with it. There, beyond the horizon, was Hima my village. There on the opposite shore lived my mother, my friend Noura, my tight-lipped teacher Miss Nailah and . . . and my father. '*Lyeesh? Lyeesh?* Why? Why?' murmured the waves. I held the white railing of the balcony tight. My heart was fluttering in my chest like a slain chicken. They seemed to be so near in the darkness yet so far. 'Keep your mouth shut!' said Miss Nailah. 'Mummy,' she screamed. She was crying for me. 'I command you to Allah's protection, our maker and breaker, daughter,' said my mother. 'I will never hold my head high as long as she is still breathing,' said my father.

I sat in the café without family, past or children like a tree without roots sipping the now cold tea. It was my lunch break and I needed to get some fresh air. The smell of starch and tobacco filled my lungs and clung to the insides of my nose, my clothes and hair, making it more frizzy. At the next table a family were having their lunch: a middle-aged mother with a wrinkle-free face and slim figure; a middle-aged father, who looked as if he were in his early twenties; and two kids, a boy and a girl, who smiled politely at their parents while eating their quiche and salad with knives and forks. 'To the homeless this sense of security was unattainable.' That was another Open University expression I picked up from a TV lecture about family dynamics. Miss Asher had advised me to consolidate my knowledge by using these words and expressions in real-life situations. 'Unattainable,' I repeated after I heard this word in order to memorize it. I went to the counter to ask for more tea. The overworked girl behind the counter asked, 'Do you have any change?'

'Change', I said, 'was unattainable.'

'You what!'

'No change. Very, very sorry.'

My mother watched over me. I held the ripe peach with my hands and stuck my teeth into it. It was red and velvety on the outside and orange on the inside. The juice began dripping down my chin. When I saw the expression on my mother's face, I laughed and continued eating. 'You are like a rabbit, munching, munching all the time.' I shook my ten-year-head and picked another peach. She put the weeds on the ground and whipped my face with the end of her sleeve. 'So hungry for life like a locust, but you must not chew whatever you come across. One day you might chew a snake and it will sting back.'

★

The rattlesnake stuck her fangs into my arms and released her venom, Mother. I sat on the bench in the cathedral close watching the sun go down. A group of children were rolling on the grass; their blond hair shone in the golden glow of the sun. I pressed my hands against my tummy to stop the cramps. It was my third day of taking the medicine, but my mountainous stomach refused to adjust. Soon after we met I opened my heart to Parvin and told her about Mahmoud lurking in the dark wherever I went; she dragged me all the way to the doctor, who prescribed some medicine to help me sleep and make me feel happier. He also gave me some cream for my sores. The mothers of the children were sitting on the grass having a cigarette while watching their children play. Another wave of nausea washed over me. I ran to the bin and threw up.

'She had one too many,' shouted one of them at me.

'Not in front of the children,' said another.

I wiped my mouth, my forehead, and lay down on the grass panting.

Parvin and I walked through the alleyways behind the cathedral close, crossed the busy street, pushed a white wood door open and asked the receptionist for Dr Charles Spenser.

She looked at us holding hands and said, 'Please sit down.' A few minutes later she said, 'Dr Spenser's room is upstairs second left.'

Parvin was reading a glossy magazine when she waved me off.

I walked up the stairs and knocked on the door.

'Come in,' he said in an elegant English accent.

I opened the door, closed it and stood right there in the middle of his office.

He pushed his glasses up and looked at me suspiciously. 'Your name is Miss Sally Asher? How preposterous!'

I nodded my veiled head.

'What can I do for you, Miss Asher?' he said and poised a pen ready to write.

'I ill, doctor. My heart beat. No sleep,' I said and pulled the white scarf back off my hot forehead.

He sat up, released the pen, adjusted his tie and said, 'Any physical symptoms?'

'Sick yes. Arms and legs see.' I stretched out my arms so he could inspect them.

He held my thin dark arm in his fat white hand and inspected the sores. 'It is psoriasis, that's all. A skin condition. Nothing serious,' he said.

'Sweat, heart beat, cannot sleep,' I said.

He dropped my hand and said, 'If your heart is beating then it must be in good condition. That's what hearts are supposed to do.'

'But I ill. Please. Today alive, tomorrow dead, me,' I pleaded.

'I told you there is nothing wrong with you. Please do not waste my time and government money.'

I turned around, held the cold door handle, pushed it down and walked out.

I made sure that I walked neither too slowly nor too quickly for Miss Asher's sake. The promenade was old and run-down, just a path covered with concrete slabs and a low wall. There were a few buildings dotted around and a kiosk selling soft drinks, cigarettes and newspapers in

Cypriot, which I did not understand. Whenever we got a paper in prison we used to have a celebration. We would sweep the floor, mop it and then spread the paper carefully on it. Noura would line her arched eyebrows, put on some lipstick and comb her shiny black hair, Madam Lamaa would tie her pink headscarf properly around her head, making sure that all her grey hair was covered, and I, the youngest and the only inmate who could read, would put on my veil. I would open the paper on the obituary page and read out all the names. '*We announce the death of our beloved mother al-Hajja Amira Rimawi. We belong to Allah and to him we shall return.*'

Madam Lamaa would say, 'If my sister dies they would never tell me. I wouldn't know anything.'

'*Munira al-Hamdan*,' I read and stopped. 'Noura, I told you about Sabha, remember? Her brother shot her during the wedding? Well, this is her mother.'

'It did not take long for her mother to follow her,' said Noura.

The derelict Turkish castle on the Cypriot beach looked dark and grim. 'The Turkish sultan had it built during the days of the Ottoman Empire in sixteen twenty-five,' said Miss Asher. 'Do you want to go in?'

'Yes,' I said.

'Castle,' she said.

'Castle,' I repeated.

The gates were big, made of sturdy carved wood. 'Islamic architecture,' she said. The smell of vegetation filled the air. There was an inner courtyard full of trees and shrubs which had not been pruned for years. A vine tree coiled up a big trellis. Miss Asher pushed her short grey hair away from her glistening forehead and pointed at the guard's small room. When we got there the guard pointed at my veil and said, 'Turkish?'

'No,' said Miss Asher.

'No this,' he said, pointing at my white veil.

'Please,' said Miss Asher.

He waved us in, but he seemed unhappy.

We went up the stairs to the sultan's quarters and walked straight into a big hall, where the sultan used to sit on his throne and hold court. The room was full of velvet chairs, settles and cushions, and a brazier with brass coffee pots stood in the middle of the room. The sultan's tribe must have had many visitors.

It was dark when I finally returned to the hostel. Parvin was pale with worry. 'Where have you been? I looked everywhere for you. You also left your pipe and necklace behind.'

'I went for a walk,' I said.

'Look, I made us some curry,' she said.

'Cannot eat. Everything that goes in comes out,' I said and sat on the bed.

'OK! I will get you some soup,' she said and rushed out.

I lay on the bed listening to the sound of traffic outside. Among the hubbub I could hear a sparrow twittering, the clanking of glass, dogs barking, then the din of the traffic again.

Parvin unlocked the door and rushed in, took off her fleece, put the kettle on and then sat on my bed. 'Potato and celery soup,' she said, 'your favourite.'

She filled a mug with hot water, emptied the packet then stirred. 'You'll love this,' she said, holding the mug under my nose.

'I cannot,' I said.

'You have to eat. You cannot take the pills on an empty stomach.'

I shook my head.

Lying there on the bed I tried to wrap myself with their warmth, their sad voices. I needed a rope to pull me up and suddenly I began hearing their singing.

'*Low, low low lowlali,*' we started singing, our voices bouncing off the stained wall, reaching out to the outside world, which we hadn't seen for years. '*My absence has been long,*' we sang together. Noura stood up, tied a shawl around her wide hips, and began wiggling and swaying to the beat of the metal pot. We raised our voices.

The guard on the evening shift began shouting abuse at us. 'You are all whores! No one cares about you. You are just cheap sluts so why don't you shut up?'

'*Low, low low lowlali,*' we sang together.

'If I shoot one of you your families would thank me,' he shouted.

When Madam Lamaa heard that, she clutched her big breasts, stopped singing and began crying. Noura held her tight and said, 'What does he know? He's just a peasant boy, so uncomfortable in his uniform.'

'A garbage collector with a rose in his lapel,' said Madam Lamaa.

'A monkey leaping about in the dark,' said Noura.

'Outside his cage he looks ridiculous,' Madam Lamaa said.

'The Japanese are coming,' said Max, my boss, one morning and ran his hand over his thinning hair to make sure

that it was gelled into place. He grew the thin strands, and
pulled them all the way up and round his head to cover
his baldness. The wave-like fringe was always slipping
down and he would curse and press it back into place.
'The Sock Shop is back in business, possibly bought by a
Japanese company.' He waved the newspaper at me and
said, 'The Japanese are coming, and they will buy my
trousers off me before I know it.' Every day he expected a
Jap to come and offer him a 'phenomenal' price for his
shop. And what would he say? The answer varied every
day depending on Max's mood. 'Take your filthy foreign
hands − no offence − off my shop and go back home,
eaters of monkey brains.' Max had read somewhere that
monkeys' brains were a delicacy in the Far East, so he
decided that all Asians were snake-, monkey- and donkey-
eaters. Another morning the answer would be different:
'This government is playing ping pong with us. One
day they say we must pay the community charge and we
say they must never introduce the poll tax. If a Jap offers a
million for this dump I will pack up and go to Gibraltar.'

'Why Gibraltar?' I asked.

'It's British, innit?'

Butter, Honey and Coconuts

RUSHING UP THE WHITE THIN STAIRS OF THE LARGE SHIP my heart started beating. A few days before I had visited a small church inland with Miss Asher. The Little Sister who received us was keen to please her. She rushed into words breathlessly, pointing at some old instruments and book-cases. She said that the *Hellena* was a cargo ship, which would take some of the belongings of the convent from Cyprus to Southampton. The captain had granted Miss Asher and 'her daughter' special permission to travel on his vessel. Cypriot families were saying farewell to their sons, tanned English husbands were kissing wives and children goodbye, sailors were pulling ropes and porters were carrying wooden chests and suitcases. I was ashamed of my tears because I felt I should try to look cheerful for Miss Asher's sake, a woman who had saved my life. When I saw tears trickling down other faces, I held the railing tight. Miss Asher was standing on the deck surrounded by boxes and suitcases. I put my colourful bundle on top of the wood trunk. The ship blew its whistle announcing departure.

★

I still would not eat. The stomach cramps were so bad I had to curl up on the ex-army bed for hours. Parvin put the mug of soup on the side table and began rummaging in her rucksack. She produced a small silver cassette player, put it on the table, looked for a socket, then plugged it in. She pulled out a plastic bag full of tapes and selected one, opened the cassette door, slid the cassette in and pressed one of the buttons. Like the aroma of ground coffee music filled the room. The lyrics were so clear and for the first time I was able to understand them. The singer sang in a husky voice about arduous journeys uphill, about heartache and pain. When Parvin joined in I realized that she knew the words by heart. The singer's deep voice and Parvin's sweet voice soared together in the hostel. Parvin pretended to be holding a microphone. 'I screwed up real good.' Her voice was loud and shrill by now. 'But I drink tea and chew biscuits. Drink and chew. Drink and chew. Drink up the soup and chew the bread then screw up agaaaain!'

When she pressed 'stop' I held the now cold mug and began drinking.

On board the *Hellena* Miss Asher slept on the bunk bed and I slept on a mattress on the floor. We also got used to eating cold food and stale bread. The dining room was small and smelly. Crockery, cutlery, napkins and sugar bowls were laid out on the side table. I was not confident about using the cutlery so I ate cheese and bread and drank tea. A nice woman with three daughters would come to the dining room sometimes. Mrs Henderson, who worked as a nurse in a British hospital in Cyprus, was travelling back home to see her family. 'I cannot bear the heat and clear skies any more. I cannot wait to feel the rain on my face,' she said and smiled. She must have noticed my discomfort, so one morning she came to my table while I was chewing the bread and sat down. 'My name is Rebecca, and these are my daughters Margaret and Lucy.'

I looked at them and said, 'Pleased to have met you,' which Miss Asher had taught me in lesson three. Her daughters tackled the food with such ease and confidence.

She said, 'I hope you don't mind me saying this, but why do you eat cheese and bread all the time?'

'I don't know how,' I said, moving my hands as if they were carrying a knife and fork.

'I will teach you,' she said.

From then on she started teaching me table manners and English while her daughters giggled in the background.

'You finally had a shower,' said Parvin one morning. 'You must be feeling better.'

'Yes,' I said and wrapped my hair in the towel.

'We have to look for jobs,' said Parvin, 'but first I must ask you about this scarf you keep wearing.'

'People look at me all time as if disease,' I said.

She sat down next to me on the bed and said, 'It will be much harder to get a job while you insist on wearing it. My friend back home, Ash, was sacked because of his turban although they said that he did not meet his targets.'

'The doctor said too much past,' I said.

'Yes, Salma, too much past,' she said as if talking to herself.

'Too hard though,' I said.

'Yes, I know, I know,' she said.

★

I looked at the dainty padded pink satin shoes hanging in the window display like a crescent. The soft dreams of babies, the pink halos, nursery rhymes and whimpers. Layla was faceless, but three years ago I decided to give her a face. I dressed her up, combed her hair, gave her a bath and kissed her a thousand times goodnight. 'In the film the guy who ran the projector gathered all the kisses that were censored by the priest and put them on one reel. When the boy he used to love so much came back to the town he ran the reel that had all the censored kisses just for him,' said Parvin. Layla would be sound asleep in her pink cot and I would bend down to kiss her. A three-year-old Layla would be chasing the hens and I would run towards her, hold her in my arms and kiss her. Layla would be crying, afraid to go to school for the first time; I would hold her, wipe her tears with my veil and kiss her. Then Layla, a teenage girl, would be telling me about a boy, like Hamdan, she had met on the way to school; I would rub her back then kiss her. 'The young man was in tears, watching all the kisses,' but I walked on back straight, face dry, muscles taut, wrapped up in my raincoat.

On board the *Hellena*, leaning on the railing, I watched dry-eyed the sea churning and surging. The ship was pushing and shoving the grey water around leaving lines of white foam behind. Under the critical gaze of Miss Asher I received Rebecca's gentle instructions about table manners and the English language. This was the small bread plate, this was the main course knife and fork, this was the soup spoon and this was the dessert spoon. I had learnt how to corner the green lettuce, cut it into pieces, shove it in my mouth and eat it unwillingly as if I were full. I had learnt how to butter a piece of bread, hold it with two fingers and eat it with the soup. I had learnt how to be patient and wait for others to start eating and then start after them. I had learnt how to wait for others to stop speaking before I started talking. I had learnt how to start each conversation with a comment about the weather.

'Good morning, Sadiq. The weather is lovely today,' I said.

He pointed his finger at me, jerked his chin sideways and said, 'Salma, Salma, you are becoming a memsahib. Soon you will be English also.'

'Stop being so sarcastic,' I said, holding my shopping bags tight.

'Well, you have even forgotten how to pray to Allah,' he said.

'What about you? Praying all the time and selling alcohol to infidels!'

'Business is business also.'

'So what do you use to keep your hair so shiny?' I asked to change the subject.

'Indian oil called Sexy,' he said and ran his hand over his sleek hair then smiled.

'Give us some then,' I said.

'You know, Salma, I would have taken you as a second wife if you were not so coconut.'

'A second wife, you must be joking,' I said and smiled.

'All we need to do is send my first wife two hundred pounds a month for her and the kids. If you help me with the payments I'll marry you.'

'I am supposed to pay you to get married to you as a second wife? Who do you think you are? Casanova?' I said and smiled again.

'Shoo, shoo, go lick the feet of your English landlady.'

In the evening, around sunset, I would walk outside and climb the nearest stairs to the higher decks to watch the Mediterranean closing in on us from every direction. I would linger on the observation deck watching the sky change its colour from glowing gold, to grim grey, to indigo then luminous black. I would just stand there hugging myself to stay warm. How the colours intermingle, disperse and then shift. It was a change of colour, and the colour of tomorrow would be like the green meadows I saw in a magazine called *Woman's Own*, which I found on one of the chairs on the deck. It had photos of plants and gardens full of colourful flowers. 'Hinglaand sweet. Hinglaand beautiful,' I said to Rebecca.

Pea-green was the colour of the hills. Parvin told me once that the farmers used chemicals to kill the weeds and make the crops look greener than normal. Since then I would look at the green hills from my bedroom window and think of the layers of poison underneath the ground. While looking at the deep green grass of the cathedral, which no doubt had been sprinkled with some fertilizer, I remembered that Liz had asked me to buy her some bread. Projecting the words slowly I said, 'Granary, please,' to the sales girl.

'Say that again?' she said.

'Granary bread,' I said.

'This one.' She pointed at a brown loaf.

I was too embarrassed to say no, the one to the left, so I nodded my head in agreement. I always felt that there was a long queue of old English ladies behind me, huffing and puffing. Of course I was an alien. It must show in the way I pronounced my 'o's, the way I handled the money, the way I was dressed. My thin ankles betrayed me. I moved out of the queue before I had even put the change back in my purse. Elizabeth would crucify me because she had asked me to buy granary bread.

I noticed that after few nights of lectures about Jesus the Saviour and the Holy Trinity, Miss Asher stopped giving her nightly sermon. I would sit politely on the floor of the narrow cabin, hug my knees and listen to Miss Asher reading me stories from the Bible. 'The wife of a man from the company of the prophets cried out to Elisha, "Your servant my husband is dead . . . But now his creditor is coming to take my two boys as his slaves."' I would listen as if listening to Jadaan, our village storyteller, whose stories of travelling to faraway lands and heroism were punctuated by playing the rebab. Whenever the fiddle struck the strings a rich thick sound, like the muffled cries of a woman, filled the yard. Miss Asher would translate some of the words into Arabic and then read the stories in the original English. Although I understood little, I really enjoyed listening to the tunes of a different language. One evening, I said to Miss Asher, as if divulging a great secret, 'I play the reed pipe. Shall I play while you read?'

Miss Asher made sure that the top button of her white frilled collar was in the buttonhole, placed the Bible on the bed and said, 'No. I am reading a sacred text. You must listen carefully and try to learn something.' She crossed herself and began undressing. I turned round and stretched on the mattress on the floor. I could feel the ship swaying here and there and through the small rounded window I could hear the rhythmic swoosh of the water.

I saw him walking down the alleyway to the cathedral close. 'Hello,' I said to Jim.

'Jesus! You startled me,' he said.

I looked at his grey eyes, his waxy complexion, his ponytail and felt that Saturday night was so distant, hidden away in one of the storerooms of his mind. I began fiddling with the strap of my bag.

'I am in a hurry, I am afraid,' he said.

'Yes, of course,' I said. I was nervous and kept shifting my weight from one foot to another. 'A cup of coffee some time?' I asked.

'I am really busy these days. See you around,' he said and hurried down the cobbled alleyway.

I waved a feeble goodbye and walked up the alleyway. I turned round and saw the back of his grey shirt, his long thin arms, his delicate fingers and his sensible shoes disappear around the corner.

Parvin had already told me about the 'see you around'. 'It means I never want to see you ever again, *adiós*, goodbye. Capish?'

I looked at my reflection in the hostel's one and only mirror. I had lost so much weight, my eyes and nose looked larger and my skin looked darker. I was so thin my trousers were slipping down. 'It's a journey, a crossing to adulthood,' said Parvin. 'The Chinese call it the little death that prepares you for the real big bang.' I was ready to go out for a walk. I wore blue jeans, a T-shirt and tied my white veil under my chin tightly. I looked again at my reflection then slowly began untying the knot of my white veil. I slid it off, folded it and placed it on the bed. I pulled my hair out of the elastic band, brushed it and tossed it around. I was so thin that my frizzy dark hair fell over my face almost covering it completely. I looked again at the veil, which my father had asked me to wear and my mother had bought for me, folded on the bed. I rubbed my forehead and walked out. It felt as if my head was covered with raw sores and I had taken off the bandages. I felt as dirty as a whore, with no name or family, a sinner who would never see paradise and drink from its rivers of milk and honey. When a man walked by and looked at my hair my scalp twitched. I sat down on the pavement, held my head and cried and cried for hours.

River Exe split into two branches forming a small island. It was a peaceful space covered with green grass, wild flowers, and on its borders birch, chestnut, oak and rowan trees grew. I sat down on my jacket listening to the water rushing down to the sea, afraid to go home and face Liz. She might ask me about Jim. He said, 'See you around.' And it sounded like: 'You sleep around.' Was I too easy, too available? Maybe I was too dark and foreign with my frizzy hair and sage tea. Was I too stiff and unwelcoming? I might be too inexperienced. My obsession with cleanliness might have put him off. I got a cheese cube and some bread out of the plastic bag, then broke the bread with my hand. I started chewing. I had borrowed *Hidden Greece* from the library so I took it out and began looking at the photos: the vine trees, old houses, cool whitewashed cloisters, women in permanent mourning and cold mountain springs.

★

Margaret, Rebecca's eldest daughter, began seeking me out on the ship. She would sing her salaam, which I taught her, and hold my hand urging me to take her to the deck and play her some music. I would blow her name into the pipe: 'M-a-r-g-a-r-e-t'. She would laugh, swinging her golden braids. I learnt more English from her than all the afternoon lessons with Miss Asher. 'Not "woord", "world".'

While playing one morning, a tall, graceful man walked straight towards me stretching out his hand. 'My name is Mahoney, and I am the pastor on this ship. I've listened to you play the pipe several times and wanted to introduce myself.'

I often wondered who this graceful man, always looking at the sea, was. 'I am Salma and here is my friend Margaret.'

He raised his eyebrow quizzically. Margaret was eleven and I was twenty-five. 'Pleased to meet you.' He shook her hand.

'Where do you come from?' he asked.

I did not know what to say, but Miss Asher had taught me to say that I was her daughter. 'Hinglish,' I said.

'I am Irish,' he said.

'Where?'

'Across the sea, silly,' said Margaret.

He looked at my face too intently. I felt hot under my white veil so I held Margaret's hand and said, 'You're late for bed.'

We waved goodbye and rushed down the stairs.

Miss Asher closed the New Testament and said, 'You came back early, you two.'

★

I sat with my cup of tea watching a show on television. The presenter was wearing a glittering green suit and must have changed her hair colour; it was warm brown this time. I sipped the cold tea and watched long-lost families being united courtesy of the show. Amanda's baby sister Molly was lost during the war, and it turned out that she was adopted by an Australian couple, and was now living in Sydney. Ten years ago she began looking for her sister. The presenter smiled and said, 'Amanda, your baby sister Molly is here with us today. COME ON, Molly!' Amanda and Molly looked at each other incredulously, ran towards each other then hugged. I switched off the TV and looked at the damp walls, the small table, the Indian mirror and the dark window. Before closing the curtains I noticed that a dark shadow was standing by the railway track. No one was allowed to get near the track. I shut the curtains and switched on the light. Water was dripping from the electric bulb onto the duvet. I tied a pillow case around the cable and rushed downstairs to tell Liz.

Liz was dozing off on the sofa with a letter in her hand. Her diary lay on the floor. On the dirty carpet I could see an empty bottle of wine and a glass. 'Liz,' I said and shook her shoulder.

She opened her eyes and said, '*Kaise* no?'

'Liz, wake up!'

She rubbed her eyes and said, 'Where am I?'

'In your home in Exeter,' I said.

She sat up and began crying. 'I haven't got my reading glasses on. Please read me this letter.' Her tongue slurred over the words. She was drunk and tired.

I began reading: '*Darling, I called you Upah because of your white luminous skin that shone in the moonlight. I wanted to celebrate you, worship you, treasure you.'*

'Stop,' she said and snatched the letter. 'What do you think you're doing? What, at this hour?' Liz's face was covered with sweat, the red veins under her skin filled up with blood.

'Let me help you up the stairs and tuck you into bed,' I said.

'No, I am perfectly capable of taking care of myself,' she said while holding my arm tight.

I pulled her up, put her arm around my shoulders and helped her up the stairs. Entering her bedroom felt like trespassing into a forbidden territory. It was a mess: ruffled sheets, dirty clothes scattered on the floor, some cold pizza on a plate and dark stains on the beige carpet, where wine had been spilt. It smelt of dust, lavender soap and denture cleanser. The large 'Victorian Mercer king bed I inherited from my grandfather' was exquisite. It was made of silver metal with a brown finish; the head- and footboards had large medallions, cast in the shape of the letters V, R and I, 'Viceroy to India', which were accented by smaller half-circle castings with flowerlike decorations at the end. On the antique bedside table I could see a bundle of letters tied up with a rubber band in an open crimson satin box. Liz caught my eye and put the lid back. 'That'll be all. Thank you,' she said.

She took her dentures out and placed them in the glass on the bedside table, untied her hair and, fully clothed, eased herself under the white frilled duvet covered with yellow and red stains. Still holding the letter she switched off the dusty old bedside lamp.

★

The next morning I looked through my window at the green hills dotted with white sheep and black cows. It was a sunny day and the river, which I could see beyond the old rail carriages, was sparkling silver. Was she out there? I rushed down the cold stairs to the kitchen and made myself some real coffee to get myself going. I had some cereal, drank some water and got dressed. I realized that I was losing weight again. The tight blue jeans, which I had not worn for months, fitted me perfectly. Mondays were the hardest because of Max's foul mood so I sprayed myself once again with deodorant. I put my fleece, *Understanding Poetry* and my pipe in my large bag. Today I would insist on having a lunch break so I could read a bit. I pulled down my T-shirt, laced up my trainers and took the tuna sandwich wrapped up in clingfilm out of the fridge and stuck it in the bag together with the coffee thermos. I opened the front door and filled my nostrils with morning air.

'Good morning, Salma,' said Postman Jack.

'Finally you got my name right,' I said and smiled.

'I am not the sharpest tool in the box,' he said and winked at me.

It must be mid morning in Hima by now. My mother would be walking through the hills piling up kindling and long dry sticks, then tying them to her back. I would get up, open the window and listen to the cock's crow and the cooing of pigeons. My mother told me once that what the pigeons were really saying was, 'Glory be to Allah!' I rushed to the well, got some water then washed my face. The coal in the brazier was lit and Mother was kneading the dough with her rough, swollen fingers.

'Good morning, Mother,' I said and kissed her forehead. She smiled and handed me her first loaf, dripping with honey and butter. I ate it while watching her flinging the dough up in the air until the large thin loaf covered the whole of her outstretched arms. She would throw it on the hot iron tin placed carefully on the outside fire. It would start sizzling immediately then it would puff up like a round brown moon filling the chilly morning air with its aroma.

I spent weeks chewing at dry bread, drinking soup, taking pills and listening to Parvin's tapes. I went through them one by one: 'Relax', 'Like A Virgin', 'Sexual Healing', 'Rock The Casbah', 'Rock With You'. I wrote down the lyrics, looked up some words in the dictionary, played the cassette again, then memorized the songs.

Parvin walked in on me while singing. 'Get the lyrics right, Salma!' She put the shopping bag on the table and said, 'No luck!'

I sat down on the bed exhausted and said, 'Relax, something will come up.'

'We must change strategy. How about you? What can you do?'

'Can farm, take the sheep to grass, take care of horses and cows.'

She pushed her straight fringe back and said, 'Countryside kind of skills.' Then she looked at me and said, 'That white dress you keep under your pillow. Who made it?'

'How did you see? Search the room when me out?'

'No, I was stripping the bed to take the linen to the laundry, stupid.'

'Did you like dress?'

'Yes, it's so beautiful.'

'I no stupid, I made. Never say stupid.'

She held my hands and said, 'I am so sorry. I was joking. I was not serious.'

'I no stupid, I family, I tribe.'

'I am sorry.'

'I no stupid, I think God.'

Completely mute and on hunger strike, I thought, while looking at the reflection of the moonlight on the barred window, about God. The night guard greeted Officer Salim, the prison governor, and shut the gate behind his speeding car. I could hear the clank of the main gate being pushed shut for the night. Ants were tiny insects crawling on this earth looking for food and shelter. They were defenceless against floods, the hot sun, famines and each other. They were exposed to the elements. We were exposed to the elements like an open wound. They put us in prison, took away our children, killed us and we were supposed to say God was only testing his true believers. But this heart, this blood-red heart, which was too hungry to beat regularly, belonged to me for I was the one who was starving it.

The *Hellena* stopped for a few hours in the French city of Marseilles. The old port was bustling with people and goods. I watched passengers rush down the gangway to meet their loved ones and could hear the cries of happiness of families being reunited: hugs and kisses and a rush of French and English words. I pulled down my white T-shirt to cover my hips, fixed my veil, put on a brave face and held the railing tight while France was receding. The seaside café with blue and green parasols was getting smaller and smaller. I joined Miss Asher on the sun deck.

Her blue eyes looked tired when she said, 'Child, I must speak to you.' I sat on one of the white chairs and prepared myself for one of her lectures. The sun was going down slowly, setting fire to the sea. 'I have noticed that you don't think about religion at all. Look around you. This vast sea must have been created by a great force.'

I looked at the sea, the wave crests breaking, the sun sinking and said, 'I have never thought about God before.'

Later in the cabin, looking out of the rounded window, my pipe dangling between my breasts together with my mother's letter and her lock of hair, I felt better. When on deck there was something in the way affluent foreign people converse and sip coffee, the openness of the view and the brightness of the sea that hurt your eyes. In the cabin, the view – small and framed – was tolerable. 'May Allah bring a good end,' my mother had said. I saw her open face, ever-smiling eyes and heard the smack of the disapproving lips. I could smell the powder of cardamom pods which had clung to her headband while grinding coffee beans in the mortar. She would run her fingers over my face, rough from weeding, reaping and grinding in querns.

At around eleven o'clock in the morning Max calmed down about the Japanese and began working while having a long chat with a customer on the phone, sucking at his cigarette. When the yellow nicotine started dripping down the window panes I knew that the boss was in a good mood and ready to talk.

I placed the silk mauve skirt on the chair and walked

towards Max. I must ask him for a rise 'that in real terms was in accordance with inflation'. Ten per cent I thought, not bothering to calculate how much a month. 'Max, I've got to talk to you.'

He pushed his metal glasses up his nose then said, 'Not now. Pass me the iron, will you?'

I picked up the steam iron and gave it to Max.

Max had always been kind to me. He offered me employment when no one did, he gave me Christmas presents and cards and helped me make skirts and trousers for myself. He also knew when I was going through one of my long silences and started telling me jokes in Pakistani pidgin English. 'Is your wife dirty? My wife is dirty too.' I did not know whether to laugh or cry at his jokes. I would compose myself and say, 'We better do some work or our customers will start complaining.'

'Max, I must talk to you now.'

'What is so urgent?'

I pulled my stomach in, took a deep breath and said in a quivering voice, 'I want a rise.'

'What? Say that again.'

'I want a rise, Max,' I pleaded.

He pressed the steam iron on the grey collar, spat all the needles on the floor and said, 'With the way things are I cannot give you a rise.'

'Business is good.'

'Yes, but there is a cash-flow problem.'

'But you always ask for cash, you never take cheques with tax and all.'

'Look, Salma, there are many young English kids out there without a job. They would jump at the chance. Count your blessings, darling.'

I walked back to my chair, placed the mauve silk skirt on my lap and continued stitching the hem. I should really count my blessings. Four years of work and no rise. Five hundred pounds a month. Rent has risen to forty-five pounds a week plus bills. About sixty pounds a month for rates, which together with other taxes added up to four hundred a month. Then I am left with one hundred to eat, pay for transport, buy books and pay university fees. If Max gave me fifty pounds more things would be much easier. I realized that I had stopped stitching and was gazing at my shoelaces which were getting longer and longer. Either my feet were getting thinner or the shoelaces were stretching.

Max was busy talking to his wife on the phone. 'Darling, I put the money on the kitchen table before I left.' He pulled the measuring tape tight around his neck. 'Who borrowed it? The dog?' I noticed that the mauve skirt had some wet spots on it. I was horrified. I vowed once never to cry in public. I rushed down the stairs to the toilet, put the lid down, pulled the flush handle and sat down face in hands like an unwise monkey. The sound of rushing and gurgling water refilling the tank filled the hollow cold space of the toilet. I rocked myself back to normality again, then washed my hands and face with cold water, tied my hair with a rubber band, took a deep breath and rushed up the stairs. I must look for an evening job.

I closed my eyes and imagined my mother's chipped hand running on my face and erasing my anger and fear like a rubber. 'It's a girl,' announced the dayah and spat on the floor. She did not expect a large tip delivering a baby girl. 'The burden of girls is from cot to coffin,' said my father.

My mother told me that she had forgotten all the pain of labour when they told her it was a girl. She said that when she looked at my swollen closed eyes open for the first time her heart had never been the same. She sat me down, untied my braid, poured some olive oil in her hands, rubbed it and combed it through my hair. 'In the name of Allah, the compassionate, the merciful,' she said and poured the cold water over my head, then rubbed my hair with soap, trying to create a lather. She washed behind my ears, under my arms, between my legs and buttocks. 'Your bath is cold, your bath is cooling, sheikh,' she sang. 'I purify you from minor and major sins,' she said and poured more water over my head then dried me with a piece of linen that my father had given her as a wedding present.

When I got dressed my father called, 'Salma, *na'iman*. Where is the bath kiss?' I kissed his hand then he held me up and put me down in his warm lap.

'My lunch break's mine and I'll do whatever,' I said hastily to Max. He sucked his cigarette and said nothing. That was a definite yes. I put my bag on my shoulders and left the shop, rushing down to the cathedral close. The sky was overcast, the sun nowhere to be seen and fog filled the air. A café in the middle of nowhere with some white tables and chairs on the pavement, without sunshine, overlooking no busy street, pretended to be a continental hotspot. It was nothing like the receding French café I saw in the harbour at Marseilles. Many professional men, in their grey or blue suits (which were definitely not made in our shop), with their newspapers and lunches, walked towards the close. Those with money go to the hotel bar and those without head straight to the lawn, sit on the grass and start munching their tuna sandwiches. A man in a black dinner jacket with tails was tap dancing to an old song.

> If I look back what do I see?
> Green trees and fresh meadows
> If I look forward what do I see?
> Falling leaves trembling in the wind
> If I look at you what do I see?
> I see the man I used to be

Old ladies looked wistfully at him and giggled when he did a difficult jump.

Parvin asked the porter of the hostel for something called the Yellow Pages and he gave her a big thick yellow book. She flicked through it looking for tailors and alterations. She began reading: 'Kings; Lord's Tailors, Exeter; Make and Mend; May, Donald; Whipple, J. & Co. Ltd, Complete Alteration Service. Lord's is at the other end of the high street. What do you think, Salma?'

I shrugged my shoulders. The pills made it all seem easier. 'Why not?' I said, 'but you have to come with me.'

'Of course, tomorrow morning sharpish,' she said and smiled.

I could see the tip of an old oak tree in the distance, wet and gleaming in the feeble sunlight. I wondered how everything grows so much without the heat of the sun. It must be the water and the fertilizing poison Parvin told me about. The Yellow Pages was left open at tailors on the table. The room was clean and tidy but the musty smell lingered. The duvet cover I bought with the few pounds Minister Mahoney (who spent his time visiting immigrants in prisons) had given me was purple with flowers drawn in silver paint on the edges. Parvin's was a myriad of orange and gold streaks. She began crying at night again and because she did not show me her tears I could not tell her how green the meadows were when the sun shone on them, how white were the clouds and how vast was the blue sky. I could not play 'Rock The Casbah' on my pipe for her. I could not run my fingers on her face. I just lay there under the duvet listening to her muffled sobs.

Crossing an unknown river far from your domain, observe the surface turbulence, and note the clarity of the water. Heed the demeanour of the horses. Beware of massed ambush.

At a familiar ford near home, look deep into the shadows on the far bank, and watch the movement of the tall grass. Listen to the breathing of your nearest companions. Beware of the lone assassin.

I continued reading, 'This piece by Suzume No-Kumo is an example of Japanese poetry, which is normally short and concise focusing on a few images.'

My lunch break was over so I drank up the cold coffee, secured the flask lid and put the clingfilm in the bin, stuck my book in the bag and walked back to work. When I listened to Hamdan's breathing I was not heeding his demeanour so I was betrayed and ambushed. As for the lone assassin, he followed me back to work. His leather sandals worn out, his feet covered with desert dust, his yellow toenails long, chipped and lined with grime and his rifle slung on his right shoulder, he kept pace with me until I arrived at Lord's Tailors.

English Tea

THE HILLS WERE DARK APART FROM THE DISTANT LIGHTS
of the mill and I could make out the silhouette of the
cows huddled together on the hillside. The river was
gliding quietly now and the trains were less frequent.
Everything was asleep, apart from the odd car. The *Hellena*
glided gently into a brightly lit land called the port of
Southampton. England looked like a tree of light. Miss
Asher laughed, fixed her collar and pulled her cardigan
over her ample breasts. Metal columns with cargo tied to
them were being lifted right, left and centre. Men in small
cars were carrying boxes from one place to another. Piles
of wood, boxes and machines were waiting to be loaded.
I felt that I had landed on another planet, where men were
working like machines and where giant lifts filled the sky.
I held Miss Asher's hand. She smiled and said, 'Soon we
will be out of here.' She was wrong. She spent a whole
night in the harbour and went in the morning to get some
help, and I spent two months in the port prison.

Walking on the iron bridge, I could see the cathedral and
the green meadows of Devon in the distance. Honestly, a

postcard. Although I didn't have their addresses, I kept sending letters and cards to Layla and Noura. An old Arab postman might feel sorry for me, and go on a mission to find them. The other day I sent Noura a postcard telling her about my new rented room in Swan Cottage, my lovely boss, and described to her the cows on the hills which I could see through my window. 'From cows to cows,' I could hear her distant voice say. What I did not tell her is that I earned so little that I ended up with nothing at the end of the month, that Jim did not want to have anything to do with me ever again, that I was still living on my own and that the railway line was about a hundred yards from my bedroom, which rattled with every train arriving or departing from the station.

It was cold but bright when Parvin and I walked to the tailor's shop. It had a sign on the door listing the charges for alterations and mending. When we opened the glass door an invisible bell rang. It sounded like the small brass bell Miss Nailah used to strike to announce the beginning and end of the school day. A bulky man in a striped navy suit, gold glasses and thinning hair came down the narrow stairs behind the reception. 'Good morning, ladies,' he said while holding pins in his mouth.

'Good morning,' said Parvin.

'What can I do for you?' he asked while sticking the pins in the sponge pincushion.

I began shifting my weight from one leg to another, while trying to maintain a smile on my face.

'My friend Salma is a seamstress and she is looking for a job,' said Parvin hurriedly.

'So you are not customers,' he said and pushed his glasses up his nose.

'No, but good worker me,' I said and smiled.

'She cannot speak English, for Christ's sake!' he said.

'Her English is irrelevant. She will be making, altering and mending clothes,' Parvin said and pulled the white dress out of the plastic bag and put it on the reception counter.

He held it with both hands, lowered his glasses, examined the pockets and the sleeves, then gave it back quickly. 'No vacancies.'

'Why don't you try her for a month without payment? See for yourself.'

I noticed that his trousers were too loose around the knees with turn-ups that were too wide.

'You are wasting my time, miss,' he said.

She stuck the white dress back in the bag and said, 'It's because we are black, isn't it? Because she is not an English rose,' she said.

His face was covered with red patches when he said, 'Get out of my shop!'

'Racist, sexist pig,' she said.

The immigration officer at Southampton port detention centre kept asking, 'What is your Christian name?'

I looked at him puzzled. 'Me Muslim,' I said. He ran his fingers around his stiff collar as if trying to loosen it. Other passengers whizzed through the immigration control counters with a smile on their faces.

'Name?' he said

'Yes. Salma Ibrahim.' I nodded my head to show him that I understood his question.

Miss Asher interrupted quickly and said that my name was Sally Asher. There was a quick interchange of words in English and showing of papers. She mentioned the word 'adoption', which she had taught me. The officer slammed his book shut, phoned someone and a policeman appeared through the sliding glass doors. I was standing there fingering the plastic plants. The policeman pushed me to one side, searched me quickly and handcuffed me. I felt the coldness of the metal cuffs encircling my wrists. Miss Asher looked at me reassuringly, but I could see that she was distressed. 'Don't worry,' she said while I was dragged through the glass doors. They ushered me through a narrow well-lit corridor and then unlocked a heavy door. They asked me to go in, unlocked the handcuffs then shut the door and locked it. The room was small but clean, with a single bed right in the corner. I sat down and waited for Miss Asher to knock on the door. There were no windows to be seen and the invisible fan whirred all night. Hours later I stretched out on the bed and tried to wrap the whole of my body with the blanket, but it was too short and my uncovered feet were frozen. There was a huge difference between the port prison and the prison room I had left behind: this room was spotless, it did not smell of urine, the walls were covered with gleaming metal sheets, it had no barred windows, it was really quiet except for the whirr of the fan, but I was in solitary.

Max gave me two sleeves to stitch before closing to claw back the hour I spent over lunch. I took the pair of loose sleeves and sewed them lightly and neatly, put them on the table, took my things and rushed out while Max was on the phone. It was a good half-hour delay. I went to the Royal Hotel and walked through the old thick doors to the reception. A middle-aged man rushed towards me and said, 'May I help you?'

It sounded like 'May I throw you out?' to my sensitive ears. 'Yes, please, I would like to see the bar manager.'

'This way.' I was ushered quickly out of the thickly carpeted entrance to a small, untidy room. 'He won't be a moment.'

Another middle-aged man, his hair oiled and combed back, gave me another mechanical smile which reminded me of the Fred impostor tap dancing for the old ladies. 'May I help you?' he said in a perfect English accent.

My chin began quivering and with difficulty I said, 'My name is Salma.'

'Yes?'

'I am looking for evening job.'

'Are you registered with a job agency, the job centre?' he asked.

I shook my head.

He was about to dismiss me, then he changed his mind. 'You don't sound English.'

'I am British of Arab origins.'

'Aha!'

Egged on by the images of *Hidden Greece*, where I could stand on a high cliff and probably see my homeland, I tried again. 'I work in a tailor's shop; I just need the extra cash, that's all.'

'Right,' he said and smoothed his slick hair.

I smiled, stretching my wide mouth to the limit.

He picked up a cigar, tapped it on the dark table and said, 'You will just collect and wash glasses between seven and eleven-thirty on Friday, Saturday, and possibly Thursday nights.'

'Thank you. Thank you very, very much,' I said and stood up, ready to rush out of the door before he changed his mind.

'Wear something decent,' he said, 'a white shirt and a black skirt.'

'No problem,' I said.

'I will see you on Friday,' he said and then lit the cigar.

When I walked out of the hotel my burning face was hit by a gentle cold breeze. She was out there whimpering, crying, looking for a foothold. I knew that wind. A sudden chill ran through me so I bent forward as if winded and hugged my erect nipples. The muscles where my ribs meet between my breasts were inflated then collapsed as if I had sunk inwards. Before I had the chance to look at her face she was taken away by the warden to one of the homes for illegitimate children. I lay on the floor bleeding like a lamb slaughtered for the grand Eid festival. Noura, Madam Lamaa, Naima and others held me down and poured cold water over my head to force me to breathe. They began praying and washing my body. 'May Allah have mercy on Salma! Alleviate her distress, God, lighten her load, widen her chest! Bless her with the gift of forgetfulness!' they chanted together. They rubbed my hair, my shoulders, my arms, my back, my legs with soap until I was covered with white lather. 'Damn your prayers, she is still not breathing.' When I was two breaths away from death, I heard a shot in the distance. Another girl, who had been released by the prison authorities, was shot dead by her young brother. I opened my mouth and inhaled, straining my lungs.

I went to Gwen's straight away and knocked on her door.

I could hear the shuffling of her feet on the floor. 'Who is it?' she asked.

'It's me, Salma, open the door.'

She slid the chain open and said, 'Oh! Hello, Salma!'

I held her tight and waltzed her through the dark corridor.

'What's happened to you?' she asked.

'Oh sorry, Gwen, I forgot about your arthritis. I got a part-time job at the Royal.'

'Doing what exactly?' she said.

'Collecting and washing empty glasses.'

'That's all right as long as it remains that way,' she said and put the kettle on.

'Gwen, I want to have a holiday, I want to go to Greece and have a look across the Mediterranean.'

'I thought you gave up on that dream a long time ago,' she said and sat down. On the kitchen table there were an open can of baked beans, two slices of toasted bread and a cup of tea.

'I must have interrupted your dinner. I am sorry.'

'It's all right, I never heat up the beans. Make yourself a cuppa, will you?'

I made myself a cup of tea and sat down. 'You know English people. Dos and don'ts, please.'

'You must wear decent clothes, but try to look classy, never wear tight short skirts, don't talk to customers and be as unobtrusive as possible. Don't tell Max. And I hope to God that you will not break any glasses on your first day.'

An old album full of black-and-white photos was open on the table.

'Have a look!' she said.

I turned the album round and looked at snaps of Gwen's memories. Pointing at a fading photo of a well-kempt man she said, 'My father. He was a great man.' A tall and thin man with intelligent eyes stood by an aeroplane.

I drank up my tea, kissed her on the cheek and rushed out.

When I got out of Gwen's house I saw Elizabeth walking stealthily across the street to the off-licence as if she were being followed.

'Hello, Liz,' I shouted.

'You have been to Gwen's?' she said.

'Yes?' I answered.

'The riff-raff stick together,' she said and almost stumbled trying to get up the pavement.

It was seven o'clock and Liz was already drunk. She staggered into the shop and through the glass I could see that she was welcomed by Sadiq's dextrous smile.

After a sleepless night in the port detention centre I was ushered out again to an office full of flickering screens and bleeping machinery. The immigration officer behind the desk looked so white and tired. His eyes were swollen and red; his starched collar dirty and his oily hair stuck to his head. He kept his hands clasped together and his back straight while observing me trying to sit up after the cold sleepless night.

'Salma, why have you come to Britain?'

I did not understand 'have you come'. So I nodded.

'Are you seeking political asylum?'

I tried to remember what Miss Asher had instructed me to say. All the trivial 'good morning's and 'enjoy your meal' were readily available, but I could not recall the exact word she had asked me to use. 'Adapted,' I finally said.

'Adopted?' he said while flicking through reams of paper.

'Yes. Yes. Adopted, Miss Asher.'

Looking at the blue lights reflected on the barred window, Noura said that it all started in a small kebab shop where she used to watch the dying lights of the capital while washing dishes all night long. The owner ordered her to use kerosene and lemon to get rid of the fat clinging to the utensils. Enveloped in a cloud of kerosene and lemon she used to spend her nights watching snatches of sky between the old dusty houses. When the first thread of light brightened the sky, she would fold her apron and wash her hands ready to go home. She must go back quickly to take Rima and Rami to school. There were no buses at that time of the morning so she had to run the three miles back to her house.

Dear Noura,

Seventeen years ago, we met in prison. You were charged with prostitution and I was accused of having sex out of wedlock. Do you remember me? You went on hunger strike and were force-fed. You smiled when I stopped mine. You also gave me your mother-of-pearl combs and a bottle of perfume. I still have them. I put them together with her lock of hair and my mother's letter in a small Chinese silk box. Your daughter must be twenty-four by now and your son twenty-six. My Layla is sixteen. In two years' time she will start university. She decided to do medicine and I said why not? I hope,

Noura, that life is being kind to you after all these years and that your children are taking good care of you so you do not have to hustle any more. One of these days we shall meet.
    Love,
    Salma

I licked the envelope with my tongue, sealed it then wrote the only address I had for Noura: the old country. Before having my dinner, I walked to the post box and posted the letter. When the blue aerogramme air-mail envelope was swallowed by the gaping red mouth of the post box my hands stopped shaking. I could go and have my dinner now.

In the early evening the cottage was cold and dark. I went to my bedroom and switched on the television. London's *EastEnders* were at it again, having fights with their parents, wives, friends, sleeping with their sisters' husbands and then making up as if nothing had happened. The evening spread itself long and thin to the end of the horizon, where I could see cows sleeping in the open meadows. The days were getting longer so a dark blue glow never left the sky, lighting up its edges with a dying flame. While eating my dinner, pasta with a tomato and garlic sauce, I watched TV. It was a holiday programme about a Greek island. Will I ever set my eyes on hidden Greece? I got really excited thinking about taking the plane for the first time in my life. 'I am flying to Spain on Sunday' was what Max said once a year when he was about to take his family to Ibiza. I would do my evening job properly. I would wear my classiest dress, keep my mouth shut, put little make-up on, tie my frizzy hair tight, and if I spoke I would speak slowly and carefully in order to sound as English as possible. I would say, 'Have you finished with this, sir? Thank you very, very much, sir.'

I told Max about Parvin's job interview so he agreed to give me the afternoon off. She had applied for tens of jobs without any luck. I said to her maybe she needed to smarten up and I opened the large plastic bag. 'A suit for you! Max gave me some leftover material and I make for you. Took your size from dirty clothes.'

She was reading the newspaper so she blew up at her fringe, looked up at me then down at the paper. Her hair was dull, her skin dry, her nails without varnish, her back bent.

'I took time off for your interview. Please, Parvin, let me come with you this afternoon.'

She finally stopped reading and said, 'I need to get ready.'

'Me help.'

She went out to have a shower in the communal bathroom and I plugged in the cassette recorder and pressed 'play'. Music filled the room. The band sang of watching over each other and broken promises.

She came back to the room in her pyjamas, her hair wrapped up in a towel. I sat her down and unzipped her pink make-up bag and put it on the bed next to her. She got a cream jar out, put it back in, then got it out again and began rubbing cream on her face. I made her a cup of coffee and began tidying up the room.

She looked at me and said, 'This song is before Sting had left Police.'

'Left the police force,' I said.

'No, Police the band,' she said and smiled.

★

The London train punctuated my life whenever it passed through the valley reminding me of what lay ahead at the end of the line. It was a spacious railway station with a stall selling flowers and a small café. When feeling tired I would go to the station and sit still in the café listening to the sounds of arrivals and departures. A black man was mopping the dull floor rhythmically then plunging the mop in the bucket full of water and bleach. The sound of loudspeakers telling us what to do and where to go was soothing. I would sip my tea and listen to the flapping of pigeons' wings caught up in the mesh lining the roof, the hellos and bye-byes of passengers, the guard's whistle and the shunting of trains. In the station, where passengers, families and friends were waiting, I felt at home. The post box in the far corner was the beginning of a thread connecting me to my loved ones overseas. The noise of the crowd, shunting and the whistles managed to frighten off the ghosts that stalked me. In transit or public spaces like receptions, lobbies or waiting rooms I felt happy, suspended between now and tomorrow.

When I heard the whiz of the bullet speeding towards the head of one of the released inmates and her heart-wrenching cry, 'Oh! Ya Allah!' I decided to stop seeking death. I dried my face and said to the dirty walls, 'Layla, I will call her Layla.' I took my reed pipe out of the bundle and began playing a reaping season tune. Salma, with tender hands and feet, gave birth to Layla, on a mild and luminous night. From then on I did not speak or have a whiff of sleep. I would just sit in the dark prison room, leaning on the wall and watching the sky through the high barred window. If it had some sheen on it I knew that it was the fifteenth of the Arab month, when women turn into ghouls and eat travellers; when my period began and I would start looking for clean pieces of cloth. I remained curled up in the dark until the inmates forgot that I was there wide awake and sore. One night I overheard Noura saying to Madam Lamaa, 'Do you think she will ever forgive me?'

'Your intentions were good,' Madam Lamaa said.

'But both options were as bitter as colocynth.'

'She will get used to the taste,' Madam Lamaa said.

'I thought if the lips of her baby touched her nipples she would never be able to forget her. If she suckled her for a year she might not have been able to let her go,' said Noura.

'But she would have enjoyed nursing her baby for a while,' said Madam Lamaa.

'May Allah forgive me, I paid Naima to take her away instantly.'

I stood up and hurled myself at Noura.

'What seems to be the problem?' said the plastic surgeon. After I moved in with Liz I went to the doctor to get an appointment with a specialist. It took five months to get the appointment and all that waiting tied up my tongue. He pulled his silver pen out of the pocket of his white coat and twisted it open. 'What is your name?'

'Salma El-Musa,' I said.

He switched on the desk lamp and said, 'What can I do for you?'

I hugged my breasts.

'Do you want a breast reduction?' he said.

Whenever I was under pressure my English would recede. 'No, nibbles reduction,' I said.

'You mean nipple reduction,' he said and waved to the nurse to stand beside him. 'Let me have a look!'

I unbuttoned my shirt, but kept it on, unhooked my bra, pulled the straps through the sleeve of the shirt until the bra was released. My nipples stood dark, erect and long in the middle of a circle of long black tufts of hair.

He pointed the lamp at my breasts and touched my nipples with his cold finger then measured them. He looked at the nurse and then looked at me and said, 'There is nothing wrong with your nipples. One and a half centimetres is longer than average, but they seem normal to me.'

'I want them reduced, cut out, doctor, please,' I said in a trembling voice.

'Why?' he asked pointing the lamp at my face.

'You cannot see other women's nibbles. Me always dark and out. Slice them. Better that way,' I said with eyes brimming with tears.

Speaking to the nurse, he said, 'I want her referred immediately for psychiatric treatment,' and switched off the lamp.

I buttoned up my shirt before hooking my bra and pulling the straps into place. When I looked up the nurse and the doctor were looking at me intently.

'Me no mad,' I said while trying to manipulate my bra up to cover my breasts.

The next day I did everything Max had passed on to me quickly and quietly to save my energy for the next job. It was difficult because Max was in a talkative mood. He was

full of praise for an old Rolls-Royce he saw in the park-
ing place. 'Oh! Our fathers and forefathers were more
skilful. If you look inside that car you won't be able to see
a trace of a stitch and there is a box for the cloth and shoe
brushes all neatly tucked under a panel. Oh! We used to be
lords and masters. Just look at us now. Look at us.'

'You used to rule the world,' I said imitating Parvin.

'Yes, the sun never set on the British Empire,' he said,
pinning the hem of some trousers at the correct length.

'Parvin said you ruled over palm, pine and coconut,' I
said.

'Yes, coconuts like you,' he said and sniggered.

'I no coconut,' I said.

'We rule over ivy-ridden buildings and white elephants
now.'

In Minister Mahoney's company I never felt foreign. I
remembered him with his small glasses, wide smile, his
funny tales and limitless compassion. Although he was a
man of religion he was so kind and understanding. He said
that I looked like a frightened puppy that morning and I
smiled.

'Dark puppy,' I said.

'Yes, there are some dark puppies around.' He held my
cold hand and said, 'Don't you worry. We will get you out
of this detention centre soon.' I pulled my hand away and
thanked him. Later on I learnt that Miss Asher, the Little
Sisters and Minister Mahoney the Quaker took the British
government to court on my behalf. My adoption papers
were in order but the immigration authorities questioned
their authenticity. Miss Asher told me that Minister
Mahoney argued my case beautifully and gave me the

script of his speech. I looked up the words in the *Oxford English–Arabic Dictionary* and read them and reread them until they began to make sense. 'Even if you want to question the adoption, which is ridiculous in itself, she should be given the right of political, social or religious asylum – whatever you want to call it. Yes, you would create a precedent, but hundreds, nay thousands of women are killed every year. You must give her shelter because if you send her back she will be shot on sight.'

I rushed to the public toilets and changed into a long black skirt, a white frilled shirt and flat shoes. I tied my hair and coiled it into a bun, then put on some light make-up. I looked like my old self, the shepherdess from Hima. The only difference was the wrinkles, as if a cock had stamped on my face on its way to its cage leaving a web of lines behind. I treated myself to a cheeseburger and a large Coke, thought about the evening job, psyched myself up, as Parvin would say, and walked to the hotel. I gathered some courage and opened the old heavy door. The receptionist gave me one of her mechanical smiles and said, 'You need to see Mr Wright, the bar manager.' I nodded. 'Next time use the side door to the bar.' She opened a door to an old dusty office, full of wine boxes, plastic glasses, mats, and there in the middle of it all sat Mr Wright, oiled and groomed, wearing a spotless black suit and a bowtie. He was speaking on the phone like the old aristocrat in the television ad who ordered Persian carpets to be flown in from the end of the earth. Mr Wright looked like an old gentleman's butler but behaved as if he were not in service. He put the receiver down and looked at me, standing in the middle of the small office and gripping the handles of my cheap black bag. His grey eyes shot an arrow of disapproval at me.

'Good evening, Salma,' he said slowly, careful not to mispronounce my name.

'Good evening, Mr Wright,' I said.

'Call me Allan, please.' With both hands he pressed his gelled hair into place, rubbed his nose and said, 'You are early today. Go and dust the glasses and bottles in the bar. I will pay you cash, three pounds an hour.'

'Thank you,' I said and almost stumbled out.

A sea of bottles and glasses extended in front of me. I put on the rubber gloves he gave me and began wiping the glasses. 'Don't wear them when you collect the glasses, just behind the counter please,' he said. Half an hour later, the customers started arriving. Mr Wright and someone called Barry were serving behind the bar and I continued dusting and polishing. Men in grey suits, salmon-pink shirts, striped ties and tired faces drank bitter and smiled. They sucked their cigars, filling the small space with the smell of tobacco. In a cloud of smoke, and among the clink and clank of glasses and chatter, I became invisible to the customers. They would see a thin dark hand taking away the empty glasses to create more space on the table for their hands and elbows.

'It is raining cats and dogs,' I said to Minister Mahoney one morning. He was sitting by the fireplace. The house in Branscombe he had inherited from his mother was old and spacious, with a 'Victorian fireplace, with poppy and swallow tiled insert. She was so fond of this fireplace.' He took off his raincoat and his walking shoes and stretched his thin legs towards the flames. 'You insist on leaving,' he said, rubbing his hands and looking at the embers. 'I bought you a return ticket to Exeter as promised,' he said. He gave me seventy pounds pocket money, the *Oxford Advanced Learner's Dictionary of Current English* and the address of a cheap hostel run by the local authorities. 'I wrote to them so they are expecting you,' he said without looking up. 'The return ticket so you can come back if you are ever in trouble.'

The ticket, yellow around the edges, was still in my silk Chinese box, which Parvin had given me for my birthday, together with my mother's letter, the lock of hair, Noura's mother-of-pearl hair combs, a bottle of perfume, a Mary Quant lipstick and Françoise's turquoise silver necklace. I got dressed and packed my things in the small bag he gave me. He drove me to the nearest railway station. It was raining heavily when we got there so he opened his raincoat, invited me to move closer, covered my head and part of my body with it and ran to the platform. He smelt of books, open fires, lavender, honey and wine. When the guard blew the whistle I tore myself away, hugged him and jumped on the train. 'Take care of yourself, child,' were his last words to me.

I had never been on a train before, so I followed an old lady and sat next to her. 'Toilet please,' I said and she pointed at the sliding glass door. I found the sign, opened the door, closed it, locked it, put the lid down, sat on it and cried.

Milk and Honey

WITH MY UMPTEENTH FILLING OF THE DISHWASHER behind the bar, I began seeing the sparkling of glasses without seeing the glasses themselves. The smell of the detergent, beer, nicotine and breath filled the small bar. I straightened my back and gave some instructions to myself: Do not cross the sea! Do not depart! You are not allowed to tonight. My mind ignored the laughter, shouting, smoke, stale smell of mats and travelled all the way to prison, which I cleaned with Noura every Thursday. Equipped with a sweeping broom, two buckets of water and mats and some disinfectant Noura swept the rooms and I went down on my knees and mopped the floor. Noura swung Madam Lamaa's large bra in the air and laughed loudly and I kept my head down trying to get the dirt out of the cracks in the cement. Squatting on the floor the guard prodded me with her stick. 'Are you leaving the corners for the spiders?'

'Nothing, but nothing, frightens me except spiders,' said Noura.

'Good, I shall bring you a bucketload of them,' said the guard.

★

Parvin was reading a glossy magazine when I told her what the GP Dr Charles had said. The cleaner at the hostel said that immigrants were living off this country, 'and the doctor said I foreign and waste NHS money.'

She blew her fringe off her forehead, folded the magazine neatly and put it back in the rack, ran her hands over her shalwar kameez then rushed up the stairs holding my hand firmly. She pushed the door open and walked into his room. He ignored us and continued writing.

'Look at me!' she said quietly. 'Just look at me!'

He took off his glasses and looked up.

'She told you she is having palpitations, night sweats, little sleep, didn't she?'

'Yes . . .'

She did not let him interrupt her. 'You call yourself a doctor! This woman is ill and you send her off without any medicine, afraid to spend some of your precious budget.'

Plump and erect in his chair the doctor seemed small, but when he stood up he was taller than Parvin.

'Sit down and listen,' she said quietly so he sat down.

'Miss Asher imagines men with rifles follow her around Exeter,' she said.

'Just hostel,' I said.

'Right, are you going to do the decent thing and prescribe enough medicine for the next three months?'

The doctor began scribbling on a small piece of paper. 'Here you are! Now get out!' he said, handing Parvin the paper.

'You also think that we waste the NHS, us Pakis. Well, I have some news for you. We are both British and soon we will be sitting in your very seat.'

I got excited and said to Parvin, 'Is OK do medicine?'

'You want us to pay tax. We will pay you in shit because that is what we're getting at the moment.' She blew her fringe off, pulled me out, down the stairs and through the waiting room.

I overheard the doctor shout, 'You are most welcome to it . . . miracles . . . no money . . . recovering . . . heart attack . . . rather live in Pakistan.'

'You're fucking welcome to it,' Parvin screamed.

The flushed receptionist ushered us out and shut the door.

Parvin's hazel eyes were filling up by the time we got to the chemist. She handed him the prescription and hid behind a shelf decked with sun creams.

'Me need rat poison,' I said.

'Oh! Please shut up!' she said from somewhere behind the stacked-up shelves.

'Fluoxetine twenty milligrams and E45 cream,' the Sikh chemist said and smiled.

Allan looked at me and said, 'You look tired. Maybe you should go home. It's your first day, after all.'

I said I was fine, but wanted to go to the toilet. When I got there I looked at my face in the mirror: strands of hair had fallen on my sweaty forehead, my eyes had sunk in their dark sockets and my face was pale. I pinned back my hair, washed my face with cold water and gently dried it with the towel. I went up and began collecting and washing glasses again. When the last customer left the bar Allan waved at me with a glass in his hand. 'Try this wine,' he said.

'A soft drink please,' I said.

He raised his eyebrows and said, 'You don't drink?'

'I am tired, that's all,' I lied.

He poured me some fizzy mineral water in a slim glass, put some ice and lemon in it and handed it to me. I sat down on the stool and drank it all in one go.

'Here you are! Twelve pounds,' he said and handed me the cash.

I realized that he had stuck to the original agreement and had not counted all the overtime I had put in.

'Thank you Allan,' I said. 'Is there anything you want me to do before I go home?'

'Yes,' he said, 'please put away the clean glasses.'

Wave after wave, fear like an electric current used to rush through my body while I lay in the ex-army bed, reducing me to a heap of flesh and bones, turning me into a slain chicken convulsing and leaping about. I would hug my breasts and rock myself, reciting my mother's letter until panic loosened its grip on my insides, until some fresh air rushed into the room, until I surfaced and began to breathe. I knew what it felt like when the chicken gasped for air and finally died.

I walked back to the hostel as tired as if I had climbed all the mountains surrounding Hima. At night I did not have to think about the possibility of walking out of my room. I lay in bed wondering. What if my family discovered my whereabouts? What if I had to walk out of this room and look for a job? What if I was ill, seriously ill? I used to hold my mother's letter, my reed pipe, and the lock of her hair Noura was able to cut off, and rock in my bed. The window was too small, the bed was small, the world was small and when I died my grave would close in on me because I was a sinner.

It was just after midnight when I finally staggered back home with aching shoulders, back, arms. 'Whatever is part of me is hurting,' my mother used to say and drink some brewed bugloss. Standing on the highest point of the footpath, which used to be the main road a long time ago, leaning on the green railing, I was able to locate myself. This country was right in resisting me; it was right in refusing to embrace me because something in me was resisting it, and would never belong to it. To be introduced first to four walls covered with metal sheets did not help. If I had been dropped by parachute in Branscombe, where Minister Mahoney lived, in that evergreen valley leading to the sea, I could have fallen in love with England. We were like two old friends now, who had become familiar with each other's anger. I should forgive Britain for turning me into moss that grows in cracks, for giving me the freedom to roam its cities between five and seven in the evening, for confining me to the space between the sole and the heel, and Britain should forgive me for supporting Italy in the World Cup, the nearest I could find to my old country.

Parvin walked through the glass door and I was right behind her. 'I have an interview this afternoon,' she said to the young woman minding the customer service counter.

The girl sized her up and said, 'Please wait here.'

A young man in a black suit, black shirt and grey tie walked towards us. The suit I made for Parvin looked a bit loose and shabby, but Parvin by pulling her back straight and keeping her chin up made it look elegant and expensive.

'Mark Parks, assistant manager,' he said and offered his left hand.

Parvin shook his hand and said, 'Parvin Khan.'

'Miss Khan, this way please,' he said and guided her through a corridor.

I did not know whether to go with her or to wait outside.

She put her arm behind her back and waved me off.

I stood there looking at the corridor and wondering whether Parvin was all right. I needed the toilet desperately, but did not dare move in case I missed her coming out. 'Can I help you?' the customer service woman asked.

'Yes. If friend come out please say urinate me.'

'I will tell her that you've gone to the Ladies,' she said and pressed the button of the money machine. A black drawer dinged then slid out.

While watching *Great Expectations* on television, I opened my *Advanced Learner's Dictionary* and read Minister Mahoney's inscription, *To Salma, may this country bring you happiness*, then looked for the letter E. *Expectation: think or believe that something will happen, wish or feel confident that one will receive.* Liz expected this country not to change, her fortune not to decline and the sun not to set on Swan Cottage. She wished that her mansion and horses had not been sold and that her servants were foreign and obedient. Gwen wanted to educate the children well so they loved their mothers, called them often, visited them and hugged them. I expected to find milk and honey streaming down the streets, happiness lurking in every corner, surprise, surprise, a happy marriage and three children to delight my heart. Parvin expected a job, marriage, stability and a family who would accept her the way she was. Parvin had a proper education, she went to a comprehensive, passed her A-levels, and was doing a sociology degree at a community college when she had to run away. She often said, 'At first everything seemed possible in this country, but the fucking orgasm does not last long.'

I was reading a leaflet about a store credit card when Parvin walked out. She raised her thumb and winked at me. I knew that she had got the job. When we walked through the glass doors, she screamed, 'Yes! Fuck it! Yes!' and jumped in the air. 'My Bedouin friend, this calls for a celebration.'

'Great, great,' I said and hugged her.

Hand in hand we walked to the best café in the city. We sat down on the stools where you could see the main street through the high glass windows. Parvin said to the waiter, 'I want a hot chocolate with cream, marshmallows and a flake bar.'

He lowered his tray and said, 'And you, madam?'

'Me want milk, with honey and butter.'

'We don't do that, madam.'

Parvin pulled her short skirt down and said, 'Surely you do flavoured milk.'

'Yes we do. Which flavour?'

'Make it caramel,' she said and smiled.

I held her hand and said, 'I happy for you.'

She pulled her hand away and said, 'Don't hold my hand or touch me in public. They will think we are from planet lesbo.'

When the hot chocolate arrived it looked so large, with a twirl of white cream on top, small pink pieces like cotton wool floated in the long glass and a chocolate bar lay in the saucer. She took the bar and began eating it and it instantly crumbled over the white cream and napkin.

The café was warm, bright, clean, elegant and full. Sunbeams lit up the counter and shone through the water jugs. The aroma of coffee and the scent of caramel, hazelnuts, walnuts and hot milk filled the air. I had a sip of my milk and honey and it tasted like Islamic paradise. We looked at the passers-by and smiled; the whiteness of our teeth was accentuated by our dusky brown skin. Before every sip Parvin raised her glass saluting an invisible audience and I couldn't help but join in. We sat there, dark, employed, with white creamy moustaches, winking and waving at passers-by.

That morning Max took one look at me then said, 'You look exhausted this morning, girl. What have you been up to?'

'I had a late night,' I said and tucked a strand of hair behind my ear.

'Who was it? One of them Arabs?'

I shook my head.

'You know what bugs me about them. They come here like an army, buy houses and cars then sell their houses and cars without us hard-working English people making a sodding penny out of it. They don't go to estate agents or dealers, no, they buy off each other.'

'I don't know any Arabs here,' I said and sat down.

'That's strange. Why not?'

I was taking in the sides of a crushed velvet ball gown. It was purple but when it caught the light it turned light then dark green like peacock feathers. I could picture its owner: a tall blonde, with an immaculate figure and long legs tucked in flat satin ballerina shoes, her hair tied with a velvet band, her lips crimson, her earrings a waterfall of pearls. She would be reclining on an antique sofa in a country mansion, sipping her champagne, surrounded by Europe's most eligible bachelors, who would dutifully kiss her hand. Her flushed cheeks were the only sign of her excitement. She would smile like a goddess made of pink porcelain, misty, smooth and expensive.

'You're not listening to me. Are you?'

Max held a needle between his fat lips, his eyes looked tired and swollen under his double-vision glasses and his grey hair was thinning. A photo of his family was stuck on the wall. He had a foot on the sewing machine and his lunch of sardine sandwiches and oranges was in a brown paper bag on the floor right behind him. The pungent smell of sardines preserved in oil filled my nostrils. He would say proudly, 'None of this brine business for me.' Sometimes when I was steam ironing legs of trousers the smell of Max's sardines was released.

'I've finished this dress, shall I hang it?'

'Yes, with the tag, girl. Write "Sharon" on it.' The goddess's name was Sharon! Not Sofia, Alexia, Nadine or even Natasha. It shouldn't be Sally, Salma, Sharon or Tracy, who were birds of a different feather, a feather restricted to certain width and height. The dress belonged to a Sharon!

I decided to spend two pounds on lunch today and went to a department store café, ordered a soup, two portions of bread and a glass of orange juice. It all added up to two pounds seventy. I took my tray and sat upstairs overlooking the entrance. I pulled out my *Marie Claire*, which was dog-eared, and started reading a piece about protecting your skin that summer when you were on the beach. The model's hair was long, very long and blond and it shone in the sun like rivers of molten gold. Her skin was even, taut and tanned, and her nipples nowhere to be seen. Which beach was she on? The sand was as white as sugar and the sea was light turquoise. The Mediterranean for sure. I sipped my carrot soup and then looked up and saw them. Dr John Robson, my university tutor, walked in with a petite woman with short blond hair, big beautiful blue eyes and a slim figure hidden under a loose T-shirt and blue jeans. She clung to him while he was choosing food off the counter. I had met him only once when I went to register for my part-time university degree. I concentrated on my soup and continued sipping. They sat down each with a tray decked with fruit and salad. I continued looking at the model, shot in mid-air, legs and hands splayed like a suspended bird. I pretended that I was reading. With the corner of my eye I saw that they had settled down and begun eating. I wrapped what was left of the bread in a napkin, put it together with the magazine in my bag then rushed out of the sliding glass doors. It was raining a gentle drizzle. The cathedral was quiet, apart from the sad sound of an organ; I pulled my scattered self together and looked at the bright colours of the window where blood was dripping down the forehead of the enamelled blue and red Christ. I walked to the altar, put a cushion on the floor, knelt down and repeated, 'May Allah have mercy on Salma! Alleviate her distress, God, lighten her load, widen her chest! Bless her with the gift of forgetfulness!'

I blew my nose then walked out of the cold cathedral.

It was still raining a gentle drizzle that you'd normally ignore and end up soaking wet. The pavements were wet, the streets were wet, the windows were wet. Looking at the warm glow of table lights behind the steamed windows of the hotel in the corner, I psyched myself up to face the wrath of Max. I was half an hour late. The minute I entered the door and shook the water off my hair, Max surprised me by saying, 'You were crying? Weren't you?' No angry telling-off, threats of being kicked out of this fine establishment and this great country, no you have no respect for your employer, no hundreds of white English kids would give an arm and a leg to have your job. Nothing except, 'Stitch this for me, will you?' I could not look Max in the eye. I could handle angry words, but kindness I could not bear. Kindness I did not deserve. He should have shouted at me, called me a foreign tart, kicked me in the stomach until I blacked out. Kindness I did not deserve.

I went back home, had a bath, shaved my legs, washed my hair, rubbed my body with cream, sprayed myself with deodorant and powdered myself with perfume. I dried my hair enhancing its body, put on black tights, a short black skirt, black high-heeled shoes, a sleeveless frilly white shirt and painted a rainbow around my eyes. I looked at the mirror and saw a clown looking back at me. I might be attacked tonight. I might be gang-raped then killed. They might find my body under the yew tree by the river. When Elizabeth saw me she said, 'Sally, you are hustling these days, aren't you?'

Allan ran his hand over his sticky hair. 'Salma!' He cleared his voice. 'You look very nice.' Last night he summoned me to his office and lectured me on my appearance. 'Our customers want to be surrounded by beautiful women; they all go to the cinema and see those Bacardi girls. You must try to look presentable like . . . like an air hostess. Whenever I take a flight, I get tucked in, taken care of by girls with lined eyes, tight skirts and full red lips.'

How can I become a Sandy, a white beautiful doll? I am only a Shandy, a black doll, a black tart, which was heavily made up and quick with her straps and suspenders. I slept with Jim, didn't I? But Gwen advised me to look like a lady.

'I see,' I said.

'Allan. Please call me Allan.'

'Yes, Allan.'

Allan liked the frizzy wild hair and the short skirt. With a stretch of his imagination he could see me now as an air hostess, cooing and flirting, tucking him in, getting him his drinks, kissing him with a lipsticked mouth. I realized from the way Allan was following me with his eyes that I had stopped being an incomprehensible foreigner and had become a woman, a body neither white nor olive-skinned nor black. My colour had faded away and was replaced by curves, flesh and promises.

Since Parvin started her job I saw very little of her. Our alarm clock was set at 6:30 in the morning. We would get up and chase each other to the communal bathroom, join the queue outside the door and wait. We would get dressed quickly and eat some cornflakes with milk, brush our teeth, comb our hair, make sandwiches and put them in our bags. Parvin would listen to the morning news and would punctuate it with, 'What a wanker! He is a dickhead. What a prick!' I did not understand much so I would chase the cornflakes around in my bowl and listen to her getting more and more agitated. She put on some weight so the suit I made for her looked really good now. Just before walking out of the room she would look at me and say, 'Have you seen men with rifles lately?'

'No!' I would lie.

'Are you taking your pills?'

'Yes,' I would say.

She would say, 'Good,' snatch her briefcase and rush out.

Madam Lamaa sat on the rubber mattress leaning against the wall and looking at the barred window. It must be summertime because it was hot that night and the sound of the shrill cries of the cicada filled the air.

'Madam Lamaa, are you thirsty? Here you are, some water,' said Noura and gave her a tin cup full of water fresh from the clay water jar covered with wet sackcloth.

'Thank you. God bless you,' she said, drank, then wiped her mouth with the end of her sleeve. She pushed herself up, adjusted her scarf to cover her grey hair and said, 'My bra size is not available in the market. One of my friends made my bras for me. I saw you the other day swinging it in the air.'

'We were just messing about. We have so much respect for you,' said Noura.

'They found me standing naked under the lamppost in the main street. They thought I was a prostitute. I am not a prostitute.'

'We know that. You look like a real *sitt*: a lady, but why were you standing in the street naked?' asked Noura.

'I gave birth to five sons, kept his house clean and

cooked him a fresh meal every day. Whenever he turned round in bed I opened my very heart for him. All of this was not enough,' she said and wiped the sweat off her forehead.

'Men are insatiable, aren't they?' said Noura.

'A few years later I began putting on weight. I developed a tummy first then fat gathered all over my body. I also began losing my hair, the sheen in my eyes, the lightness of my step.'

'What was it? *Sin il ya's*: the age of despair?'

'The doctor said yes it is *sin il ya's*: the menopause. Sleeplessness, palpitations, night sweats, and dark hair everywhere, my upper lip, around my nipples, on my tummy.'

'So?'

'He stopped sleeping with me. "You are disgusting," he said and never turned towards me ever again. Then I heard the old tongues wagging, "He is looking for a second wife."'

'Here is some more water,' offered Noura.

Madam Lamaa drank and wiped her mouth and face with a handkerchief. She clutched her large breasts and said, 'What if he chucks me out of the house? What if she comes and lives with us under the same roof? What if he makes me become her maid, her servant after all these years? What if my boys begin to like her? Fear took hold of me and I would spend all night looking for stones and bad grains in rice, searching for migrating birds in the sky, pursuing answers.'

'That fucking cicada!' said Noura then added, 'They threaten us with taking on a second wife to keep us in our place.'

'One night I went to the storeroom, opened each sack

and scattered the rice, the flour, the sugar, the lentils, the dry fruit all over the place. I took my clothes off and walked out of the house as Allah had created me and stood under His vast sky looking for stars. The judge said that it was a lewd act and here I am without a friend, a loved one or a companion,' she said and turned away.

'I wish I were rounder, fatter like you,' I said.

She covered her face with both hands.

'That fucking cicada!' shouted Noura.

When my dark hair almost fell in the drinks of customers they would look up with their puffy eyes, wet their lips and smile. I would smile back and collect the empty glasses. There were very few women customers, and they were all better covered than I was. Come and have a look at my cleavage, at my round bottom, my long dark hair and thin ankles! Why don't you? Allan saw me pushing the hand of an elderly man away from my backside. He didn't like the liberties the old man was taking. When I went back behind the bar to feed the glass washer Allan said, 'Stay behind the bar, Barry will collect the glasses.' I gave Allan a thank-you look. Behind all that groomed look, sticky hair and bowties, Allan was a real gentleman. At the end of my shift I helped myself to a cup of coffee, sat down on one of the upholstered chairs, took off my shoes and put my feet up. Allan was bolting the heavy wooden door. He rubbed his hands together, pulled up another chair and sat down.

'You don't need to wear high heels.'

'Thank God!'

He smiled and said, 'If it were down to me I would have just let you wear whatever you want. It's the manager of the hotel, Mr Brightwell. He goes on and on about our image.'

'It does not seem right when I am walking among drunken men. I like something more modest.'

'If Mr Brightwell comes to the bar and sees you looking scruffy he won't like it.'

I sipped the dregs and pulled my trainers out of the bag. The walk back home took me thirty minutes. I normally enjoyed it, but tonight it seemed like a heavy chore. I wrapped my mother's shawl around my shoulders, zipped my bag and put my hand on Allan's arm. I was grateful to him for giving me the job and for keeping me behind the bar beyond the reach of the drunken eyes and hands. 'Goodnight Barry. Goodnight Allan.'

We sat in the café drinking tea and arguing. After we moved out of the hostel I did not see much of Parvin. She was busy with the new job. I watched her flushed face while she chewed at the end of her plastic pen.

She looked me in the eye and said, 'Why literature?'

'Because I need to know English. The English language.'

'You can study language without reading literature.'

'No, stories good. Teach you language and how to act like English Miss.'

She blew some air up at her fringe and said, 'But, Salma, this BA is not in English Language. It does not teach you English. It is about Yeats, Joyce, feminism, Shakespeare, for Christ's sake!'

I sipped some coffee. 'I want know about Shakeesbeer. I want know things,' I said and pulled my earlobe down.

'Upon your head. All right. Let us fill in the form. Name? Sally Asher.'

'No. Salma Ibrahim El-Musa.'

'Is this what's written in your British passport? You need to be accurate or else you will pay a fortune as an overseas student,' she said and poised the pen over the line after name.

'No, but I want Arab name.'

'You cannot. They will deport you,' she said and began writing Sally Asher.

I knew she was lying but I kept my mouth shut. She was the one who was filling in the form.

'So you want to apply for a BA in English Literature?'

'Yes,' I said and looked through the window at the white clouds changing shape. The strong wind brought them all together then dispersed them in minutes.

'You need a decent address. The community hostel will not look good.'

I looked at Parvin's face, her curled and lowered lashes hiding her hazel eyes, her generous mouth and wide forehead. The clouds became dark and dense. The café looked dingy without the sunlight. I put my jacket on and said, 'I have to look for somewhere to live.'

'I need to move to somewhere closer to work,' she said then blew up at her straight long fringe.

'We get a house together?' I said.

'That will be too expensive. What we can reasonably get is a room in a house,' she said and chewed at the end of the pen.

'Let's go,' I said, 'I do not want Max to tell me off.'

'Mark will be wondering where I am,' she said and

looked at the narrow shred of blue sky between the rushing clouds.

My feet were covered with blisters so it was hard to enjoy my midnight walk back home. Think about the green hills, the sheep and cows that were asleep, the old man in a Hawaiian shirt and safari hat with a plastic card urging us all to express ourselves. Although it was windy the sky was clear, as if darkness were rising rather than falling. The top of the hills were lined with a brightly lit strip and darkness was imprisoned right in the middle of the sky. Curtains were pulled closed, blinds pulled down, and the whole city was breathing evenly. It was asleep. The house on New North Road, which I looked wistfully at whenever I passed by, had a new red-brick wall around the garden. I closed my eyes, breathed in the fresh smell of recently cut grass, and dreamt of living inside, being either the daughter or the wife of the owner; my three blond English children were safely tucked in their beds and my husband was sipping his brandy and watching a late-night horror film. I had just had a hot, bubbly bath, changed into a clean cotton nightie and was about to go to sleep in my safe, wide marital bed, between sheets that smelt of lily-of-the-valley conditioner, when my husband walked in with a dagger in his hand bent on stabbing me.

When I got to our street I saw a body lying on the pavement. It was Liz splayed right opposite her front door. She smelt of cheap wine. Her navy jumper was filthy, her skirt pulled up showing most of her thighs and her white cotton pants; ladders ran up her tights and her shoes were

nowhere to be seen. Her face was pale and her shut eyes
had sunk in their dark sockets. When she breathed out
the sound was between a snore and a grunt. I knelt down
and began slapping her cheeks gently. 'Liz, wake up!' I
whispered. 'You don't want to be seen like this.' Finally she
began stirring then woke up. I wrapped my arms around
her shoulders, pulled her up and led her indoors. 'Thank
you, love,' she mumbled. I put her in her bed, covered her
with her dirty embroidered frilled duvet and turned
her head to one side to stop her choking on her vomit.
The crimson box on the bedside table was full of old
letters held together with a rubber band and a diary with
Elizabeth's name printed on the green silk cover. I put
everything back in the box and secured the lid.

Lying awake I could feel the vibrations of trains flying by.
Through the half-open curtains I could see the moonless
sky, vast and clear. Why did I sleep with Jim? Why did I do
it? He did not even acknowledge my presence. Was it the
sage tea? Was it just a body wriggling away with fear? It
must be my long dark frizzy hair and crooked nose. I
looked at the wardrobe and saw the familiar face of
Hamdan, the twin of my soul. He was tall, strong and dark.
I stretched my arms out to him. He walked towards me
and said, 'How is my little slut, my courtesan, my whore?'
My body welcomed his weight, his rough hands, his
urgency. I filled my nostrils with the scent of his musk-
covered face, his oiled hair, his waxed moustache. Like a
bone-dry desert I welcomed the heavy rain. I was back at
the Long Well filling the bucket with cold water, pouring
it over my head then gasping for air. Hamdan held me
tight. When the bright light of the morning began rising

layer upon layer I covered my stiff limbs with the duvet and floated into sleep.

The dining room of the *Hellena* was empty when Miss Asher and I went in. They served pork and potato on Sunday and they also served wine. We were halfway to Southampton now. Miss Asher poured some wine in her glass from the decanter then had a sip and said, 'It is good wine. You must try it.'

'It forbidden in Islam. You lose control and make all kinds of sins,' I said.

She ran her finger around the rim of the glass and said, 'Do you see me committing any sins?'

'No, but I different. I Muslim. I go crazy. Allah says so.'

'Sit down, child! Have something to eat!'

'Don't eat pork. Filthy animals.'

'Christ said, "Nothing that a man eats from outside can make him unclean." But I can assure you there is no pork in this food, only meat.'

'Cannot eat meat, I Muslim. I eat halal meat only. Slaughtered the Islamic way.'

Miss Asher was showing annoyance. 'Eat the potatoes then!'

'No, cooked with pork.'

'There is nothing else on offer.'

'Can't eat, miss home.'

'I know, child. But you must eat to remain strong, strong for your daughter.'

'Can't reach out for the food. Muslim, me,' I said hesitantly.

'God is love, he loves you, child. He will forgive you no matter what.'

'Allah punish me. Burn me in hell. Close the grave in on my chest.'

'Not the Christian God, he is love. He loves and forgives. Jesus died on the cross to wipe out the sins of mankind.'

'God loves me? Don't think so.'

'Jesus Christ loves you, child. It says so in the Gospel. Here is a copy. Read it sometime.'

I took the Gospel and put it on the table quickly, afraid of the contact with the Christian text.

'Do you have to wear this veil? God has made you perfect and he loves every part of you, including your hair.'

'My hair is *'aura*. I must hide it. Just like my private parts.'

'Christ was put on the cross for the sins of mankind. He died on our behalf. All our sins will be forgiven.'

'Christ not put on cross. It appear so. Christians think so. Not true.'

'What a load of nonsense. How can I purify your mind of such drivel?' she said.

'Angry you?' I said.

'No. Well, you also think so many things. Not necessarily true. One day you will see the light. One day the truth shall set you free.'

'I cannot take off veil, Sister. My country, my language, my daughter. No piece of cloth. Feel naked, me.'

'Christ was crucified. He loves you,' she said.

'No crucifixion, no love me,' I said.

Miss Asher stood up and slapped me on the face. Holding my smarting cheek I ran to the cabin.

★

The sun was shining on the green hills that reminded me of Hima's. I used to fondle the soil every day, but now sealed in an air bubble I lived away from the land and the trees. I just looked at the postcard view and thought how distant the river was although it was only yards away. I had divorced my farmer side, but on mornings like this I felt the palm of my hands itching for the scythe and to touch the mud and vines. Wearing my slippers and bathrobe I tiptoed to Liz's bedroom and pushed the door open. She was still asleep and breathing evenly. What a relief! I went to the bathroom and while sitting on the toilet I remembered that my paper on Shakespeare's sister was due. Apart from some scribbling I had nothing to show. All that business with Jim had set me back. I had to explain the delay to John. I scoffed my breakfast, drank some coffee quickly, scalding my tongue, and ran out of the house.

'Good morning, Max.'

He lifted his head, which was stuck between the pages of the *Sun*, and answered me absent-mindedly. The boss was not in a bad mood this morning. I began working and thinking about how to say sorry to my tutor. He was tall and tanned, which was unusual, but Parvin told me that they send them to Cyprus twice a year to teach there. He had dark thinning hair, a goatee and wore tiny half-moon glasses which were always hanging at the bottom of his pointed nose. When he was saying, 'The Open University has a mission of bringing higher education within the reach of the entire nation,' I was watching his glasses, which looked as if they were about to fall off any minute. He lowered his head until his big grey eyes were gazing at me directly, above his reading glasses, and said, 'Where do you come from?'

With a strained voice I said, 'I am English.'

'I am English too,' he said, smiled, then walked away.

It was like a curse upon my head; it was my fate: my accent and the colour of my skin. I could hear it sung everywhere: in the cathedral, 'WHERE DO YOU COME FROM?'; in the farmers' market, 'Do you know where this vegetable comes from?' Sometimes even the cows on the hills would line up, kick their legs in unison and sing, 'Where do you come from, you? Go home!'

I headed towards the steam iron and began flattening rebellious hems, collars and sleeves. In that tiny room, overlooking the city centre, enveloped completely in steam and smelling of starch and nicotine, I stopped locating myself. I became neither Salma, nor Sal nor Sally, neither Arab nor English. Puff – like magic I would turn into a white cloud.

My nipples were erect so I rubbed them with the palms of my hands gently. She must be crying for me. I recognized that wind. She must be out there calling me. Noura said that souls were soldiers of our master Solomon and they had a sophisticated system of communication. After his father's death Solomon became king. He begged Allah for a kingdom as no other, and Allah granted him his wish. He could command the winds and understand and talk to birds and animals. Allah instructed him to teach both men and jinn to mine the earth and extract its minerals to make tools and weapons. He also favoured him with a mine of copper, which was a rare metal in those days. Prophet Solomon even understood the ant when she cried, 'Run to your homes and hide, otherwise, unaware, Solomon and his army will crush you.' He smiled because he knew that Allah had intended to save the ants. Then Noura stopped talking and looked at the barred window.

'That's it?' I asked.

She cleared her voice and said, 'Prophet Solomon died suddenly leaning on his staff. People did not realize that he was dead until the ants ate his staff and his body crumbled down.'

Dal and Willow Trees

PARVIN'S MAN WAS THE ASSISTANT MANAGER OF THE department store where she worked. He was stocky but not fat, with thick blond hair, big blue eyes, a wide, thin, almost lipless mouth and wide jaws. She introduced him to me with a voice full of pride, 'Meet Mark my fiancé!'

Since I moved out of the hostel I had not seen Parvin. Months had passed without even a phone call. I was a Bedouin and perhaps she didn't want to be seen with me now she was professional and all.

'Pleased to meet you,' I said and stretched out my arm.

He pulled up the sleeve of his jacket and offered me a metal hook instead of a hand made of flesh and blood. Parvin raised her eyebrows, urging me to shake it. I held the cold metal hook in my hand and bowed.

He went to the counter and ordered some salad and juice. Parvin winked and asked, 'Isn't he cute?'

'Yes, but he is white,' I said.

'So?' she said.

'And . . . and . . .' I whispered.

'He had cancer and they had to amputate his hand. He is in the clear now,' she said.

163

'Great, good, congratulations,' I said.

'He is a good manager. He knows everything about sports gear. He will never go bust 'cause the English love sports,' she said.

I nodded. She was not wearing much make-up and her face shone in the midday sun. Mark came back with a tray decked with food for the three of us. 'Parvin told me you love salad,' he said and sat down. He looked at Parvin and when she raised her curled eyelashes and looked at him her eyes were full of approval.

'Oy, not so fast, miss!' he said when she began scoffing the salad.

Mouth full she said, 'I am hungry.'

He asked me what I did for a living and when I mentioned Lord's Tailors he said that he might come to our shop to order his suit for the big day.

'We be delighted to serve you,' I said and smiled.

When we finished eating they both went silent and looked at me.

I drank some water and said, 'What? Is spider crawling my head?'

'No,' he said, 'but we want to ask you something.'

I tucked my hair behind my ears.

'Will you do us the honour of being our bridesmaid?'

'Maid? What I do?' I said.

'No, it is not like that. You will be the maid of honour, my best woman, like, second in charge,' she said.

'You don't want me. You want a nice-looking Englishwoman,' I said.

Parvin stood up and hugged me. 'I don't want anyone but you, you daft Bedouin.'

★

I did not go to the university very often because I felt that everyone knew everything about anything; they had read books I could not understand, they spoke a language I could not speak and they looked down upon me because my English was bad. The minute I began walking up the hill towards the university my heart would begin beating rhythmically like a pestle pounding coffee beans in a Bedouin mortar. I felt small against the old large building with towers and high ceilings. When I finally entered the building I was trembling. With shaking hands I showed my instructions to the porter. He led me down a spacious room full of sculpted busts, posters and conversing students to a narrow staircase. 'Up those stairs, then turn left,' he said.

By the time I found Dr Robson's office I was in a state: my heart was pounding, my shoulders were aching and coffee was dripping through the rucksack. I felt hot and sweaty but before I burst into tears I knocked on the door.

'Come in,' came my teacher's prompt answer.

'My flask must be broken,' I said to his thinning hair.

He looked up and saw the coffee dripping on the carpet. He stood up and got me a towel out of a sports bag and said, 'Use this!'

I put the towel on the floor and placed my sack carefully on it.

'Now get your stuff out.'

I was reluctant to let this stranger see my personal belongings. Everything I had in the bag was cheap and scruffy and would look even more so soaked in coffee. I began pulling out my jumper, the ultra-short skirt, the see-through blouse, the make-up bag, *Marie Claire*, the file on which I scribbled my apology. I wrote it all down to get it right: 'Last weekend I started a new job and I was extremely busy. I could not finish my essay. Please accept my sincere apology.' Gwen had added 'extremely' and 'sincere' and an 'ed' to 'start'. I hesitantly pulled out some underwear and finally the broken flask.

He held the frame of his glasses and said, 'You need a new flask.'

'Yes I need,' I said.

A poster with a naked woman turning her back to the world was stuck on the wall behind him. Her head was bent towards her curled body and all we could see was her back clearly outlined.

'Right,' he said. 'Let me have your essay.'

Looking at my personal belongings scattered on the floor I struggled with the elusive words. Out with it. 'I haven't done it.' There, I said it.

'Why?' he asked gently.

'I busy,' I said.

'Is it family- or work-related?'

'Is family,' I lied. 'My daughter go to university. She is doing medicine and I have to cook for her and look after her . . . I also work in the evening.'

'Next Monday I want the essay on my desk,' he said.

'Yes,' I said while collecting my clothes and sticking them in the wet sack. 'Yes,' I said while offering him the broken flask. 'Yes,' I said while walking backwards towards the door. 'Yes,' I said and shut the door.

'Sally, wait,' he called.

I did not answer. My name was not Sally.

One evening after we ate the *mjadara*, a risotto with onion and lentils, Noura, while looking at the barred window, said, 'One day Rami fell ill and I took him to hospital. He was in a coma for four days. I used to go to the kebab shop to wash dishes at night and then rush to the hospital in the morning. I never prayed, but that night I prayed for the first time. "God of the universe, God of humans and jinn, God of earth and limitless skies, have mercy on this child and deliver him. Please, God, if you cure him I will wear the veil, pray five times a day, fast, give the *zakat* to the poor and go to Mecca to do the pilgrimage." In the morning Rami got better, but I had lost my job. It turned out that Rami was diabetic and needed two insulin injections a day. Someone told me about the "House of Perfume", so I went and instead of wearing the veil as I vowed I began taking off my clothes. You know why I am here, Salma, because I broke every promise I had made to Allah. My husband decided to take the children to live with him and his second wife. And here I am in Yildiz palace.'

'Yildiz palace?'

'It's the palace of the sultan on the shores of a lake in Turkey.'

'Islah prison and Yildiz are identical. Aren't they?' I smiled.

'Especially the ostrich-feather mattresses and the gold ewer,' she said and laughed. The sound of her laughter was somewhere between a titter and a sob.

Allan said, while I was putting glasses in the large drawer of the tumbler washer, 'I must teach you some social tricks. When I am finished with you people will mistake you for a princess.'

'Are you sure?' which was exactly my answer to my first

167

teacher, Minister Mahoney, the kind Quaker priest. After eating my breakfast, which tasted like sawdust, I drank the cold coffee, brushed my teeth and tied my hair back. Then I heard a knock on the thick detention-centre door. It must be Miss Asher, I thought, while trying to straighten the ruffled sheets. Then in came a tall man, with blue eyes, wide smile and grey hair. When he said in Arabic, '*Al jaw bardun huna*: the climate is cold here,' I recognized him. He was the ship's pastor. His Arabic sounded stiff and classical like Miss Nailah's textbook so I laughed.

'*Haya bina ya Salma*: let us go, Salma,' he said.

'*Ma'ak?*' I asked

'Yes, *na'am, ma'i*, with me,' he said and opened the door.

A Bedouin shepherdess would be turned into a princess, full of smiles and brightness, sparkling, straight-backed and flat-stomached, no way.

'You are basically well mannered, but a bit rough around the edges,' said Allan.

I smiled to Allan while thinking of Islah prison, where I was lying in the filth, having a bath once every two weeks, washing the cloths I used whenever I had my period in a bucket full of soap and water, eating with my hand, and dreaming of a spring of fresh water, like the one my mother used to take me to on donkey-back when I was really young. The spring was so clear you were able to see every pebble, big or small, even or uneven, in the bottom. The water was jetting out of the hillside covered with grapevines. Ripe watermelons sliced in half were floating in the ice-cold water like the fuchsia oleander flowers that grew along the stream all the way to the mill at the bottom of the valley. 'Our tribe has given this spring as a wedding gift to the bridegroom's tribe. Alas, it's no longer ours,' she said.

'I don't know how to speak to people,' I said to Allan while sipping the dregs of our closing-time cup of coffee.

'You speak well,' he said while stealing a glance at my tired legs. I did not like it when Allan reminded me that he was a man. I wanted him to be just a friend without desires and stolen glances.

'Yes, but today I made a fool of myself when I went to see my university tutor.'

Allan ran his fingers over his waxed hair, straightened his bowtie and said, 'Are you a university student?' There was admiration, confusion and condemnation in his tone.

'Yes. First year English Literature, part time, though,' I said the same way Dr Robson would have said it to me in his untidy office.

'Oh! You will be reading Shakespeare then.'

'I am reading about his sister for the women and culture module.'

'Oh dear! So Shakespeare is not important any more!' he said.

I did not know why he was or was not important so I put my jumper on, my trainers and said, 'I am off.'

'Goodnight,' he said and sucked on his cigar.

When I switched on the landing light, I heard moaning upstairs. 'Liz, is that you?' I cried, rushed up the stairs and knocked on her bedroom door.

A feeble 'Come in.'

I opened the door and saw her lying in bed, flushed, sweaty and breathing heavily. 'Liz, are you all right?'

'It must be a fever, ayah,' she said.

'Have you been to the doctor?' I asked.

She looked so thin and pale curled up under the sheets. 'No,' she said. Her late husband's black-and-white photo smiled at her from the bedside cabinet.

'I need some port,' she said.

The bottle was almost empty on the smudged silver tray and the glass looked misty with stains. I poured what was left of the port and handed it to her. She pulled herself up and drank it in one go.

'Ayah, there is no better ayah than you,' she said while looking at the lace curtains fluttering in the wind.

'Yes,' I said and sat down on the bedside.

'You know, ayah, I wish I had never set foot in India. Everyone looked up to me and served me. Servants carried me to school, you dressed me, Hita cooked for us, Mr Crooked Hands took care of the garden, Riza guarded the gate.' Her eyes drifted off to a place known only to her. She swallowed hard and said, 'Hita used to make the best chaat, dal, onion bhajis. He would set a tray and bring it to me in the garden while I was playing with Rex. "Here you are, Princess Upah," he would say.' She looked at the cupboard and said, 'It had to be him, Hita *jaan*; it had to be your father, Hita *jaan*.' Liz turned her head, looked at the peeling William Morris wallpaper, fingered the intricate silver frame and ran her hand over the fading black-and-white photo of her late husband, and finally focused her eyes on me and said, 'What are you doing here?'

'I heard something so I came up to see if you're all right.'

'Get out! Shoo! Shoo! Get out,' she said waving her hand towards the door as if she was trying to shake off some dirt. The smell of cheap wine, dust; betrayal, damp, tears; broken promises, dirty sheets, false teeth and disinfectant followed me all the way to my room.

It must have been love. I was sitting on top of a pile of sheaves of wheat, scoffing my butter sandwich, when Hamdan walked out of a dust cloud and sat next to me. I could see our wedding camel caravan crossing the village, carrying us to our own dwelling.

He pulled a hair out of his moustache and said, 'How is my mare?'

I fixed my veil into place and said, 'Fine.'

'I want to see you,' he said and fixed his white-and-red-chequered headdress.

It was hot and dry with clouds of dust blown about by the wind. The songs of the harvesters died out, the reaping and threshing season was over and piles of wheat, barley and lentils lay spread out on the threshing floor at the hill top. I swallowed hard then said, 'I am pregnant.'

His cockiness collapsed and he turned into a man troubled with a bent back and a trembling voice, 'You cannot be. How?'

'I don't know,' I said and stuffed the last morsel of bread into my mouth.

When he finally looked up at me he was a different man, his brown eyes burning with anger rather than desire. He cleared his voice and said, 'You are responsible. You have seduced me with the yearning tunes of your pipe and swaying hips,' he said and raised his arm about to hit me.

I shrank on the wheat pile and covered my head with both arms.

'I've never laid a finger on you. I've never seen you ever before. Do you understand?' he said, wrapped his kufiyya around his face like a mask and walked into a cloud of dust.

I sat there listening to the barking of distant dogs, the moo moo of a cow in labour, the rustle of leaves and the susurration of the whirling wind.

Liz did not usually allow me into her room, but that morning I knocked lightly then entered like a trespasser. Liz was sleeping soundly in her exquisite iron bed. The silver tray with crystal cocktail glasses was on the antique chest of drawers. I was relieved to see some colour back in her cheeks. I looked at the fading picture of her husband, who died in the war, on the bedside table. The crimson satin box was still open. I tiptoed to have a look and saw the bundle of letters held together by a rubber band and a diary with green silk covers with a photo of the Queen printed on it. I opened it and read, *Monday 5th September 1931, Janki ayah bought me bangles from a pedlar in all the shining colours of the rainbow, but Mama wouldn't let me wear them much. 'Too Indian,' she said.* Liz turned her head to the other side. I put the diary back in the box and walked quietly out of the room. I rushed down the cold stairs to the kitchen, put the kettle on and sat on the stool waiting for everything to get warmer: the wooden cupboards, the stainless-steel cutlery, the antique crockery, the pile of old *Homes & Gardens* magazines in the bamboo book holder, the misty ceiling and the dusty mugs hanging on the hitching hooks screwed to the edges of the wooden shelves.

I stepped out of the house and breathed in the clean

morning air. Although we were in the middle of the summer, it was still raining lightly. The persistent light drizzle took the edge off the heat and penetrated the soil all the way down to the roots of plants and trees. Through the large glass shop front I could see Sadiq spreading his prayer mat on the floor. He stood on the edge, placed his hands behind his ears and began the *takbeer*. The door of the shop was closed so I placed my ear against the letter box and listened. '*Allahu akbar, allahu akbar!* With hardship goes ease. Lo!' Sadiq knelt down, prostrated then placed his forehead on the mat. My father stood up and placed his hands under his ribcage and began reciting. It was November and we had not seen a single drop of rain this year. He began the *tasleem*, turning his head to the left shoulder to greet the angel sitting there recording sins, then turned it to the right to greet the angel recording good deeds, then he waved to me. I walked towards his outstretched chipped hands. He held me up and then sat me down in his lap saying, 'Good morning, my little chick.'

Sadiq suddenly opened the door and said, 'Good morning, memsahib! Do you want me to teach you how to pray to Allah also?'

I waved a hello and crossed the street quickly.

Walking on the green pedestrian bridge I could see the thin clouds lit by the morning sun reflected in the river like large balls of flames. I saw the river split into two branches forming a small island. It was a peaceful space covered with green grass, wild flowers, and on its borders birch, chestnut, oak and rowan trees grew. The white sea-gulls flew in and out of the water and the dark green trees glistening like a sea of gems as if the rain was not water but pure sparkling olive oil. 'Too much past,' the English doctor had said, 'and not enough future.' I held the railing of the bridge and looked up again in time to see a dark figure lurking among the trees, wounded, his honour compromised, his eyes emitting sparks of hatred, the ends of his red-and-white-chequered kufiyya stuck in the black round robe securing it over his head, his rifle aimed at me ready to fire. I took a deep breath, put my bag on the ground between my legs, held the iron rails tight and opened up my chest, ready to be killed. He put his rifle down then slung it on his shoulder, pulled the end of his headdress out signalling the end of hostility, and walked towards the balls of light. When I finally shut my eyes salt stung their rims. I filled my lungs with fresh morning air travelling down from the green hills, picked up my bag and resumed my walk to work.

During my lunch break I went to the public library to look for books or articles on Shakespeare's sister. Imitating my university tutor, I began 'deconstructing' why libraries were intimidating: a) because the system of classification and borrowing was too complicated for me, and b) because the sight of so many books reminded me of my ignorance and backwardness. I felt so guilty when I entered the library because I had been wasting my time reading trivial magazines. In *Cosmopolitan* there was an article about women addicted to chocolate, which had chemicals similar to those produced when falling in love, but there wasn't a single word about women like me addicted to glossy magazines. Whenever my morale dropped a notch or two I would go to the newsagent and buy some chewing gum, a bar of chocolate and a glossy magazine. I would eat and read, chew and read until the packet was just pieces of silver paper scattered on the table and the magazine dog-eared and falling to pieces, its perfume sample pulled open and wiped clean.

A young girl with big eyes and a ready smile saw me hesitating and walked towards me. 'Can I help you?'

I wanted to pretend that I knew it all and give her a haughty thank you, but I remembered my tutor, the spilt coffee and said, 'Yes.'

'Let me explain the classification system for you,' she said politely.

When I realized that we were heading towards a computer, I was about to run towards the entrance. The place was unfamiliar and the pain of having to learn yet another new thing hit me hard. I remembered the expensive visit to the dentist, who is not subsidised by the NHS any more, and his persistent needle drilling right into my heart.

She pointed at the flickering light-blue screen and said, 'You can see the words "subject", "author" or "title". Just type the first letter and press enter. What are you looking for?'

'Shakespeare's sister,' I said.

'Aha!' she said. 'It must be the article by Virginia Woolf.'

I smiled a knowing smile. I had never heard of her in my whole immigrant life.

'My advice to you is to look under feminist theory.'

I sat on the chair, straightened my back and touched the keyboard. I pressed 'subject', 'enter' and then typed with my index finger 'feminst theory'.

The librarian was watching me. 'You have misspelled feminist. Add an "i"!'

I did, pressed 'enter' and a long list of books and articles suddenly appeared on screen. I was lost in the desert without the official tracer by my side. 'What shall I do now?' I asked.

'Choose one introductory book such as Mary Eagleton's *Feminist Literary Theory*!'

'This one?' I asked and clicked on it.

'Write down all the details and come with me please!'

She took me to a large hall lined with shelves decked with books. It reminded me of Minister Mahoney's library, where we celebrated my release from immigration prison and where we used to drink tea and discuss the weather. 'Books, Salma, are our only consolation. How can we forgive and forget without books?' he said.

'Here you are,' she said.

'Thank you very, very much,' I said to the smiling librarian, hugged my first borrowed books and rushed back to work.

It was raining heavily in Branscombe when I decided I should leave. It was my turn this time to insist on leaving. It had been almost a year since I moved in with Minister Mahoney. 'A guest must not burden his host for more than three days.' My English had improved partly because I liked the sound of it and partly because of my devotion for my Quaker host. I used to have a shower, wear a clean dress, tie my hair and wait patiently in the reading room for my evening lesson. I would look at Minister Mahoney's face and wonder why he had never got married. He must have been in his early fifties. The golden light of the fire was gleaming on his flushed face, peace-loving eyes, approving nod and his thin, long fingers. The *Cambridge Grammar* was open on conditionals. My mother had said to me many times that if you plant 'if' 'I wish' would grow. I said, 'Minister, I am not in the mood for studying tonight.'

'Are you OK?' he said concerned.

'Can you see tired I am tonight?'

'Yes I can see *how* tired you are tonight,' he corrected me.

'Nothing but we must war, we must war on radio. I cannot sleep.'

'The Friends are opposed to the war and are committed to peace,' he said.

I cleared my voice and said, 'If I could help you, I would. If I could stay in this house, I would. I must leave. My stay has finished your hospitality.'

'Aren't you happy here?' he asked.

'Yes, you are so kind. Like . . . father to me,' I said, choosing my words carefully in order not to upset this honey man.

He looked away and said, 'Can you manage on your own?'

'You told me Exeter the best southern city for jobs. I try,' I said.

'If you try you might fail.'

'Yes, but also might succeed.'

'But if you fail you must try better to fail better.' He smiled and left the room.

In the evening all was quiet and still apart from Liz knocking about in the sitting room. I tidied up my bed, wiped the wobbly table, pushed it close to the window and put a piece of cardboard under one of the legs to balance it. I put the table lamp on it and switched it on.

Gwen gave me the complete works of Yeats as a birthday gift. I read a few poems then put the book down. I fingered the rough jacket, folded it back, inserted it between the yellow pages like a bookmark. I placed my hand over the book and pressed hard, hoping that the words would cut loose, scatter, then find a way to my head. I wanted to understand all the words, see why the human child suffers, find a cure for weeping.

He must have been a bat, a night person, a scholar who liked the darkness and the quiet. They used to use lanterns then. I opened the feminist book as if it were fragile, made of fine glass, and looked through the index: Virginia Woolf. I began reading about having a room of one's own and enough money to be able to work. My mother had nothing of her own, her brother took her share of the farm; when her husband died Shahla was thrown out of her house so she came to live with us; and all I had was a daughter of my own, who cried and cried for me. My mind drifted to the bleak mountains with the few dusty shrubs, a field of black iris, some olive trees, to a world full of weeping, so I pulled it back to the black-and-white words on the page. Halfway through I saw a reference to Shakespeare's sister. The language used was too difficult for me so I began looking up words in the dictionary: 'escapade', 'substantial', 'guffawed', 'morbid'. I didn't know that 'offspring', which I came across while flicking through the pages, meant children.

While trying to put the pieces of the jigsaw together, I heard a sudden slash. It must be Liz. I rushed downstairs and found her standing in the sitting room, riding whip in hand, with three empty wine bottles rolling noisily on the floor. She was wearing her riding breeches and boots, a red

FADIA FAQIR

scarf knotted around her neck and her straight grey hair tied in a ponytail. Her frenzied eyes looked past me through the window. The crash was the sound of her riding whip hitting the bottles and carpeted floor. 'Liz. What do you think you're doing? Give me the whip!' I said and walked towards her to ease the whip out of her hand, but I was too slow so she caught the muscles of my forearm. I held the leather handle with one hand and the shaft with the other, pulled to the left, to the right then pushed and pushed until Liz let go of the whip and fell down. By now my arm was bleeding so I rushed to the bathroom, bandaged it, then ordered a taxi. While on the landing waiting for the taxi I heard Liz's laughter, then she said, as if talking to one of her Indian maids, 'Slaves must never breathe English air.'

'That looks bad,' said the taxi driver and handed me an old newspaper to cover the back seat. By the time I got to Casualty blood had seeped through the bandage and was oozing out. I was welcomed by neon lights and tired nurses. While examining the winding cut the nurse said, 'An incisive wound, I see. We must report it to the police.'

'No,' I said, 'there is no need to. I making salad and lost control of the knife.'

'It is a suicide attempt that went wrong then.'

'No. It was accident. If it suicide I wouldn't be here.'

She pulled her short hair behind her ears, looked at her fob watch, pushed up her silver-framed glasses and smiled. She must be used to hearing people's lies by now.

After filling in a form she asked me to wait in a narrow corridor full of chairs. The walls were painted lime green and the chairs and carpet were grey. Looking around me I

179

realized that my condition was not as urgent as others. A young man had a big piece of cotton covering his right eye; another's face was bruised and bleeding.

'This is a neat cut,' said the young exhausted doctor, 'how on earth did you manage to do that?'

'I was chopping carrots you see . . .'

'Look, we must report this to the police.'

'Please not,' I pleaded, 'I just lost control of the knife and it was really sharp.'

I could see that two emotions were fighting each other around his eyes, his sense of duty, which required reporting the incident to the police, and his exhaustion, which stopped him from challenging my story. He gave in to his fatigue.

When he unwrapped the bandage he said, 'You need stitches.' The wound ran from my elbow to my wrist, neat and winding like a snake. I gave in to local anaesthetic and travelled out of the decaying hospital, out of Exeter, towards Southampton, took the ship back to Lebanon then travelled by car to Hima, where my father with his wrinkled dark face, my mother with her beady patient eyes and Layla with her curly dark hair and her white dress were all waiting for me behind the barbed wire. We embraced and kissed and then I peeled one of the oranges they brought me and pushed it in my mouth. Orange juice and salty tears dripped down my face and became mixed together, then hit the ground one bitter-sweet salty liquid. My mother ran her chipped fingers through my hair and my father hemmed, coughed then said, 'How are you, daughter?' Then he hugged me, filling my senses with the smell of musk, fertile soil and coffee with ground cardamom pods.

The doctor was surprised to see my eyes fill up with tears. 'Surely it is not that painful,' he said.

I wiped my eyes with my left hand and blew my nose. For a second the professional mask slipped off the doctor's face so instantly he pushed it back into place. 'Do you have relatives here?'

'Yes,' I lied, 'my parents and daughter.'

'You must come back to get the stitches checked and the bandages changed the day after tomorrow. The antibiotics: three tablets a day and . . . and take it easy.'

When I finally waved down a taxi the sun was about to rise and the orange electric lights were going off one by one, leaving the streets covered with the grey light of the morning. 'Eighteen stitches, but don't worry, they will leave no mark.' The driver drank some coffee while speeding through the empty streets. I pulled my purse out with my left hand and gave him the money. 'Thank you, miss,' he said and drove off. Miss in Hima was reserved for virgins, Mrs for married women or widows, but there was no title for those who had sex out of wedlock for they simply got shot.

Gwen would be asleep and I didn't want to disturb her so I had to open the door of Swan Cottage and tiptoe to the sitting room. Liz was lying face down on the carpet of the hall. I wouldn't be able to take her to bed so I turned her head sideways, made sure she was breathing then covered her with a blanket. How could I allow them to report the incident to the police against this old drunk woman? Why create problems for her? Why create problems for me, Salma not Sal or Sally, an outlander, who must not confront the natives? You begin to climb the stairs without leaning on the railing; you throw yourself in bed

181

after you lock your bedroom door; you switch off your table lamp and think about Shakespeare's sister; you adjust your mirror and drive on exploring this new land; you sleep between the cold sheets not knowing where to put your arm, how to adjust its position so you would not feel the pulsating pain, so you would close your eyes and drift away.

After finishing my late shift at the hotel I walked to the high street as if drawn by a steel rod to the kebab van parked by the tower. I sat on the bench inhaling the smell of falafel rissoles bubbling away in the hot frying oil and listening to North African Arabic.

'*Hadi? Belhaq miziana*, but that one is as ugly as your grandmother, *vraiment, haraq w makhabel*,' an old man said.

'Wha'?' the young man replied. '*Ma nifhamsh*. I don't understand the Arabic.'

'I said Yasin has no papers and no brains,' the older man said.

'He is a "ten-pee" then,' the young man said.

'Yes, you slot the ten-pee coin in a public phone, call immigration, finish him off,' the older man said.

They threw a fresh batch of falafels in the frying pan. The aroma of crushed chickpeas, garlic and parsley balls hitting the hot oil wafted to my nose again.

Khairiyya parked the car by the uneven pavement, switched the engine off and got out. From what she told me I assumed that we were in the main road of one of the villages of Levant. She walked to the small grocery shop with a few wooden boxes full of fruit and vegetables laid out neatly on the tiled platform. I grabbed the handle, turned it, lowering the window, then stuck my head out and sniffed and sniffed, filling my heart with the smell of freedom. The warm and gentle air full of the aroma of rich food being fried felt like precious Indian silk against my face. I deserved to be dead, but I was not only alive, I was free.

She headed towards the large cauldron balanced over a brass kerosene cooker on the wooden table and said something to the man with a white cap busy stirring the contents of the vessel with a large spoon. He fished out some crisp brown balls and tucked them in the pockets of slit pitta bread. With his right hand he pressed the bread against the table, squashing the brown balls, dripped a ladle full of white sauce inside the sandwiches, added some lettuce and tomato slices, wrapped them with a piece of thin white paper then placed them gently in a brown bag. Khairiyya gave him some money, picked up the brown bag and walked back. 'Here you are – a falafel sandwich!' she said and handed me one of the wraps.

I tore the soft tissue off and bit into my first falafel. The crisp balls broke under my teeth filling my mouth with the flavour of garlic, cumin and crushed coriander. 'What is it?' I asked.

'It is made of chickpeas, fava beans, parsley and onions with some tahini sauce,' she said and bit into the white bread.

The taste of falafel and the aroma of rich spicy food filled the car and the dusty wide road.

My scalp twitched as if someone had blown cold air against the back of my neck so I looked back at the mirage at the end of the dusty road and saw my grandmother Shahla in her black Bedouin madraqa crossing the road in

THE CRY OF THE DOVE

a cloud of dust carrying a leather bag full of milk. I breathed out and shook my head.

'*Mkhabil gultilak*,' said the old man in the kebab van parked on the side of the main street.

'Wha'?' said the young man.

'The top floor of his head is empty,' said the old man.

'Nobody want buy falafel. Only chips, chips,' said a third man, who might be Yasin, and sniffed.

'They are English, what do you expect?' said the young man.

'Look at the young sir,' said the old man.

'Stop fucking pointing at me. I am Algerian me,' said the young man.

'You? Algerian? And my goat blond,' said Yasin.

They laughed.

'Yes, I cannot speak the Arabic, but I am Algerian,' the young man said.

The smell of crushed cumin, black pepper and coriander filled the busy high street. Sitting on the bench in the dark I could not be seen, but I could hear the sound of police sirens, a man throwing up in the rubbish bin and a group of young men singing, 'ENGLAND ENGLAND MIGHTY MIGHTY ENGLAND.' A woman shouted, 'Get off me, you drunk git!'

I had a last sniff, vowed never to come back here again, and walked home.

The ringing of the payphone in the hall woke me up so I rushed down the stairs and picked up the receiver before Liz could hear it. Max was shouting, 'Where the hell are you? The department store are asking for all the trousers back.'

184

I lost my tongue. How on earth was I supposed to finish fifty trousers in one day? It was not a straightforward job. They had turn-ups too. When I finally composed myself I said, 'There was an accident. I cut my right arm and had it stitched. Give me just today. I'll come to work on Monday.'

'You mean two days' leave.' Max had included Saturday, which I normally took off.

'Right, two days then,' I said.

He surprised me by saying, 'I hope you'll feel better soon. With no family and all.'

'Thank you, Max. See you Monday,' I said and put the receiver down.

Weakened by the nausea and the vomiting I saw tiny spots of lights swimming around when I suddenly got out of the ex-army bed. In the hostel, which was so inhospitable they switched off the heating after nine in the morning, I stood in the middle of the cold room looking for answers, a foothold, for something to grab, for an anchor. I rummaged in Parvin's rucksack looking for her plastic bag full of cassettes. I picked one that had 'When Doves Cry' written on it in purple ink. I plugged in the cassette player and slid the tape in the pocket then pressed the 'play' button. I held the pen in my hand ready to write down the lyrics. A taut sharp voice sang of courtyards, violets in bloom and doves crying. This was followed by a barrage of squeaks that sounded like a drawing of breath followed by sobs. I looked up the words I did not understand in the dictionary and read and reread the lyrics until I memorized them. Then I rewound the tape and played the song again. I stood up and held the back of the chair to steady myself and began dancing to the music, stepping in then stepping out the way they do on television. Then I began jumping then landing on the tip of my toes then relaxing my toes until the bottom of my feet touched the cold carpet then jumping again in the air higher and higher until my hair flew off my shoulders. Parvin walked in on me.

'What the hell do you think you're doing?!'

'Why do we scream at each other?' I asked her.

'I am not screaming,' she said.

'Maybe you are just like my mother,' I sang.

She put her briefcase on the table, kicked off her shoes and sat down on the edge of her bed. She placed her bowed head between her hands.

I stopped singing and dancing and sat next to her and said, 'I tired. I ill. I look for flowers in bloom.'

She held both of my hands and said, 'If only you weren't losing so much weight.'

'Conditional sentence. I see. Express wish,' I said like a schoolteacher.

When I turned round, I realized that Liz was standing right behind me.

'Good morning.' She smiled.

'Good morning,' I said and was about to rush back to my room.

'What happened to your arm?' she asked.

I looked at Liz's dishevelled hair, swollen eyes, her hand pressed to her forehead, her pointed nose and said, 'Nothing.' Standing there in the hall she looked tired, washed out.

'What is wrong with your arm, Sal?'

186

'Nothing, a minor accident,' I said. She genuinely couldn't remember last night.

'This late-night job you're doing is dangerous,' she said.

I knew what Liz was thinking: a lower-class immigrant slut, hustling down on the quay, must have been stabbed by her pimp. All of that was written on her hangovered face. 'I must go now,' I said.

She parroted my accent. 'I moost go noo,' she said and smiled.

It did not sound like me, it sounded like a programme on television about masters and servants, some sort of a northern accent. Come to think of it, it sounded like Dr John Robson. I rushed up the stairs and shut my bedroom door.

With three days' break I would be able to finish my essay on Shakespeare's sister. I began writing, *Why was I asked to write about Shakespeare's sister not Shakespeare although so much has been said and written about him? He must have had friends and women to help him. Nobody talks about the women. I remembered the stories of Abu-Zaid El-Hilali, the hero whose adventures were memorized by both the young and the old. Nobody ever mentions his wife, daughter or mother.* I spent the whole morning writing the seven pages the tutor asked for, using some of the stories I was told as a child as examples. Between sipping cold coffee, peering out of the window at the crisp clear morning and writing, I finished the essay. The conclusion was about my own experience as an alien in their land. They, and I, think I don't live here, but I do, just like all the women who were ignored in these tales. Comparing my essay to the book it sounded like a gossip column in the *Sunday Sport*. That was it. I cannot write like them. If I were able to I wouldn't be stitching hems.

I dozed off to be woken up around lunchtime with the forceful knock of Liz. She must have sobered up. She opened the door and had a pine tray, covered with an embroidered white cover, a bowl of soup, slices of brown bread and a cup of tea. She stood above my head smiling benevolently like an angel. I said thank you and attacked the food. Gratitude. The smell of lavender filled the bedroom. She must have had a bath. 'Are you going somewhere?'

'Yes, must dash. I am going to see my doctor.'

The way she said it gave you the impression that she was off to see her own private doctor in Harley Street where the stars go, but I knew that she was, just like me, registered with the local NHS practitioner.

Dear Noura,

Greetings from Exeter. I am not feeling very well. My landlady, who is alcoholic, took me for one of the ponies she used to own and hit me with her riding whip. The wound was coiled around my arm like a snake. With no one to make me soup apart from the landlady I feel sorry for myself. I wish you were here to run your hand on my head. I wish many things. Layla has passed her A-levels and will go to university soon. She will come home weekends and we will drive to Dartmouth and spend the day swimming in the sea. I see you smiling. Yes I learnt swimming in the city baths, where you queue for days, pay thirteen pounds and then are given a swimming course. The instructor is in her fifties now, but looks so young. She said swimming keeps your skin taut. That is why we age so fast in Hima because we have no water to drink let alone swim in.

Noura, I hope that you, Rami and Rima are in good health. How is Rami's diabetes? I keep an eye on new remedies for it here. They are experimenting on the pancreas of a pig, but you might not want pig cells implanted inside your Muslim child.

You never know fate might bring us together again.

I licked the addressless envelope and stuck it together.

If you looked carefully you would find hundreds of letters thrown in dustbins or being blown here and there by the wind, either alongside the post office or in the streets and alleyways of the old country, their black ink smudged or wiped away. The yellow paper, litter, empty plastic bags, dry leaves would be dispersed then gathered, then dispersed again until they found a sheltered corner to rot in. The old white Greek houses shone against the azure sea broken only by the mane of frothy white waves. I would save up and travel to Greece, the nearest I could get to my home without being shot. Standing on a high cliff by the sea I would shout thousands of salaams across the Mediterranean.

I watched a chat show about men who go out with younger women. 'Husband snatchers!' a woman in the audience shouted. Talk about sisterhood, I thought. Noura used to tell me about the husbands she used to render her services to. I used to say, 'Here in this country, you cannot be serious?'

She would laugh, one of those laughs her customers paid so much for, and pat my cheek. 'Chick, you are so naive.'

Then the warden would come and say to Noura, 'Leave this girl alone. Your obscene laugh gives me the jitters. I seek refuge in Allah. This is not a whorehouse.'

'Oh! Yeah! How come you always call us whores?'

Naima's patience was running out.

'By the way, I gave a blow job to your husband,' said Noura.

Naima slapped her with all her might.

Noura ducked to the ground and started crying, tears of pain and humiliation.

Naima shut the door and spat, 'Scum, that's what you are.'

Madam Lamaa, who was convinced that she was scum, got up in time to hear Naima's last words. She placed her hands on her ears and began sobbing.

Gwen came to see me on Saturday. I phoned her and told her that I had not abandoned her, but I was not feeling very well. She came despite her dislike for Liz, and brought me a second-hand copy of a novel I had been looking for. She sat on the edge of the bed and asked, 'Who did this to you?' pointing at the bandaged arm.

I waved to her to move closer and whispered, 'Liz was drunk and hit me with her riding whip.'

Gwen tucked the ends of her short grey hair behind her ears, then sighed, 'How awful! The woman has gone mad.'

'I lied to the doctor and told him I cut my hand chopping salad.'

'Did he believe you?'

'No, but he was too tired and overworked to care.'

'You must move out.'

'I cannot.'

'I am so sorry, Salma,' she said then hugged me tight.

It was the nearness I had been waiting for for days so I began crying.

'What's wrong with you now?' she said in her head-mistress voice.

'Nothing, I just want to be with my family,' I said like a child.

'But you know that you cannot be with your family – that is if you still have one back there.' Gwen regretted saying this as soon as she did so.

I pulled the neck of my nightie up and said, 'It doesn't matter . . . any more.'

'No, it doesn't,' she said and ran her fingers over the duvet cover. 'Look what I brought you. Your favourite haloumi cheese,' she said, pulling a slab of white cheese wrapped in plastic out of her cloth bag. The smell of mint and brine filled the room.

'Where did you get it? It's hard to find.'

'The delicatessen in town ordered it for me,' she said.

I looked at Gwen's neat grey hair, her flushed red face, golden glasses, V-neck pink blouse and smiled.

'That's better,' she said.

Turkish Delights and Coconuts

I WENT TO THE UNIVERSITY AGAIN, TO SUBMIT MY ESSAY TO my tutor. It was neatly packed in a mauve plastic folder Gwen had given me when I finally joined the Open University. I chose to wear a dark flowery second-hand skirt and a long embroidered white shirt, which Parvin had given me for my birthday. I ran my fingers down my skirt, made sure that my hair was neatly tied up, spat on a tissue and wiped the dust off my shoes, then knocked on the door and got an instant and thunderous, 'Come in,' which froze my limbs. With trembling fingers I opened the door, but could not drag my feet forward on the Persian carpet.

'Come in,' he said in a gentler voice.

I stood by the door and said, trying to imitate Liz's accent, 'Here is the essay!'

'Ah! At last,' he said and looked at me from above his sliding half-moon glasses. He took the folder and placed it on top of the pile on his desk. I was still standing up, so while flicking through it, he said, 'Sit down!' I caught a glimpse of the same novel I was reading on the shelf behind him and made a mental note to tell Gwen.

'I see you don't have your flask today. Would you like a cup of coffee?' he asked. He took off his reading glasses, folded their handles gently and put them in a soft leather box.

'Yes, thank you,' I said, expecting the coffee to be produced straight away.

He stood up, pulled his blue shirt down over his trousers, stuck his hands in the pockets of his jeans and said, 'Let's go then.'

We walked on grass, among flowers, shrubs and trees whose names I did not know. Had he asked me about that tall tree with flowers erect like candles I wouldn't have known what to say: 'Beech, horse chestnut, oak,' which I memorized recently without matching the words to the shape of the trunks and leaves. Had he asked me about that dog chasing a stick I wouldn't have known what to say: 'Dalmatian, Rottweiler, Alsatian,' which I memorized recently without matching the names of species to the actual dog. When I closed my fingers over my empty palms I realized that they were wet with the sweat of ignorance.

A man in a red worn-out velvet jacket, a bowtie and glasses walked towards us on the footpath and when he was close enough to be heard said to Dr Robson, 'Whey aye, man!' and smiled.

Dr Robson said under his breath, 'Arsehole!'

'What did he say?' I asked.

'He is taking the piss,' he said.

'Why?' I asked.

'I come from a village called Aycliffe. A northerner,' he said and ran his fingers through his thinning hair.

I was about to cross the distance between us and grab

his hand, but I remembered that my palms were so sweaty. Shahla would have sucked her teeth loudly and said, '*Tzzu*!' The eye can never be higher than the eyebrow.'

The building was totally hidden behind trees and shrubs. We rushed up the old stairs to the entrance. Dr Robson opened the door for me and I entered as if I were a lady. The café's walls were made of shining glass and when I sat down I felt as if I were outdoors in the magnificent garden inhaling the scent of flowering trees. The smell of coffee, clean flesh and clothes wafted to my nose when Dr Robson came back carrying a tray with two mugs of steaming coffee and a piece of flapjack. He smiled and asked sweetly, 'Sugar?'

'No thank you, Dr Robson,' I said while still looking at the delicate blooming tree.

He followed my eyes and said, 'Please call me John. It's a Japanese dogwood tree.'

I sat on the edge of the chair nearest to the entrance pretending to enjoy this cup of coffee with him.

He searched my face and then asked, 'What is the name of your daughter?'

I choked on her name. 'Lay ... Layla,' I said and swallowed hard.

He stretched back, stuck his hand under his loose shirt, rubbed his belly and said, 'Do you have a big family?'

'Yes,' I said and shuddered as if I had caught a cold. My thin cotton shirt felt sticky and damp. I must leave before the fabric sticks to my sweaty back. He sipped his coffee, then fingered the lip of the cup. 'Is it time-consuming taking care of a family?'

'Yes,' I said.

'Yes, John,' he said.

'Yes, John, cooking for them, and all,' I said and stuck a rebellious strand of hair back into the elastic band. I found it hard to address him as John. In the old country teachers were never addressed informally.

'Thank you for the coffee,' I said and stood up.

He took a final sip and said, 'I'll see you next Monday, same time.'

I sighed with relief, pulled my top off my back and rushed out.

While walking down the hill I saw a tree in full bloom, its delicate white flowers swaying in the wind. 'Dogwood, dogwood,' I repeated. I began writing a letter in my head. *To whom it may concern: My name is Salma Ibrahim El-Musa, I was in Islah prison for eight years. During the first year I gave birth to a baby girl and she was instantly taken away to a home for illegitimate children. I wonder if you can help me locate her. My postal address is . . .* Then I tore the imagined letter up. How could I reveal my true identity and address? I would risk being traced and killed. How could I ignore Layla's cries, her calls, her constant pleading? I stood at the bottom of the hill and looked back. It was green with grass, weeds and shrubs, but suddenly like magic everything was erased and it turned into a dry brown mountain covered with silver-green olive trees, plum trees and grapevines. I sat down on a flat stone, put my head between my hands and breathed in. What was better: to live with half a lung, kidney, liver, heart or to go back to the old country and get shot? To learn how to numb this throbbing pain or let it all end swiftly? A swarm of bees was sucking the nectar out of some purple irises with bright yellow hearts. When I turned my head again the hill was covered with the black iris of Hima.

When I got back to work Max was in a foul mood, cursing the Japanese all the time for coming to this country and buying factories. I tried to be invisible, like Casper, and do my job briskly and lightly like a summer breeze. Many people were losing their jobs; I was lucky to have one, I thought, and stitched, sewed, ironed, until my nostrils were lined with starch. At the end of the day Max sat next to me and asked, 'How is the arm?'

'It's fine, thank you.'

He put the pins and needles on the sewing machine and took a paper bag off the dirty floor. 'This is from the family. A coconut cake,' he said and ran his finger over his gelled hair to make sure that the fringe-like wave was still stuck around his head.

'Thank you, that's really nice of your wife,' I said.

'She said you must like coconuts, being foreign and all,' he said and smiled.

'Yes, very, very much. Thank you,' I lied. The first time I saw a coconut was several years ago when Parvin bought one in the market 'to cook with the chicken'.

'It's all right, bint,' he said and walked away.

Allan was surprised to see the wrapped arm. 'What happened to you?'

'A small accident,' I said and smiled.

'When?'

'A few days go,' I said.

'Are you sure you want to work tonight?'

'Yes,' I said.

'I will get you some rubber gloves to wear. Keep them on when you collect glasses.'

The bar was crowded and the smell of cigar smoke, beer and stale breath filled the air. I concentrated on collecting glasses then lining them up in the drawer of the dishwasher. One of the customers, thin and respectable, suddenly shouted, 'We're not in a fucking operating theatre. Jesus, what are those gloves for? I don't have Aids you know.' I stepped back and bent the elbows of both arms to stop him from pulling off the gloves.

Allan was angry so he rushed to the man and asked him to leave. 'Out,' he said.

I felt awkward. Allan was overreacting. My immigrant survival kit said, 'Avoid confrontation at any price.' 'Allan,' I pleaded.

Ten minutes later the thin respectable man was back with Mr Brightwell, the manager of the hotel. Heart thumping I knelt behind the counter to feed the dishwasher. I was about to lose my job. There was a hushed silence. The manager walked towards Allan and said, 'Let me introduce John Barker-Rathbone OBE, chairman of International Enterprises Limited.'

It must be serious, I thought, although I did not understand what OBE stood for.

'Allan, I would like you to apologize to Mr Barker-Rathbone.'

Allan cleared his voice and said, 'Sorry, sir,' then walked behind the bar.

'Where is the rude barmaid?' the manager asked.

I raised my head slowly, waving my yellow rubber glove in the air like a flag and parroted Allan, 'Sorry, sir, very, very sorry, sir.'

'Why are you wearing gloves?' he asked.

I showed him my bandaged arm.

'You should be at home resting.'

I was shaking by now, sure that I would get the sack. I looked for Allan, but he was busy serving customers. Pulling my rubber gloves up I said, 'I am all right, really,' and smiled.

The manager was about to say something then he changed his mind then he changed his mind again and said, 'When will you get rid of the bandages?'

'Tomorrow,' I lied.

The manager walked out and Mr Barker-Rathbone OBE went back to the same table and resumed his drinking as if nothing had happened.

After closing, legs spread on chairs, over our usual cup of coffee we began chatting.

'He must be a rich son-of-a-bitch,' said Barry, referring to Mr Barker-Rathbone.

Imitating him I said, 'Jesus, I don't have Aids!'

Allan joined in. 'Then the dark iceberg came crashing down.'

Then Barry said from behind the bar, 'An avalanche of disease.'

I asked Allan, 'What does OBE stand for?'

'Order of the British Empire.'

'So it is a title like sir,' I said. And I thought about the perfect English/Irish gentleman, my only sir, Minister Mahoney OBE.

The sun shone on Minister Mahoney's house in Branscombe. Shelves decked with old books, the worn-out sofa, the old radio in the corner and the Bible with his reading glasses on top of its leather jacket. He used to teach me English to 'equip me to tackle this harsh environment'. The most beautiful language was the language of peace and reconciliation, he would say, and read me Portia's speech about mercy. And now like my father I searched the sky for clouds and the gentle rain for kindness.

It was a 'glorious' summer evening in Branscombe and Minister Mahoney was cooking pasta in the kitchen while listening to Sunday jazz. I was sitting on the soft sofa in the sitting room listening to the sounds of home: pasta bubbling away in boiling water, mushrooms sizzling in the frying pan, water gurgling out of a carafe, laying the table, stirring, checking, whistling then singing along. The lyrics were about longing to meet a caring person, someone who will watch over his loved ones.

Noura, there were no nightmares that afternoon. I looked through the patio doors at the orange rose tree in the corner lit by the golden light of the setting sun, sniffed the aroma wafting from the kitchen and listened to the bouncy but sad voice. I held my breath, released it and snuggled against the soft leather of the sofa.

I was not working that evening, so I decided to treat myself to a trip to the Turk's Head. My arm was still thinly bandaged, so I struggled to keep it out of the water while having a bath. I began the atrocious routine of trying to make myself look younger. The pine bath and the close shaving was followed by covering my whole body with cocoa butter, spraying myself with deodorant, working mousse into my hair, bending down to blow dry it. The awkward position pushed my blood pressure up. Head dangling like a chicken, oiled as if about to be roasted, hair sweeping the carpet, I started shaking. I could see the grime lining his dusty toenails sticking out from under the curtains. I threw my hair back, stood up firmly and straightened my spine ready to face him, but he had disappeared again. I pulled the curtains open and there was nothing behind them except my steaming washing folded neatly and wrapped around the radiator.

My Bedouin mother would have smacked her lips and said, '*Tzu*'! You look like a slut.' To convince Mother that respectable women here wore clothes that made them look like sluts would be impossible. She used to cover even her toes with the end of her long black robe when sitting down, 'Don't let the men see your ankles.' My thin and ugly ankles were not a turn-on as a buxom actress had once said. It was late evening, but the summer sun was still shining, turning everything into gold, the trees, the river and the hills. I wrapped my mother's black shawl around my shoulders and walked on to the Turk's Head. I quickened my pace when I got to the big Royal Mail hangar, where they sort out the mail for the whole of Exeter. I must be well known there, the crazy lady who never wrote a complete address on her letters. The sun by now looked like a wound at the end of the horizon, dripping clear blood all over the place. The water caught fire, the way the village creek used to do in the summer. Our crop of wheat was being gently cooked to maturity so the old men, the women, the young men and the children would say, 'Isn't the sunset beautiful?' Old women would say, 'Thank Allah for his kindness. Your crops could have been plagued by locusts or could have rotted away.'

I stood on the riverbank, reluctant to enter the pub, happy just to watch the wound heal and the sun sink behind the hills, but the noise of animated chats, the smell of cigarette and cigar smoke and beer, and the jolly sound of the jukebox welcomed me. I sat on my usual corner stool and asked for lemonade. After the first sip, I began looking around to see if Jim was there so I could avoid him. Right behind me, in the raised smoking area, Dr Robson . . . John, my teacher, was sitting with a group of young men and women who looked like students. He saw me and raised his glass to me. I raised mine. At that very moment, I realized that Jim was heading towards me and it was too late to avoid him. I'd told John that I was a family woman and now look.

'Hi.'

'Hello,' I said, looking at my glass.

'Are you following me?' he asked.

I remembered steaming cups of sage tea on the side table, the hurried breakfast and bumping into him in town. I also saw him in a café with a petite blonde woman, whispering to each other. I looked at him without saying anything.

'If you are stalking me I will sort you out,' he said.

I was shaking when I said, 'What are you saying?'

John was watching from the distance when Jim wiggled his finger at me and walked away.

I put the drink down and rushed out. John was right behind me. 'Are you all right?' he said and pushed his glasses up.

'I am fine, J . . . John,' I said.

'What happened to your arm?' he asked.

'Nothing really. Just a scratch,' I said and walked away.

The last thing I needed was for John to show me any sympathy. I trudged on like a doll held together by plastic screws and any human kindness or sympathy would melt them away leaving me a heap of disjointed limbs. It was a moonless night, but the huge electric lights were like tiny sick moons floating on the water. Their artificial light, which lit the whole area all night long, made everything look unreal, as if we were all actors in a sci-fi film. I wrapped my shawl around me and wished that I were somewhere else or dead. I craved the silent, pitch-black nights of our village, with no noise whatsoever apart from the rhythmic chirruping of the cicada, the distant barking of dogs and the perfume of honeysuckle and white *ful*. The dark sky enveloped you, covered you like a duvet stuffed with ostrich feathers and under it you could close your eyes and have a deep, sound sleep.

Whenever I left the house Liz shouted after me, 'You've begun visiting your customers in their houses when their wives are away. Courtesan!' She was in a bad mood. Since she saw her GP she hadn't stopped swearing. He ordered her to stop drinking, and said to her that her nervous system and her liver were being eroded 'slowly but surely' by alcohol. The first evening she tried not to drink, but come ten o'clock she was at Sadiq's shop begging for a bottle of cheap wine. She would pay him later. I didn't know what to do. I knew that a niece of hers called Natasha lived in Kent, but what would I say to her? 'Call the AA, your aunt should be committed to an alcohol treatment centre.' How could I, me the immigrant tenant, tell the middle-class English what to do with their aunts?

*I shall never forget that day as long as I live. Daddy
walked in earlier than usual ruffled and tired. He was
always well groomed so it seemed odd. He went straight to
the library, pulled the curtains shut and lay still in the
dark. He asked the ayah to wash his head with water and
vinegar then rub some willow-tree oil on his forehead. She
told me that while she was massaging his head he kept
repeating, 'Serving His Majesty the King-Emperor is a
badge of honour I shall wear with pride until I die.'
I ran out to fish for news. The gardener told me that there
was a public gathering in the maidan. Hita's father was
addressing the crowd. The British opened fire. 'People say
that your father, miss, shot Hita's father and left him
dying there.'
    I ran out looking for Hita. When I finally found him
he was holding the bars of the iron gate tight. His eyes
were wide open and his jaws clenched.
    'Hita, Hita jaan,' I pleaded then placed my hand over
his. He pushed it away as if I had leprosy and began
shaking. He released the bars slowly and walked out
through the gate. I never saw him again.*

Before going to work, I found two letters on the landing
addressed to me, which had never ever happened before. I
usually got orders in the post: pay your overdraft, pay your
rent, but I rarely received a proper letter. I opened the first
one and saw John's signature. *I do apologize for Monday. Can
we meet on Friday instead? I have to be out of town.* From the
sinking of my heart I realized how psyched up I was to
meet him. The second was a white decorated card inviting
me to Parvin's wedding in three weeks' time. Reception,
Reed Hall, University of Exeter. Four years ago we were

scavengers looking for leftovers in garbage bins and whenever we found a mouldy sandwich we would run to the park to eat it; 'The Paki beggars are back,' they used to say at the White Hare, and now she is getting married to Mr Mark Parks, a handsome white English man with a metal hook for a hand.

That evening Allan was caressing my arm. 'It looks much better now, Salma, you don't need the rubber gloves,' he said.

I looked at his wet-gelled hair, his bowtie, his shiny shoes and thought that it would be nice to have him as a brother. He was honest, discreet and protective. Would he watch me or watch over me? Was I a potential shame or a loving younger sister? What are brothers like with their teenage sisters in this country?

It was coming. I could see it in the way he collected the glasses if he was free, the way he kept an eye on me, the way he offered me coffee at the end of the evening. 'Sugar?' he would say as if he was calling me that.

I did not need any complications at work. 'No thank you.' I stopped before using his name, which I normally used freely. I stretched my legs on the velvet upholstery and sipped the coffee. It was coming. I could feel it.

'Salma, would you like to have dinner with me next Wednesday?' he said and adjusted his bowtie.

He knew that I did not work on Wednesdays. I swallowed hard and said as kindly as possible, 'I don't think so, Allan. You're like a brother to me.'

I could see that the message had got through to his eyes; he lowered them to hide the hurt.

We drank the coffee in silence then Allan sighed and said, 'Do you have any brothers?'

'No,' I lied. I could hear distant barking, cars whizzing by, a radio singing somewhere. I got up and said, 'I must go home.'

Mahmoud was a few years older than me, thin and regal in his wide, long white body shirt. He would look at me and try to twist his wispy short moustache then curse. His silver dagger, which had an engraved handle, a blood groove and a leather scabbard, and his cudgel were fixed to his ammunition belt.

'He thinks he is the sheikh of the tribe. He walks like a turkey cock, legs wide apart. He was circumcised late, that's what it is,' Shahla would say and suck on her teeth.

He would wave his cudgel in the air threateningly whenever I moved. But sometimes he would come home from school carrying a small brown bag full of Turkish delight and Mary's biscuits, which was practically the only food that the village store sold. He knew that I loved shaking off the sugar powder, flattening the delight with my hand and then placing it between two biscuits like a sandwich. Sitting on the edge of the well in the courtyard he would watch me eat the biscuits with a mixture of love and disgust. He was a gentle brother. He was the desert police on patrol. Shahla would suck at her old long pipe and say, 'Watch your step, girl.'

When I opened the front door the smell of naphthalene hit me. I tiptoed to the sitting room and there she was reclining on the dirty sofa in a crimson and cream sari embroidered with gold and with a crown of dry flowers on her head. Her face was smeared with a rancid dark yellow butter that she had scooped out of a silver box. Her hand, bruised and limp, rested against her heart and a letter. 'I just got married to Hita. Isn't it splendid?' she said.

The heavily embroidered sari resting on her left shoulder glittered in the dark, but you could see her dirty cotton underwear above the skirt. The tilting crown pulled her grey fringe back showing the red lesions on her forehead and the spidery thin red veins on her cheeks. She rubbed her eyes and said, 'My father, how on earth would he have known?' then began crying.

'You look lovely in your sari, Liz,' I said and put my hand on her convulsing back.

She tried to suppress her tears, but they burst out in one howl followed by rhythmic sobs. 'He wrote me letters asking for forgiveness, once, twice,' she said.

I held the back of her head against me and said, 'Shush, shush. It's all right. Shush.' I could feel the warmth of her head against my tummy and the tears running down my arms.

Her hot tears melted the butter creating a crooked line down her face and her kohl was smudged around her red swollen eyes.

I ran to the kitchen and brought a towel, soap and some warm water. 'Let me wash off the make-up,' I said gently and began rubbing off the yellow butter with the wet kitchen towel. She sat quietly while I scooped off the butter then rubbed her face gently with soap and water. She looked up and said with difficulty, 'My father shot him then shot himself.'

'Shot who?' I asked.

'His father! He didn't know. He wanted them to say

"salaam" this and "salaam" that, and he refused. My Hita's father,' she slurred.

Her face was clean and even red when I said, 'Would you like to have some rest?'

'The bride will retire to her bedroom. Charles, you may kiss the bride.'

When I put my shoulder under her arm and pulled her up the stairs she was obliging like the black cloth doll her ayah had made for her. She slipped under the dirty white duvet. I turned her head sideways, opened her mouth then said, 'Goodnight, bride.'

She sighed then went to sleep instantly.

I rushed downstairs, put the lid firmly on the silver box, wiped it clean, then rubbed the dark butter off the sofa and coffee table, opened all the windows and doors, tipped the wine down the sink and washed the tray and dirty glasses.

I sat down on Elizabeth's armchair and read Hita's letter, which was crumpled on the floor.

I dreamt for months of the day I could rub my body with your oil, Elizabeth. I mixed sandalwood powder, turmeric and oil in a bowl while reciting carefully the names and titles of your family and mine. I took off my clothes and rubbed my chest, back, hands, lips, fingers, toes with the oil until my skin turned yellow and soft. I sat there waiting for my sweat and blood to seep through the oil then I scraped it off, put it in a silver box, added more oil to it, mixed it until it was an even fine paste then stored it for the big day when you will rub your delicate white skin with it until it turns dark yellow, until you become mine.

Lemons and Monkeys

THE SMELL OF PINE BATH OIL PROMISED A HANDSOME, rich man in the garden, under my bedroom window. Under the influence of the fumes of the concentrated herbal bath I forgot that I didn't have a window over-looking a garden. I stretched my body in the hot water and relaxed my muscles. All of that bending to stitch, iron and feed the glasses into the washer has stiffened up my neck and shoulders. Soon I will be thirty-one, hunch-backed, grey-haired and alien. Soon I will be begging Sadiq to marry me and I would be happy to send two hundred pounds a month to his wife in Pakistan. A face dripping like wax looked back at me in the Indian mirror. I pulled the straps of the bra up, put on a black dentelle shirt, which I had bought from a charity shop and mended, and a long embroidered black skirt, which used to belong to Parvin. One day in the hostel she had gone mental and thrown all the contents of her wardrobe on the floor. 'I cannot bear it any more. Take this, and this. Take all,' she screamed. I never wore the black low-heeled shoes wrapped in soft tissue paper and hidden among the jumpers. I bought them on a whim then realized that only old women wear sensible shoes in this country. I longed for my grandmother's worn-out flat plastic green shoes. 'I walk in streams, ponds, on dry land and they are quality. Your kind father buys me two pairs a year from the capital, a single dinar each,' she used to say.

Leaving the house in stiletto shoes I overheard Liz on the phone whispering, 'She's got more money. She buys fresh brown bread and Earl Grey tea. Sally must be hustling.'

I sat on one of the benches outside the Waterfront restaurant, where they served you dustbin-lid pizza, and drank my Diet Coke. The newly built flats overlooking the river looked empty, no one in them, no one could afford them. Like houses made of biscuit and icing sugar, they looked bright, sparkling, but easy to crumble. The waterfront was full of people, young Italian kids studying English, Spanish girls doing tourism, American students, local skinheads with their large black dogs in their slashed black jackets and Union Jack T-shirts. I watched the Goodtime ferry carrying people across from one side of the river to the other; its lights ebbed and flowed in the water.

Suddenly the fine hairs on the back of my neck stood up. I knew that breeze. She was out there crying, looking for a foothold. I knew that wind. A sudden chill ran through me so I bent forward as if winded and hugged my erect nipples. The muscles where my ribs meet between my breasts were inflated then collapsed as if I had sunk inwards. I was drowning. Her dark hair stuck to her head, her soft tummy was sticking out and her feet were tiny. When Madam Lamaa slapped her bottom she cried for air.

I counted the fingers of each hand: one, two, three, four, five. I counted the toes of each foot: one, two, three, four, five. Her soft fingers curled up around my forefinger like a tender vine that had just burst open. Seconds before her soft lips touched my nipple Naima snatched her away, wrapped her in a blanket and rushed out. She was hungry and my breasts were brimming with milk. I howled at the barred window. The inmates stopped me from hurling myself against the wall. When I came round Noura and Madam Lamaa were holding me down. 'It's for the best, love. It's for the best.'

My legs were covered with dry blood and my tummy was sticky with milk and tears.

Even the bouncers in Dansers were middle-aged. I paid four pounds and walked in. I looked at my reflection in the long mirror by the entrance. My hair was frizzed up, my face glistened with sweat and my skirt creased. I pushed my hair back and entered the half-empty club. I felt that all eyes were on me, X-ray eyes that could see everything including my shameful past. I rushed to the bar, ordered two Diet Cokes to save myself the journey back, walked to one of the tables in the corner and sat down. It was on a raised floor surrounded by a wooden banister so I felt as if I was sitting in a pavement café watching passers-by. The disco mirror balls reflected the red and green flashing lights and scattered them all over the dance floor, which was empty apart from two middle-aged blondes in tight short white skirts dancing around their handbags. One elbow resting on the palm of one hand, the other hand rotating in the air, and when they were about to fly off a sudden throwing of the right leg in the air caused a forced landing. I recognized drowning women like me instantly.

I imagined myself standing there in the middle of an old dance floor wriggling my hips to the beat of a desert drum.

'Where do you come from?' asked a young man in an England T-shirt and black trousers, which shone with too much ironing.

He looked like a football fan so I said, 'I don't speak the English.'

He looked at me with his big blue eyes and said, 'Go on. You do speak English.'

'No, I don't.'

'Where are you from? Barcelona? I've been to Barcelona. Right, Italian?'

I did not answer.

'I know why you are not saying. Because you are from Argentina,' he said and walked away.

Had I told him I was Arab he probably would have run faster. A Bedouin from a village called Hima, whose blood was spilt by her tribe for any vagabond to drink it. I straightened my back, pulled my tummy in and shut my mouth. Like a key witness in a mafia crime case I changed my name, address, past and even changed countries to erase my footsteps.

Gwen said that it was so important to trace back your family tree. The roots hold you tightly to the ground. One must accept and be proud of who you are. She was trying to construct a history of her family when I asked her about her father.

'My father at some point moved to Merthyr Tydfil and

was training as a Mining Deputy. He gave up this idea and I know was in Wolverhampton for some time. He rowed, played rugby and was in the Territorial Army among other things. In nineteen twelve he went to work near Johannesburg in South Africa where he was deputy chief engineer for the first iron and steel works set up there. It is now part of Kvaerner.'

Out of a muslin handkerchief she produced a grey ingot, rubbed it gently and said, 'The small part of the first ingot I have is almost three inches by just over one inch and about an eighth of an inch thick. On one side it has "USCO", United Steel Corporation, I believe, and "INGOT No 1" and on the other "1/9/13" which is the date it was cast. He also left me one of the original ingots before it was cut just after it was cast. All the bigwigs were watching.' She poured some more tea in the fine china cup with English roses meticulously drawn on one side. This was a special day. Gwen was sharing her limitless love for her father with me.

At Dansers a middle-aged, dark-haired man with a beer belly stood in the corner sipping his drink slowly and watching me. Women approached him and he politely sent them away. He walked towards me. 'Would you like to dance?' This coming from a decent-looking man, with solid practical shoes and clean white shirt, probably a teacher in a comprehensive, must not be rejected.

I hesitated then said, 'I am sorry I am tired.'

The seagulls this morning looked like a fluffy white cloud soaring over the green plain; some would fly away from the flock, others would stay close to their clan, others would dive hastily in the water, yet others would stand on a tree and watch all that dancing in the air as if they didn't have the same white feathers, wings and pills.

The smell of beer and nicotine filled the now crowded club. 'Give us a kiss, you bitch!' a man cried.

'Go fuck your mother!' she answered.

A man on the dance floor, who had been approaching women all evening and being rejected, unzipped his trousers and was mooning the dancers with his Union Jack boxer shorts.

I was about to finish my second drink when a handsome, well-dressed, dark-haired man walked right in front of me, waved then winked urging me to follow him. I imagined myself making love to this Italian plumber on the leather seats of his yellow sports car. Then when the fun was over he would comb his hair, zip up his trousers, button up his shirt and say, 'Must do a runner. My wife will kill me.' I begged myself to follow him, to act human, to give in, but Salma and Sally refused to budge, to run after him, to seek refuge. I was a convict, an immigrant, trash, and a one-night stand with a plumber was more than I deserved. If I were them I would not let me into their clean fragrant houses. I was contagious and everything I touched turned into black tar. The sight of a man and a woman French kissing, who were, up to a few minutes ago, complete strangers, was nauseating. It must be all that Coke I drank on an almost empty stomach. If they came to me and said, 'Would you like to have some fresh air,' as in Victorian dramas, I would have said yes. I sucked the ice cubes, wrapped myself with my mother's black shawl and walked out of the cloud of smoke. There was a chill in the early morning air, but the pungent smell of beer was slowly being overpowered by the aroma of rich food being fried.

I sat on the bench inhaling the smell of falafel rissoles bubbling away in the frying oil and listening to the conversation in Arabic. I could also hear some old French songs in the background.

'Yasin, why this to happen to me?' the old man said.

'Kismet, *naseeb*, fate, man,' the younger man said.

'Why it to be my son, *ya rabbi*: my god?' the older man said.

'Allah test his true believers,' said Yasin.

'Amen,' the older man said.

'Also he still young and might grow out of it,' said Yasin.

'In the war of liberation in Algeria I joined the resistance. We kicked the French out of our country. We lose millions and now the European bastards claimed my son. He no longer Arab, no longer a man.'

He threw a fresh batch of falafel in the frying pan. The aroma of crushed chickpeas, garlic and parsley balls hitting the hot oil wafted to my nose again.

'I blame his English mum. She tied his hair with ribbons and dressed him up in girls' clothes,' said the old man.

'She just spoilt him. Arab mums much worse,' said Yasin.

'He is not my son and I don't want to see him ever again,' said the old man.

'He your only son. You don't mean that.'

I pricked up my ears and sniffed.

'I will divorce that bitch, I will,' said the old man.

'*Doucement*, my friend, *doucement*,' said Yasin.

'Nice handlebar moustache, Mokhammad!' cried a young English man from across the street.

'Don't listen to them! The moustache suits you,' said Yasin.

'Fuck off, English poof! Bugger off, faggot! Bugger off, cabbage-eater,' shouted the old man.

'Your blood pressure *haj, y'ayshak*,' said Yasin.

The smell of crushed cumin, black pepper and coriander filled the busy high street. Drunken young men and women staggered back home in the early morning light. I could hear the cooing of pigeons and police sirens in the distance. I filled my lungs with the smell of home, tightened my mother's black shawl around my neck then got up and joined the herds walking down the hill.

'I haven't seen you for ages, you never call me,' said Parvin. We decided to meet in the café at one. I took extra care with my appearance. Parvin with her hazel eyes, long straight black hair, sharply cut fringe, dark shiny skin looked like a model in her mauve shalwar kameez and white trainers. We hugged and kissed each other on the cheek like we do.

'You look fine,' I said shyly.

'You don't look so bad yourself,' she said while inspecting my face closely. She was looking for 'signs of paranoia' as she used to say. She smiled when she found none.

She insisted on buying me lunch. 'Are you sure you don't want dessert?'

'I'll have lemon cake,' I said, grateful.

She paid for both trays and we carried them upstairs and sat among the overgrown rubber plants.

Parvin looked at me and said, 'You're my bridesmaid so I want you to be there early to help me get dressed,' she said, munching her salad hurriedly.

'At what time?' I asked.

'If you can come by ten o'clock in the morning it will be great. Don't get dressed. Bring your stuff with you. We'll get dressed together. Oh, by the way, bridesmaids can wear anything provided it's lilac.'

I ate the lemon cake slowly and carefully. 'Parvin, are you happy?'

'Yes.'

The smell of fresh lemon rind reminded me of lemon plantations on the outskirts of our village. In the spring when the trees were in full bloom, when they looked like decorated brides, the wind carried a strong perfume that went straight to your heart.

'What about your family?'

I never saw Parvin cry after that night in the hostel. Her tears were not for public consumption, she used to say. 'What about them?'

'Are they coming to the wedding?'

'They don't know where I am,' she said and chased the carrot salad with her fork.

'And if they find out about Mark and the wedding . . .'

'It would be too late by then.'

If I hadn't known Parvin I would have thought that she was completely composed, but she lowered her eyelashes to cover her eyes, bowed her head so far down until her fringe covered most of her face and toyed with the napkin, folding and unfolding it.

'Have you told Mark about your family?'

'Yes and he is going to tell his family that my family are in Pakistan and cannot come to the wedding.'

'Why don't you try to reason with them?'

'I think about it every day. They wouldn't approve.

Although he agreed to convert to Islam to put my mind at rest he is still a white English man.'

'They might approve if he is a Muslim,' I said.

'Once a Christian, always a Christian,' she said, folding her napkin again.

'Good Pakistani men don't climb on trees,' I said.

'You mean "grow",' she said, correcting me.

We laughed.

While chasing the last bit of lemon cake, I thought that the real monkeys were Parvin and me, good at climbing trees without help and then coming out of them just like that. I reached out across the white tablecloth and held Parvin's elegant hand. 'Don't worry! The wedding be fine.'

After work I rushed to Gwen, who must have been in the kitchen when I rang the bell. I could hear her approaching the door with difficulty. She opened the door and her pale face smiled.

'Hello, Gwen, you look pale,' I said and kissed each cheek.

'These legs are killing me. I must lose weight,' she said while running her hand over her coiffed grey hair.

I hugged her and said that she needed some exercise. 'What about a walk now?'

It was still early and the sun was breaking gently through the clouds. She put her rain jacket on, her flowery scarf and struggled with her walking shoes. I didn't offer to help, she would be offended. We walked down the road. 'When you have arthritis the liquid that lubricates the joints runs out and they begin rubbing bone against bone,' she said. The pain was drawn on her face, but she kept walking. 'But if I don't keep moving I will become an invalid.' I held her arm, trying to encourage her to lean on me. She pulled it away and continued leaning on her walking stick. Her forehead was sweaty when we got to the first bench by the river. Gwen sighed with relief when we finally sat down.

'Out with it. What's the problem?' she said.

'Parvin has asked me to be her bridesmaid. I do not have a lilac dress. By the way, she did not invite her family.'

'So?'

'She should have asked one of her department store girlfriends. They would know what to do.'

Gwen was drawing lines on the grass with her stick. She looked at me with her ageing eyes and said in her head-mistress voice, 'It's time for you to pull yourself together: a) her family are not yours and it was up to her to invite or not invite them, b) she has asked you to be her brides-maid and no one else and c) I have an old lilac and mauve dress that I put on once almost forty years ago at my sister's wedding. It's in good shape, you can have it altered if you like,' she said and looked over at the river.

'Really? Great, great,' I said.

The swans were waltzing across the river as if there was nothing wrong with the world. I looked at Gwen's sweaty face, her short grey hair, her overweight body and her swollen legs stretched on the lawn and hated her son Michael for not visiting her. Shahla would have said, 'You give meat to someone without teeth, and earrings to someone whose ears are not pierced.' I stood up, got my bamboo pipe out, and blew a tune, which I practised so many times while sitting here on the riverside, enjoying the sunset. I tried to imitate the graceful movement of the swans, introduced the sudden cries of seagulls and the sound of running water. I stood in front of Gwen as if performing in a royal show under the patronage of Her Majesty Queen Elizabeth. When I received my citizenship, when I became a British subject, I had to vow allegiance to the Queen and her descendants. Gwen was my queen so when I finished I bowed to her.

She clapped her hands laughing. 'You know how to play that thing. You never told me,' she said.

'Now you know.' I smiled.

'Yes, now I know.' She smiled.

Max noticed the troubled expression on my face and said, 'What's wrong now?'

'Parvin is getting married and she wants me be her maid.'

He gave me a I-wish-you-would-get-married-one-of-these-days-too look and said, 'That's nice.'

'They're an elegant family and I don't know what to do,' I said.

He spat out some needles, ran his fingers wet with saliva over his hair to make sure it was still held in place and said, 'Whatever you do do not throw up on her shoes. My niece was invited to her university friend's wedding. You know, la-di-da kind of people. Horses and boat races. The daft bugger saw all that free booze and began guzzling it. First sherry and champagne, then beer followed by wine, then port and whisky until Bob's your uncle the five-course dinner was plastered over the bridegroom's mother's silk chiffon dress.' He sniggered. 'No, it gets worse. The daft bugger went to the wedding to find herself a posh husband,' he laughed.

What he did not know was that alcohol had never

passed my lips ever. I was a goddamn Muslim. But what if
I got too nervous and vomited all over the floor?

'If they are toffee-nosed then keep talking about the
weather and saying "ma'am" to his mother and you
will be fine. By the way, I wouldn't worry too much
because very few will be sober. If you remember what
went on in a wedding then it must have been crap,' he
said.

Gwen's dress – altered, dry-cleaned and wrapped in plastic
– was rustling in the breeze. I hooked the hanger on the
edge of the old wardrobe top to keep it crease-free and to
look at it before I went to sleep. It was mauve, strapless,
figure-hugging with a heart-shaped bodice and a wide
georgette lilac coat with long sleeves and a high collar. A
big magnolia flower made of both the mauve satin and
lilac chiffon was pinned to the side of the collar. I
shortened the satin dress to just below the knee, took it in
at the back slightly and left the wide flowing top as it was.
It was just beautiful. I opened the suitcase on top of the
wardrobe and brought Layla's white dress out for the first
time in months. I spent hours making that baby-girl dress.
I spent hours trying to imagine what a water lily would
look like on a luminous jolly night, a Layla. I tried to
make the shape of the dress similar to that of a lily. I was
willing the life of whoever wore it to be happier and
whiter than mine. The zigzagged hem, the flowery collar,
the small rose-like pockets, the tiny puffed sleeves all
wished her well. I pulled up the fine plastic covering
Gwen's dress, slipped the shoulders of the dress off the
hanger, hung Layla's white dress on it then slipped
the dress and the lilac coat on top. I stuck the metal hook

through the hole in the plastic wrapping and hung the two dresses at the edge of the wardrobe. The fine mauve satin and the few pearls stitched to the collar of her dress gleamed together in the darkness.

Liz was bedridden. Her tummy was swollen, her arms were bruised and she looked as pale as the old wallpaper. I heated some soup out of a can, sliced some bread, placed them carefully on a large tray and took them to her bedroom. I knocked on the door and she said, 'Come in, Janki ayah.'

I placed the tray on the bedside cabinet carefully and noticed that her black-and-white wedding photo with the intricate silver frame was nowhere to be seen.

She was still wearing the same sullied white cotton underwear. I pulled her up and put the pillows behind her. The silver box with the foul cream was under the pillow. She looked up at me and smiled. The yellow of the butter that I scraped off her face had seeped into the whiteness of her eyes. I placed the tray in her lap and smoothed the dirty duvet. With trembling fingers she held the spoon and tried to scoop up some soup. After a few attempts she put the spoon down defeated so I sat next to her on the bed and began feeding her like a child. She swallowed the soup with difficulty and looked up, 'Is Hita making coconut ladoos, ayah?'

'Yes, Liz,' I answered.

'Yes, Upah,' she said.

She drank half of the soup and slid back under the duvet exhausted. I ran my hand over her straight grey hair and said, 'Do you want me to contact anyone? Shall I call your niece?'

'Where is Charles?' she asked. 'Still in the country?'

'Yes, ma'am,' I said.

'Running, running also,' shouted Sadiq from across the street. 'Where go? Stock Exchange market? The price of your shares falling?'

'Good morning to you too,' I shouted back.

'Or going to your English boyfriend?'

'I don't have an English boyfriend. I am a Muslim,' I said and smiled.

'All coconuts have English boyfriends. Muslims by name only,' he said.

'There are Muslims and Muslims,' I said.

'There are one Islamic,' he said.

I crossed the street and stood by him on the pavement in front of his shop. 'What do you want me to do to prove to you that I am a Muslim? Pray five times on your doorstep?' I said.

'That would be nice also,' he said and sniggered.

'I love the new hairdo. It's like the crest of a rooster,' I teased.

He jerked his chin sideways and said, 'Don't be smart aleck also. Just because you crossed the road to university just once does not make you professor,' he said and pointed towards the hill.

'How is the wife and kids?' I asked.

'As fine as can be expected. No good being apart,' he said.

I held his right hand then released it.

He pressed his forefingers at the corners of his eyes, smiled and said, 'My tummy ache. I've been having too many hamburgers and I fancy a curry, *yaar*.'

'Falafels are bad for you,' I said and smiled.

'I can try,' he said, winked, slanted his head sideways then ran his hand over his gelled hair, destroying the carefully constructed upward-tilting fringe.

Rubies and Dry Bread

PARVIN'S FACE, THE TEAR-SHAPED PEARLS AROUND THE low-cut draped neckline of her silk cream dress and the crystals and pearls embedded in the rhinestone leaves and flowers of the tiara glowed in the faint light of the setting sun. Dark, regal and composed in her silk sheath she held the sword handle with Mark ready to cut the cake. He said something to her. She smiled, looked up and kissed him on the cheek. His parents, Sarah and Jenny his sisters, relatives and young friends cheered them on so they counted to three and sliced the cake in one swoop destroying the waltzing lilac bride and groom made of icing sugar. The aunt in the large bright red hat with white flowers said, 'I made it myself. Parvin chose the colours. They must be the colours of the prairies of Pakistan.'

'Don't be ridiculous. She is British,' said Mark's mother.

Earlier his mother was suppressing her tears when the registrar read a poem entitled 'Himalayan Birch', which Parvin had chosen for the occasion.

A single slim trunk
Branches that bow in a storm
Green, leathery leaves with a soft centre
Glittering against blue sky
White bark scarred, bleeding
Heart wide-open
Bandaged, but upright she stands . . .

Parvin looked at me through the veil and smiled. I lowered my gaze, breathed in, composed myself then looked up and smiled back. She kissed me on both cheeks the way we do and walked next to Mark holding his left hand. The hook was pressed gently against her back when she walked to the decorated sports car outside. They waved to us then drove off jingling their way down to married life. Mark's mother's flushed face gleamed in the faint light of the dusk. 'I am so glad he found happiness after what he has been through,' she said and wiped her face with her embroidered lace handkerchief.

I was filling up so I said, to stop myself from crying, 'Ma'am, it's a glorious sunset!'

Speechless she nodded her head and squeezed my hand.

She was emerald, turquoise encased in silver, Indian silk cascading down from rolls, acacia honey in clear glass jars, fresh coffee beans ground in an ornate sandalwood pestle and mortar, the scent of turmeric, a pearl in her decorated dias, a single white jasmine, standing there alone, head high, with nothing to prop her up except his artificial hand.

I could only see a faint light in the hallway of the Reed Hall, but the surrounding grounds were dark with the exception of some faint electric lamps lining the footpath that led towards campus. I sat on the stairs for a long time until it was pitch black then drank my first glass of champagne ever – on an empty stomach. Max's story about his niece put me off the food and I thought if I was going to throw up then it would be less of a disaster if it had no bits of food in it. 'Damned is the carrier, buyer and drinker of alcohol,' I heard my father's voice. My hand trembled carrying the forbidden drink to my lips. It had been almost sixteen years since I last saw them. It was only me, the dark haunting trees, the vast moonless sky and the pipe. I blew a tune so nostalgic it would have fractured your heart. The made-up woman with the meek voice dressed in satin and georgette was not me. I had nothing to do with that nineteenth-century mansion, the thick even lawns, the wide stone stairs, the naked statues, the old trees. I was a shepherdess, who under a shameless sky guided her sheep to the scarce meadows, who cried whenever she felt like crying, who kicked off her shoes whenever she felt like taking them off, and who weeded and made love like a whirlwind. I ran barefoot on the lawn playing the pipe and dancing then falling flat on my face, rolling downhill, walking uphill, singing at the top of my voice, '*Min il-bab lil shibak rayh jay warayy*: from the door to the window he follows me. He is always right behind me. Nowhere to hide. If I have sip, if I spill my tea, if I drop the cake on the plate. *Min il-bab lil shibak*. Stop fucking watching!' I fell on my face again, and began crying as if an invisible jinni had come out of his bottle. My grandmother Shahla used to stroke my hair saying, 'Put the jinni of tears back in the lamp, my flower. Your tears are gems.' I sat on the grass crying. Back shaking, head bent, teeth jittering, stomach convulsing, hands and legs trembling, I rocked my body rhythmically to my grandmother's burial song, 'Where is his grave? Where is his dagger? Where is his face? Bring me a lock of his hair!' she chanted when she heard that her father had died, scooped more sand in her hands and scattered it all over her head and body. A cloud of dust with a black centre. 'Where is my daughter? Is she alive or dead? My eyes are hungry for her face! My ears are tuned to one call, "Mama", my nose sniffing for her scent. Bring me a blanket she had wrapped herself in, shoes she had worn, a lock of her hair!' I chanted. A hazy cloud with a mauve centre.

Crossing an unknown river far from my dwelling I observed the demeanour of horses, looked deep in the shadows in the distance and watched the movement of trees. I listened for feet crunching dry needles and scales. Suddenly I felt human breath on the back of my neck.

'Mahmoud?' I sobbed.

Gwen straightened her apron, tucked her short hair behind her ears and said, 'He did not know they were rubies. My father I mean. He brought those dusty stones with him all the way from South Africa and put them in his workshop in the garden together with other pebbles and pieces of steel. One of his friends had told him that he got the rubies from a miner and wanted him to have a few so he had put them in the pocket of his winter coat and forgot about them until he arrived in Swansea.'

She buttered a scone, put it on a fine plate and passed it on to me.

'You see he forgot about them again until one day when he was looking for his binoculars he saw them on the shelf hidden in a brown paper bag. He held one in his hand and began filing it to see whether it was a ruby or just a rough stone from the mines. He couldn't find anything that resembled rubies under the grey surface of the gemstone. He continued cleaning, filing, scraping all afternoon until he got fed up and threw them all on the floor. Later on he discovered that rubies must be cut in a certain way to get to their red heart. You know, Salma, he spent most of his later years looking for the rubies on the floor of his workshop, the shed, the garden, everywhere. I would watch him through the window on his knees looking for the damn rubies.'

She paused for breath, drank some tea and said, 'A few weeks before he died he found one. Yes, he found one rough ruby.'

I felt the warmth of a soft jacket on my shoulders so I looked up and saw a familiar face that I couldn't place. 'Mahmoud?' I sobbed.

'No. It's me, John,' he said and wrapped me in his jacket.

'John who?' I asked.

'John Robson. Your tutor,' he said.

Suddenly my tummy muscles convulsed and I threw up on his legs and shoes. I was shaking, breathless, ill. 'Toilet,' I wheezed.

He lowered his shoulder until it was under my arm, balanced himself and pulled me up. I was about to pass out when I finally felt the ground under my bare feet. He helped me walk across the lawn, up the stairs, through the door, down the corridor to the ladies' toilet. I stood there disorientated until he said, 'Go in!'

Another surge of nausea made me run to the toilet,

stick my head in it and throw up again. I don't remember how long I sat there on the cold tiled floor, how long before I heard his voice call, 'Sally! Sally! Are you all right?' I placed my hands on the toilet seat and pushed myself up. When I was finally able to walk to the washbasin I could not see half of my face in the mirror; as for the other half, it was covered with dry leaves, mud and grass, my eyes were swollen and red, my hair was half tied up, half loose on my shoulders, and Gwen's dress was smeared with green and brown streaks. I washed my face several times with soap and water, unpinned my hair and wove it into a braid, and gulped loads of water straight from the tap. A flickering light blotted out my right eye. I steadied myself and walked out slowly.

John was sitting on one of the sofas reading a news-paper. My black bag, shoes and pipe were on the floor. He stood up and said, 'Are you OK?'

'I think it's a migraine,' I said.

'There are bedrooms upstairs. I can call the duty porter and get you one,' he said. He folded the newspaper and stuck it in the rack.

'I still have the keys to Parvin's room. She wanted me to pack her stuff.'

'You can stay there till ten o'clock tomorrow morning,' he said, held my hand and led me up the carpeted stairs. I unlocked the bridal wing and he helped me get in and placed my bag and shoes on the floor. The bed and two armchairs were covered with T-shirts, jeans, make-up, rollers, hairpins, underwear, towels. I placed my hand on my tummy and sat on the bed. The nausea was coming back. 'I'll go and get you something for that,' he said and rushed out. I took off Gwen's dress to see whether it was damaged and how it could be repaired, put on my jeans and T-shirt and lay on the spacious bed. John was back with a tray full of stuff. I could see half of his face, his bloodshot eye, his goatee, his slipping glasses. 'Some yoghurt, herbal tea, a bottle of water and a tablet for your migraine, madam,' he said and placed the tray on the bedside cabinet. I was too embarrassed to look at him so I kept tracing the ink lines of the painting of the Japanese lady on the wall. Strangely enough I ate the yoghurt, drank the tea, took the bright pink pill. Sitting on one of the armchairs he watched me eat. 'Can I get you anything else, Sally?' he asked.

'Salma,' I said. I slipped under the white sheet and blanket, turned round and went to sleep.

'My father returned home in nineteen fourteen because of the political threat from Germany and was at first in the cavalry, but was not sent abroad. He was then put on the drawings of the first tanks and his brother Archie was one of those working on the construction. Winston Churchill came to watch the first trials and my uncle swapped the wellingtons Churchill wore for the occasion for those he wore and is said to have handed his own over to the people asking him for the wellingtons Churchill wore! I don't know what he did with the originals. Knowing him, he probably sold them later on! For the last part of the war my father was in the Fleet Air Arm on airships and I also have photos of the airship carrying a plane slung below it. These were experiments to try and help aircrafts fly over Germany carrying bombs and still have enough fuel to fly home again.'

Gwen stopped talking, stood up and went to the bedroom

then came back with a black umbrella. When she opened it the handle was made of a rusty, uneven piece of metal.

'Believe it or not, it's part of an airship,' she said.

Liz was in no condition to cross-examine me. She was still in bed. I made us some porridge, two cups of tea and took the tray up to her bedroom. It was messier and stuffier than ever before. Her dirty clothes were scattered on the floor, some cold pizza was rotting on a plate, and the dark red stains on the beige carpet were dry. It smelt of dust, lavender soap, denture cleanser and medication. I pushed the bundle of letters on the bedside table and the silver box to one side and put the tray down. Liz woke up, looked around with her yellowing eyes and said without dentures, 'That'll be all. Thank you.'

'I thought we might have breakfast together,' I said hesitantly.

'You did, did you?' she asked, her older self returning.

'The wedding was beautiful,' I enticed her.

Streaks of blood whirled in the glass full of cleanser when she took her dentures out. She stuck them in her mouth then bit, tied her hair, ran her fingers over her puffy face, eased herself out of the white frilled duvet covered with yellow and red stains and looked at the bowl of porridge. I placed the tray in her lap. She began to eat.

I sat on the edge of her king-size bed and ate my porridge.

'How was the wedding?' she asked.

'It was splendid. The weather was great. The sun shone on them to the end,' I said.

'Did they show you the howdah and the seven saris on the Shubbeah?' she asked and had a sip of tea.

'What is a Shubbeah?' I asked.

'You display the bridalwear and underwear on it. What about the bridegroom? Did they put him on a silver footstool and rub his face and arms with her butter?' she asked.

She grabbed the bundle of letters held together with an elastic band and said, 'Is Daddy still hiding in the library?'

I placed the tray on the bedside cabinet, wiped her face with the kitchen towel and said, 'You should have some rest now.'

'Don't tell me what to do,' she said, broken.

Noura's nose was bleeding after a forced feeding. It was my fifth day on hunger strike after I gave birth. There was nothing left to live for so I began hitting myself hard on the face, stomach, legs. When I was exhausted I would lie on the filthy floor and refuse to touch the bread and soup brought and put under my nose every lunchtime, until Noura staggered back to the room after a forced feeding. Naima and another warden dragged her through the iron door then threw her on the mattress. Your face and arms were bruised, blood mixed with snot was dripping from your nose, a white liquid was stuck to your lips and your eyes were shut.

Poking at me with her stick, the way I used to poke my lazy donkey, Naima said, 'What about this one? Is she still on hunger strike?'

'Noo,' whispered Noura.

When they locked the door, Noura opened her eyes, smiled at me and wheezed, 'Please eat.' Her voice was both broken and strong, but there was something frightening about it as if she had come face to face with the travellers'

232

ghoul. I stood up, untied my bundle, read my mother's letter again and looked at the window. She wanted to come to see me, but my father and brother must have forbidden her from crossing the threshold of the house. I bit into the dry piece of bread. In the dim moonlight coming through the barred window you were able to see me chewing at the now wet and salty bread. A faint smile was drawn on your face when you turned your head towards the wall.

I watched the English sun setting behind the hills, leaving a glowing light behind, which floated on the water, fingered the tops of trees and shone on the hair of people walking their dogs. They would smile and whisper their greetings. It was a peaceful space covered with green grass, wild flowers, and on its borders birch, chestnut, oak and rowan trees grew. I sat on the grass overlooking the steep slopes the water was rushing over and I tried to blow a simple tune, which would be in harmony with the sound of water, the gentle breeze fondling my hair, the barking of distant dogs, the sound of cicadas hiding in the long grass. That tune would be the English Sally, standing erect, head high, back straight, waving a white handkerchief to the sun. Then a shepherd's piece saying goodbye to the day, kissing the sun and crying over its departure, there was so much stamping of feet, yanking of hair and rending of garments. That was the Arab Salma sitting on the ground, swaying her upper half and sprinkling ashes over her head. Then a last tune, a tree neither of the East nor of the West, olive oil in a glass lamp, doves cooing, white upon dark, dark upon white, light upon light just where the sky meets the dark outlines of the trees, lambs and hills at the end of the horizon.

★

I kept thinking about the next tutorial with John. To go or not to go. To fake a sickness, break an arm or simply say I have a family emergency to attend to. I was trying to compile a BBC2 *Newsnight* vocabulary: 'on the other hand', 'therefore', 'despite the fact that the hostage-taking is universal it is mainly an Arab problem'. I looked up the words in the dictionary, wrote them down several times to memorize them then jotted down my speech, 'I think it is time for me to say goodbye and go to another tutor. However, you have been very good, helpful, although you are a northerner. On the other hand I can bring a sick note and you can continue supervising my project. But if you have no respect for me I cannot work with you so sad and broken also. And I don't know where the hostages are. Hope I am clear.'

'Hello, Max,' I said.

He pushed up his bifocals, pointed at the photo and asked, 'Look at this. The Princess in a bikini! How on earth are we going to see her as royalty?'

He wanted a discussion and I obliged. 'She is woman. Human like us,' I said.

'Like you? Like me? Don't be ridiculous! She is royalty. Blue blood. Allegiance to God then to them.'

'I see,' I said trying to assuage him.

'Naked, stark bleeding naked,' he said.

'She has her swimming suit on.'

'Do you call those stripes of Lycra a swimming suit?'

'Nosy photographers,' I said, 'she wanted to have quiet holiday, that's all.'

234

Our discussions always ended the same way, either with 'Sal, you have a long way to go,' or 'Sally, you have a lot to learn,' so this time it was: 'Sal, you don't know anything about us, the British, do you? How we feel when we see our princess naked in a newspaper.'

I always give him the pleasure of giving in to his logic. 'I guess not.'

'I don't blame you, being foreign and all,' he said and lit a cigarette.

John looked at me in my long wide shorts, my old T-shirt and rucksack full of an uneaten lunch as if I had just landed from Mars. I sat down as ordered. He looked professional and acted as if I'd never vomited on the legs of his trousers and shoes, as if he'd never stroked my hair before I went to sleep, as if he'd never brought me a bright pink pill. He talked to me as if I were an ant crawling on his academic floor. The problem with my *Newsnight* English was that I could not pronounce most of the words. I tried to twist my tongue around 'supremacy', but couldn't, so I sat there as if dumb and deaf listening to John telling me how 'ignorant, simplistic and subjective' the writing was, as if the essay had written itself. I swallowed hard in order to stop myself spitting out some of my newly acquired English vocabulary. If I were not ignorant I wouldn't be in his office listening to him tear my first essay apart; however, I didn't know much about academia or the hostage crisis. He went on and on. Looking at his slipping half-moon glasses, his balding head, his blue blood-shot eyes, his peppered goatee, his bent back, his white spindly arms covered with fine dark hair, his white T-shirt, I said, 'I have to go now.'

I snatched the essay he was waving at me and walked out. 'Do you still want a degree?' he shouted at my back before I slammed the door.

In the shower of abuse I just had, I noticed that he kept mentioning project Pallas. I went to one of the porters who pretended that he was sorting the mail when he saw me heading towards him. 'Hi!' I said.

'Hello, madam,' he said from behind the sliding glass window.

'Pardon me, sir,' I said, 'what is project Pallas?'

'This way, miss,' he said and led me down a dark corridor then opened a big door leading to a large well-lit room full of flickering computer screens.

'Is that it?' I asked.

'That's it, madam.'

'That's it?'

'Yes, madam. You learn how to use a computer.'

We were not very busy that afternoon. Max was chatting up female customers and I was trying a spaghetti stitch on the 'new ultra-high-speed cylinder interlock sewing machine'. Suddenly he called me using my Arab name in its full length, his tongue stumbling over it, 'Salmaa!'

I almost fell off my chair. He kept me in the background and never called me to the front of the shop while he had customers around. 'Yes, Max,' I said.

He ran his hand over his gelled hair to make sure it was stuck around his head, cleared his voice and said, as if he was delivering a speech in the Houses of Parliament, 'To reward you for years of good service I have decided to give you the ten per cent rise you asked for.'

I couldn't believe my ears, but I was at the same time

resentful that he made the announcement in front of Mrs Smith of the Royal Mail of all people. The whole town would hear the news by tomorrow morning: 'He is ever so kind, Max is, giving a rise to his black apprentice.'

I knew what Max expected of me so I said, 'Max, you've been always kind to me. Thank you very, very much.'

Mrs Smith was folding her frilled green umbrella and unfolding it, totally enjoying the spectacle. Max had been trying to have her as his 'bit on the side' for months now.

I filled my eyes with thank yous and looked up at Max's face. By now he knew that I was a sentimental fool, and that I took things to heart. The only sign of receiving my gratitude was the rub of the nose which I have come to know very well.

I inhaled more starch-leaden steam, held the wooden handle of the heavy iron and ran it like brisk wind over the blue jacket on the table.

Max's motto was 'cash in, cash out' so at the end of every month he handed me a bundle of creased bank-notes. He left me my salary on his new sewing machine so I took the envelope that had my name on it and saw the British National Party leaflet on the floor next to his chair. I swallowed hard and pretended not to have seen it. I thanked Max and rushed out of the shop to breathe. Don't be stupid, I said to myself, ink on paper cannot harm you. It was not Max's fault. Maybe Max's brother-in-law had given it to him. He believed that all foreigners must be loaded in ships and dumped 'like the bananas they are' on the shores of Africa.

When I went back home that evening, Liz was in re-mission. In her riding boots and breeches she walked like a general around the sitting room, the neck of her polo jumper folded down, her hair tied back with a leather band, a bamboo stick in her hand. Since the incident the whip had been carefully hidden between my winter jumpers in the wardrobe. I could see how beautiful she must have been in her youth. White rings circled the blueness of her eyes, a spider of fine blood veins spread on her cheeks and nose, her belly bulged out of the tight cream trousers and her breasts hung flat under her blue jumper. I was holding the Queen Anne silver-plated sandwich tray that I had just bought for Parvin as a wedding present. When she saw me peeping through the slightly open door she snapped her fingers and called, 'Bint, get me my dinner! Yes, I am talking to you. Don't pretend that you cannot hear me.' I didn't know what to do: to enter the sitting room and pretend that I was Elizabeth's Indian servant, or tell her where to go. She must be missing her horses, whose photos fill the walls of the landing; she must be missing Peshawar or wherever she used to live before the war; she must be missing Hita her lover, her father or even Charles her late husband, but I couldn't help her. If I pretended to be her Indian servant, she would sink even deeper into her drunken world. It would be easier for both of us if I did that, but I couldn't, I shouldn't. I left her giving orders to imaginary bints and wallahs and went upstairs to my room to wrap Parvin's present.

Although Parvin had called him a racist, sexist pig Max gave me a job when no one would. If I had not approached him that morning I would have gone without food. I stood outside Lord's Tailors shifting my weight from one leg to another and rubbing my hands. I spent months rehearsing going up the stairs, knocking on the door, and saying that I had experience in an institution in my country and that I had just moved to Exeter and was looking for a job. I tried to memorize all the sentences I needed in English for the manager to think that my English was good. I wiped my face with the embroidered handkerchief Minister Mahoney had given me for Christmas and walked up the stairs. My knees were too weak to support me so I held on to the banisters. The glass door looked misty. I pushed it open and walked in. The same man who chucked me and Parvin out was sewing, talking on the phone and having the odd suck on his cigarette at the same time. He stopped when he saw me standing there shifting my weight from one leg to another. He ran his hand over his head and said, 'Sit down.' I sat down looking at the sewing machines. How could I tell him I had experience when the only machine I worked was a manual Singer? When he put the receiver down, he looked at me.

'Good morning, very sorry, did not find job,' I said.

'Good morning,' he said. 'You're the white dress lady?'

'You remember?' I said.

'You made that dress?' He gesticulated while projecting the words slowly.

'Yes,' I said, my hands stuck between my knees.

'Do you know how to stitch?'

'All them,' I said.

He threw a pair of grey trousers at me and asked me to stitch the hem. I wiped my hands, concentrated on the ironing lines, and began stitching. I did the cock's feet, which was not normally used for hems, just to show him that I had experience. He would glance at my shaking hands and shake his head. It took me five minutes to do one leg. He had a look at the even line, the criss-crossed threads holding the hem tight into place, then pointing his fore and middle fingers in the air like a V sign he said, 'How about two pounds fifty an hour?'

'Yes,' I said and nodded.

'You're hired. Come back tomorrow at eight a.m. sharp.'

At first I did not grasp what he had said then I realized that he had offered me a job. I was too tired and too hungry to smile. I bowed with gratitude and walked out before he changed his mind.

I put on a pair of clean jeans, a blue T-shirt and tied my hair back with a band. Apart from some cream I wore no make-up. After experimenting with an old computer Allan had in his office, I was slightly more confident about the whole business of learning. I wanted to show John that I was not an alcoholic, not a barbarian, and that I had been raised well by my parents, back there in Hima, and neither he nor the Pope could raise me again. When I opened his office door, he smiled a pale smile and asked me to sit down. I must be a chore for him by now, one of those housewives in part-time education. I smiled back and asked him directly, 'What do you like about Margaret Atwood's book?'

I noticed by the twisting of the mouth to one side that he was caught by surprise. 'Which book?'

The English were a precise race, not like us, we leave most of our sentences unfinished and they get understood from the gesture, the angle of the head, the choice of the words. '*The Handmaid's Tale*?'

'An interesting book, well written,' he said rubbing his chin.

'You should have recommended it instead of *Justine*. It was very, very difficult. Good difficult.'

He smiled as if I were a child describing a day at the circus. They never say it, but most of them treat me as if I were a baboon climbing trees. Gwen told me why once. Because I use 'very' a lot. 'There was nothing that was very, very good,' she said. 'You are very, very dark,' I once said to Parvin.

'I don't know how to knock "very" out of your English,' she answered.

John looked at me above his half-moon glasses, still rubbing his goatee as if I were a puzzle. I came from dark countries, with blood feuds and hostages. If I were him I wouldn't teach me.

He finally looked up, took off his glasses, placed them in a small old case, closed his newspaper, folded it slowly then said, as if talking to the back of the woman in the poster, 'You lied to us.'

I was blushing and lost all the English I'd memorized. I felt hot and decided to give up the degree altogether. I looked at the Persian rug.

'On your application form it says single but whenever you're behind you claim that your daughter or your family are in trouble.' He slapped the desk with his folded newspaper and continued, 'You have no daughter and no husband.'

I had expected the attack to come from a different angle, from the direction of my lack of intellect and poor education, and me not knowing how to use a computer, but I did not expect to be hit directly on the nose like that. I sat up on the chair and straightened my back. I didn't know how to handle the attack. I must quit this degree or transfer to Sociology or Anthropology.

When he stood up and walked around the desk, I ducked, expecting him to hit me, but puzzled by my reaction he just sat next to me where I could smell the cleanness of his freshly washed shirt and said, 'You have no daughter or husband.'

Looking at his Persian rug, the wildness of its patterns, the brightness of its colours, I whispered, 'Just a daughter.'

Musk Roses and Dogwood Trees

MAHMOUD, MY BROTHER, WAS GIVEN A LOADED RIFLE TO kill Daffash's best stallion. My father's voice roared, 'They killed our horse, we must kill theirs or else they will start shooting down the men of our tribe.' My brother was late that night, but when we heard the shots fired Mahmoud galloped back to the dark courtyard. 'Bless you, my boy! The horse is a member of El-Musa family. His blood had to be avenged.' And we congregated in groups, families, clans, tribes; our honour must be protected, our blood must be avenged; eating together, sleeping together ten to a room or a tent, our destiny shackled together in a chain. Welcoming the morning faint light on my face, the gentle drizzle, I realized that for better or worse I had broken the metal ring tying me to my family. Here was I in my new country, walking to work with a rucksack on my shoulders full of bits of paper, books, a coffee flask and a haloumi cheese sandwich. I had earned everything I had apart from the money Minister Mahoney had given me. I walked shackled to nothing but my nightmares. If you had no family, you killed no horses.

★

'So, please, where do you come from?' John asked then sipped some coffee. We were sitting in the staff club.

I looked at the grey peppering his receding hair, his tired blue eyes, his large ears, stocky fingers, the glasses case in the pocket of his ruffled shirt, his spindly arms covered with fine dark hairs and shook my head. 'No, not me. You, where do you come from?' I asked.

'I come from a small village in the north-east of England called Aycliffe. My mother has a small stone house by the river,' he said and pulled his glasses out of the leather case.

'Do you have cliffs, sheep?' I asked John.

'It is almost flat, but we have plenty of sheep, dogs, hens. It's rural,' he said and placed his hand on top of mine.

Minister Mahoney's mother used to use a Victorian coal-powered iron to iron her husband's shirts. It must have been very hot and heavy. I suppressed a gasp. 'Scorching hot, John. Plenty of goats where I come from. Vines and olive and plum and almond and fig and apple trees.'

'It sounds paradisiacal,' he said and put on his reading glasses.

'In some ways.'

'Why are you here?' he asked.

'Why are you here?' I asked.

'I am here because I couldn't find a job in the north. So here I am marooned in this humourless south.'

'Marooned?'

'A person isolated in a desolate place, unable to leave.'

'Good. I marooned on this island UK,' I said and looked away through the glass walls of the café. It was raining and the white flowers of the dogwood tree glittered in the sunset.

Dark pink and red oleanders lined the stream all the
way to the mill. My mother and I walked to the next
dwelling to visit her cousin. It was so hot you could see
the cracks in the ground teeming with black ants carrying
dry husks. That afternoon my mother said, 'Let us sit down
by the cold spring to rest our limbs.' She walked through
the dense field looking for a ripe watermelon. When she
found one she freed it from its vine then hit it hard
repeatedly against the sharp edge of a rock until it split
open. We sat, legs in the cold water, eating the red flesh of
the watermelon and chewing at the small black seeds. My
mother spat them out and I chewed then swallowed them.
She plunged my hands into the cold water to wash off the
sticky liquid then washed my face. 'Mother, the water is
cool. Can I swim?'

'If they see you they will kill me. Only a loose woman
takes off her clothes and swims in public. Men might see
you,' she said and pulled up her black face mask, hesitated
then added, 'Be quick!'

I took off my long orange shirt but kept my green
pantaloons on, then jumped in. The water was so clear and
cold my legs seemed broken as soon as I stepped in it. I
plunged my head into the water right above the glistening
pebbles and swam towards rays of light. The cold water
against my hot skin was such a shock that I cried out with
excitement. My flesh was so alive with wanting.

'Shush, broken-neck! We don't want the men of the
tribe to hear you,' she said.

She should have said no, but she said yes.

'Why didn't she say no?' I asked John.

'Who?' John asked.

'My mother,' I said.

'Sally? Are you all right?' John asked.

I pulled my hand out of his grip, turned my head, looked at his blurred eager face and said, 'I am fine. It must be the coffee. It's very, very hot.'

Pressing my hands on the windowsill I looked through the dusty glass at the mill in the distance and the dim sheen of the river. I normally meet John in Reed Hall after work, but today he was back in Aycliffe village visiting his mother. While watching the trees bloom we would talk and talk about literature, types of wild flowers, kinds of birds, and about being ill at ease. He did not feel comfortable in the south and I felt 'like a fish out of water', which was one of Parvin's favourite phrases, in this new land. One day he had a phone call from a neighbour telling him that his mother had bronchitis. 'She coughed so much we took her to Casualty.'

My fingers slowly slid across the coarse tablecloth and held his rough thumb. His hand was trembling when he said, 'I must go to see her.'

'Yes, you must. Waste no time. See your loved . . .' I choked.

'You must miss her terribly,' he said and held my hand.

'Me miss her horribly,' I said and wiped an irrepressible tear.

He held his nose with his thumb and forefinger, cleared his throat and said, 'I want to tell my mother about you, if you don't mind.'

I relaxed my shoulders, placed my hand where my ribcage met, and nodded.

The trees in the distance looked like thin, dark limbs extending upwards towards the sky. Hamdan refused to marry me and disappeared. He said that I was a slut, cheap, 'damaged goods', which is what Parvin said describing herself, and a liar. Jim might be thinking, Sally foreign slapper. Sleeps with everyone and offers them sage tea. His mother might warn him against foreign women carrying disease. The trees seemed like hands extending towards dark clouds. I sighed. John's northern heart might be warm enough, spacious enough, to take on a Bedouin woman with 'baggage', as Parvin would say. And what about me, tired and all? Could I offer him an oasis with a pond full of fresh water and palm trees laden with sweet dates? Perhaps not. Some shade for his tired heart might be enough, I thought, and let go of the windowsill.

'At the end of my tutorial he gave me a box, tied up with thick red satin ribbon. "It's for you," he said, "open it!"'

The sunlight coming through the large café windows turned Parvin's hazel eyes into clear honey. She looked radiant and contented.

'When I opened I almost cry. It was full of sweet things from the Middle East: a packet of dates, baklava with pistachio nuts, halva and Turkish delight. He said that he knew little about the Levant, but he happy to learn.' I ran my hands over my frizzy hair, rubbed my chin and said, 'Parvin, John want to marry me.'

'How sweet,' she said and meant it.

'He also said that he happy to become Muslim. He no believe in God, but it will be "nominal". What means?'

'Not true. In name only,' she said.

'I told him Muslim is difficult. You don't want Muslim.'

'Muslim is fucking complicated,' she said and sipped some coffee.

'But he read so much about it and he knew what he was doing. I said that I damaged goods, which what Elizabeth said. I said warning: I wounded animal. I might flip.'

'Did that put him off?'

The sunlight seemed as if it were woven in Parvin's dark hair, her eyes were luminous, her skin healthy, the engagement solitaire ring and wedding ring shone on her fine finger.

'John has his own problems too. No saint. He wants to marry me. That's that.'

'What about you? Do you fancy him?' she asked.

'Not capable of love. Too tired, too much past,' I said.

'You never stop talking about him. I bet you'll marry him,' she said.

'No, I not marry him,' I said and drank some caramel-flavoured milk that Parvin had ordered for me.

She stopped folding and unfolding the napkin, looked me in the eye, and said, 'Salma, I bet you'll marry John.'

'My brother brought me bag full of biscuits and Turkish delight,' I said.

The florist smiled when I asked for scarlet musk roses. Carrying a bunch of English red roses I took a taxi to the crematorium to attend her funeral. She died suddenly in her sleep hugging the silver box full of rancid butter. Liver failure. A shiver ran all the way to my toes when I got out of the car. It was a 'glorious' day, warm in the sunny spots, but cold in the shade.

Her relatives arrived in shiny black cars and her friends followed the procession. The women were all dressed in black: black dresses, suits, black hats and big black sunglasses. The men looked uncomfortable in their grey or navy suits. A young woman stood by the entrance shaking hands, tall, back bent, in a black dress-and-jacket suit, her blond hair tucked neatly under a black cap with a net covering her forehead and puffy red eyes. She must be Natasha. Her mother's wheelchair blocked the entrance. I approached them and introduced myself. Liz's sister, tiny and flushed with suppressed grief, held my hand tight and said, 'Thank you for taking care of her.'

'Don't thank me for upholding my duty,' I said, translating from Arabic.

When we were ushered to the small chapel for the burial service I saw the bunch of red roses in a glass vase over the polished mahogany of the piano. The sunbeams lit up the room and were broken by the glass vase into numerous little rainbows. I sat down, leant on the small rail cushion and moved away the Bible.

Very few pairs of eyes were uncovered, the rest were hiding behind big dark sunglasses, hats or nets. Lips were tight. Tears were shameful.

When my aunt died, women in black madraqas, veils, headbands, removed their face masks, wailed and swayed for three days. They washed her in the storage room among the wheat and barley, wrapped her in yards of gauzy white cotton, placed her in a makeshift coffin and the men carried her on their shoulders all the way to the mosque. My mother and grandmother refused to stay at home and followed the procession all the way to the top of the hill. Other women remained behind, skinning the slaughtered goat, breaking the *jamid*: dry yoghurt pieces against clay jars, cooking the meat, their tears sputtering on hot baking tins. The synchronized banging of chests and rending of garments could be heard in the mosque across the valley. When she finally came home in the evening my mother was covered in ashes, her robe split all the way down to her waist, her vest smeared with snot and mud, her head uncovered. She had lost her voice so she pointed to the clay jar in the corner. I brought her a cup of water. She drank it and went out again. Under the moonlight I could only see the outline of her dark body rocking back and forth with grief.

The speech was delivered by one of her husband's friends with a poppy in his lapel. He praised her husband, his courage, his sense of humour then said at the end in a BBC accent, 'Elizabeth and Charles are united at last. Let us pray for them.'

'Upah and Hita are united at last, let us pray for them,' I said under my breath.

A blonde girl in a white suit played a classical piece on the piano, one of Liz's favourites. She used to like classical music and say to me, 'Divine music. I guess you don't know much about our music.' She would be sitting in the kitchen, listening to Radio 3, sipping her Darjeeling tea out of a fine china cup, flicking through *Homes & Gardens*, although we had a place you just about could call home and no garden. She would smile at me and say, pointing to an expensive antique dining room, 'Isn't that splendid?'

'Splendid.' I would try to imitate her accent.

At the end of the piece the chaplain pressed a button and the pine coffin slid through a hole in the wall then an electric curtain jolted then whizzed shut. No digging of graves, lowering makeshift coffins, reciting of the Qur'an. Nothing apart from the sniffs and sighs of the well-dressed mourners.

I was filling up so I walked out quickly before my Bedouin howls shook the birds in their trees. Natasha followed me and said, 'Sally, thank you for everything you've done for her. We are hoping to put the house up for sale. We will come to collect some of the furniture soon.'

'How soon?' I asked.

'In a few weeks.' She stopped talking and was about to walk away to join her family when she pulled the net of her hat down, hesitated and then said, 'My aunt was fond of you, Sally.'

My chin quivered so much I could not say anything. Elizabeth used to talk about the musk roses and flame, jacaranda and hibiscus trees of India. I sheltered my eyes with my hand and walked through the garden looking for a flowering acacia tree, then I realized that I wouldn't recognize it so I sat under a horse chestnut tree, which is the only tree in this country I could name. Alone, surrounded by jars full of pacemakers, tooth fillings, gold wedding rings, remnants and ashes, I held my heart tight.

Through the small rounded window of the aeroplane carrying me to Greece – which soon would be no longer hidden – I saw the white fluffy clouds happily floating in a brightly lit sky. Their shapes shifted from horses galloping away, to waves fighting and overcoming each other, to seagulls forever soaring above the river. A long well, cold water, seeds popping open, a body breaking free, yielding, 'I wish I had never set my eyes on you', '*Cest la vie, ma fille!*', 'Jesus died to save us all', 'You are on your own, Salma', a gun slung on a shoulder, grime-filled toenails, 'Enough, shoot me!', throwing up in the bin, Rock The

Casbah, 'too much past', doves crying, sniffing falafel, '*Min il-bab lil shibak*', right behind you, get married to Sadiq, eating dry bread, Noura's blood and snot running down her chin, a heart-wrenching howl.

'Anything else, madam?' asked the air hostess.

'No thank you.'

Suspended between earth and sky in the small aeroplane she tingled her way back to my heart. I knew that air. Layla was calling me. A sudden chill ran from the roots to the ends of each hair on my body and my chest collapsed as if I were drowning. He held my hand and said, 'Your hand is sweaty. Are you OK? Are you afraid of flying?'

'No, I am not afraid of flying,' I said defensively and held on to his hand.

She was tired, whimpering, hungry, looking for a foothold for her tiny feet. I was closer to the old country so I looked through the circular window, put a hug and a kiss in a bottle and cast it among the clouds. The waves might carry it to the opposite shore. An old Arab fisherman might find it covered in sand and sea salt and take it to her. My familiar smell, tender nipple, warm ribcage would reassure her, make her feel safe and protected. One day she would stop crying.

My husband's T-shirt was soaked when he said, 'You have to let go of her, darling. You never know, one day you might be reunited.'

I had been trying to let go of her since she was born. I kept trying and failing then trying better to fail better.

Layla was emerald, turquoise encased in silver, Indian silk cascading down from rolls, fresh coffee beans ground in an ornate sandalwood pestle and mortar, honey and spicy ghee wrapped in freshly baked bread, a pearl in her bed, a lock of fine, soft black hair, tiny wrinkled fingers like tender vine leaves, pomegranate, pure perfume sealed in blue jars, rough diamonds, a dew-covered plain in the vast flat open green valley, a sea teal at the edges and azure in the centre, my grandmother's Ottoman gold coins strung together by a black cord, my mother's wedding silver money hat, a full moon hidden behind translucent clouds, the manes of white thoroughbred horses, the clear white-ness of my eye, my right arm, and the blood pumping out of my broken heart.

Layla was standing there behind the translucent white clouds, a thoroughbred mare, her taut body dark, coffee with cardamom, her eyes bright amber, Hamdan's mouth, ripe pomegranate seeds, her hair cascading on her shoulders. She smiled, a pearl in her cot, and walked away among the vines, glittered through the soft tender leaves, a column of diamond dust. My limbs were severed. The fig tree branch, pregnant with fruit but hollow, suddenly collapsed. A displaced amputee, full of past, future and phantom pain, I picked up my arm and waved at the dust grains ever floating in the sun rays.

That night was so hot that I kept tossing and turning under the white tulle mosquito net. I drank the cool sherbet my ayah had left earlier on the bedside cabinet. Daddy was out on a hunting trip with some of his Indian friends. Rex barked and barked at the darkness. I got up gasping for air and looked through the window. The tamarind tree, laden with seeds, shone in the moon-light and the smell of ripe mangos filled the air.

253

THE CRY OF THE DOVE

John said, 'Stop teasing us,' and kissed me.

'Ayye!' I said.

Bare-foot in my white cotton nightie I walked to the kitchen to look for ice. We bought a large slab yesterday from the ice wallah and I hoped that there would be some pieces left.

Blocking Hamdan out, our persistent love-making, I received the gentle kisses of my husband. He ran his fingers over me lightly as if I were fracturable. 'Onyx,' he said.

Hita was sitting on the balcony of the kitchen looking at the darkness. When he saw me he smiled. I stood there, a seventeen-year-old girl, white, untouched and brimming with need.

The sun was flickering through the leaves of almond trees. I could hear the barking of shepherd dogs and the buzzing of bees.

'I want some ice,' I said to Hita.

'I don't have any ice left, Upah, but I have made kulfi. Do you want some?' he said and ran his fine fingers over the uneven wood of the kitchen table.

'It's still outside,' I said.

'Perfect night for a thunderstorm,' Hita said while scooping up some ice cream, fresh lime-green pistachio nuts and cardamom seeds.

I wanted to be overpowered, killed, but John treated every part of my body equally. He explored, stroked, examined, fondled. I bit, scratched, squeezed, screamed until he said, 'You're hurting us.' Hamdan would have said, 'Tighter, harder, closer.'

We ate kulfi together listening to the thunder. His wide chest, brown sugar, shone whenever lightning lit up the kitchen. He stood up, crossed the sea dividing us, held my head tight between both hands and kissed me hard on the lips, so hard I could taste his tart blood.

254

In his arms I sought forgetfulness, oblivion, the colour of new seeds.

He became the master and I the slave girl attending to his every need. He whispered orders and I, the English lady, obeyed.

Our skins had melted away exposing pulsating veins, throbbing heart, twitching livers.

'I cannot have enough of you,' John said.

Walking on the beach, hand in hand, you would have thought that we were an ordinary couple. There was nothing unusual about us apart from the darkness of my skin. Sitting on a cliff in Santorini, overlooking the deep turquoise sea, I watched a young Greek boy in an old white boat fishing. He threw the rod up then dropped the fishing line in the sea. John was reading a fat book about Greek mythology. I just sat still. I did not sniff the air or look for clouds or riffles. I just sat still. The boy hooked more bait and cast the line again in the rippling water. The white cliffs and clean fine sand framed the calm green-blue sea leaving the opposite shore out. Finally I saw a fish wriggling in the air. The boy jumped with glee, stood up, released the fish and put it in a large net basket.

'It should be OK, having a swim, I mean.'

'Yes,' John said mechanically.

'They not think I am a loose woman,' I said.

'No. Why should they?' he said.

'I want to learn how to swim,' I said to the opposite shore, to Hima.

'You can do a course when we get back,' he said while still reading.

I took the book out of John's hand and closed it. His thin toes looked ridiculous in his big brown leather

sandals. I stroked his thinning hair and kissed his tired eyes.
'Salma!' He smiled.

Coming out of his lips, my name sounded right. I
taught him how to pronounce it, which letters to stress
and which letters to let go.

Max did not approve of my marriage to a Geordie. 'Up
north they think the French are monkeys,' he said, slapped
his knee and smirked. 'They tortured the poor sod until he
squeaked a confession to being a French spy.' Max pushed
his chair back and roared with laughter. When he finally
stopped he said, 'I don't blame them for hating the damn
froggies.'

I bowed my head and continued running the machine
on the hem.

'They're also stingy. They want to make a buck out of
us southerners,' he said and ran his hand over his gelled
hair to make sure that the laughter had not shaken it out
of place.

It was hot that day and the place could have done with
a fan or an air-conditioning system, but Max insisted that
five days of sunshine did not justify the expense. My sweat
dripped between my tender breasts all the way down to
my swollen belly. I wiped my forehead with a tissue and
listened to a doctor on Radio 2 talking about a man finding it hard to get it up.

Max pricked up his ears.

I pretended to have not heard him.

'What is he talking about? We are so virile in the south.'
He smirked again.

I rubbed my belly where the baby had just kicked me
and passed the twentieth pair of trousers to Tracy to iron.

She winked at me.

I smiled.

'I am married to a Scotsman,' she said.

'Northerners are terrible, aren't they?' I said.

We laughed.

The doctor said that the sperms in England were too weak to climb up to the egg.

'What if the sperm count is OK, but the "you know what" does not "you know what"?' he asked the old radio on the windowsill.

I suppressed my laughter.

'I did not promote you to laugh at me,' he said, threw down the trousers he was altering, and dug into his sardine sandwich.

Although I had been in her bedroom several times it still felt like trespassing. It was a mess, ruffled sheets, dirty clothes scattered on the floor, some mouldy soup in a bowl, dark stains on the beige carpet where wine had been spilt. It smelt of dust, lavender soap, denture cleanser and damp.

I put the bundle of letters tied up with a rubber band, the silver box with the rancid butter and her diary in the crimson satin box, closed it and hid it in my wardrobe on top of my winter jumpers.

When I pulled the curtains open the velvet and lace released clouds of dust that floated in the sunrays down to the ground. I stripped the mattress, pillows and duvet, unhooked the curtains, rolled up the rugs and lace tablecloths, now yellow with age, and placed them on the landing. I vacuumed both sides of the satin mattress, the silver metal of the head- and footboards, the V, R and

I and the metal frame, then wiped it with polish. The vacuum cleaner sucked in the cobwebs in the corners of the ceiling, the dust on top of the antique wardrobe, which was on Natasha's list of furniture that must be kept in the family, the mouldy food crumbs under the bedside cabinet, Liz's web of straight grey hair on the carpet by the chest of drawers where she used to put on her make-up and comb her hair looking at her reflection in her grand-father's oak barley-twist shaving mirror. I shampooed the carpet, polished the furniture, cleaned the window frames and panes and the door, dusted the William Morris wallpaper and hung the new curtains.

When I finally lay down next to John under the duvet covered with cotton of the Nile, a wedding gift from Sadiq, a half-moon like a slice of lemon was shimmering through the curtains, promising to be full soon. I slept soundly as if Elizabeth's bed, which she inherited from her grandfather, who inherited it from his grandmother, was a thick handmade mattress, stuffed with sheep wool combed with a Bedouin card, and covered with colourful hand-loom wool rugs made by the women of Hima in the dusk.

Last time I was pregnant it was out of wedlock and this time it was with a foreigner. I placed my hand over the stretch marks waiting for a kick from his tiny feet. In prison I lay on my back on the mattress hoping that my swollen tummy would disappear, hoping for the pregnancy to dissolve like sugar in hot mint tea. When shame lay heavy on my chest I dreamt of an earthquake, similar to the one my grandmother described. 'The earth began cracking, then split wide open. First it was thirsty then it was hungry. It began eating dry and green. It was as if the Almighty had hit the ground with his force splitting it right open. What is left of it are the Dead Sea and the Red Sea,' she said. So I dreamt of drowning in the Dead Sea or disappearing down a ravine. Then the crack would heal and I would be no more. But one cold morning the skin of my tummy stretched out and I felt a kick against my womb. I began eating after that because the baby was blameless, but I was the one who deserved to die. I imagined her swimming blindly in the dark waters of my womb and suddenly my heart was overwhelmed. How could I die myself without killing the baby inside me? But how could I bear to live with all that shame?

When they scanned my tummy they told me that it was a boy and it was in good health. Perhaps we would call him Imran, harmonious cities and civilization. 'Imran,' I whispered, 'the light in your mother's eyes, the air she breathes, her heart pumping, pumping love and pain, land safely on a carpet made of silk, in a jar full of honey, in a garden covered with fragrant white jasmine flowers. Come to this world safe and whole for your good English father and your Arab Bedouin mother are eagerly waiting to see your moon face.'

That Sunday King Edward Street was full of cars being washed, clothes being hung on lines and children playing frisbee and cycling in the middle of the street. Last week our offer for number 15 was accepted. I unscrewed the two rusty nails, freeing the wooden sign that says 'Swan Cottage' and waved it at Sadiq. He raised his index and middle finger in a victory sign then hastily stuck his arms to his sides and bowed his head. He must be sad because Elizabeth was not only his friend, but his best customer.

He looked like a ghost gesticulating in his white shalwar kameez behind the dusty glass of his shop window.

'I will buy curtains, neither of here nor of there,' I said.

Parvin fluttered her eyelashes and said, 'I don't know what you mean?!'

John and Mark were negotiating the antique rosewood wardrobe down the stairs. Parvin said that Mark would like to help and that his amputated hand never stopped him from carrying on normally with his life. He could hold on to things even better with the metal hook.

She was sipping her herbal tea slowly. When she got pregnant she gave up tea and coffee. Imran was sucking his thumb and babbling in the baby carrier, strapped to my chest, when the doorbell rang. It was Gwen, flushed and breathless, carrying a small suitcase.

'Are you OK? You're not going to hospital, are you?' I asked while kissing her on each cheek.

'No, no, my hip is fine,' she said and put the suitcase on the kitchen table, sat down on one of the chairs, wiped her forehead and sighed. We could hear John and Mark's grunts as they struggled with the wardrobe. 'You have two strong men out there,' Gwen said and giggled.

'Hands off!' said Parvin and winked at me. She had finished eating the slice of fruit cake I offered earlier. With her fine fingers she chased the leftovers on the kitchen paper towel then put them in her mouth.

I ran my hand over Imran's head, over his thin dark hair, counted his fingers, his toes, his eyes, and placed my hand gently over the tender cavity in his skull.

Filling the kettle with water I said loudly, 'Coffee, anyone?'

'Yes please,' sang John, Mark and Gwen.

Gwen's coffee was the way she liked it, strong, with little cream and one coffeespoon of brown sugar.

The winter sun was feeble, but it managed to light up part of the corridor and hall. Gwen fiddled with the draw-bolt locks, pressed them open and lifted the top of the brown leather suitcase.

The old dusty suitcase was full of baby clothes: some white, embroidered with shiny fuchsia threads, some pink, some lilac, with ducks, horses, bears running or flying on the yokes, lace-trimmed briefs, cotton bodysuits, white and blue knitted cardigans, one with picot edging and a satin ribbon, and the other with netted jasmine-shaped flowers sewn to the edges with a matching hat, a flower-print dress set with smocked yoke and matching knickers, socks with lace trim, booties with a bear design and bibs with clowns and fairies embroidered on them.

'I bought some, made some for your Layla. But she must be sixteen by now, grown up, perhaps even engaged to be married,' she said and bit her tongue.

The white dress which I made for Layla with its zig-zagged hem, the flowery collar, the small rose-like pockets, the tiny puffed sleeves was in the suitcase on top of the wardrobe upstairs together with the return rail ticket Minister Mahoney had given me, my mother's letter, the lock of hair, Noura's mother-of-pearl hair combs and bottle of perfume, Françoise's turquoise silver necklace, the Qur'an, the Mary Quant lipstick from Madam Lamaa and a black madraqa. I spent hours trying to imagine what a water lily would look like on a luminous jolly night, Layla. I tried to make the shape of the dress similar to that of a lily.

When Gwen shook the yellow and red baby duck

plastic rattle and said, 'It used to belong to my prodigal son. I kept it all these years,' I walked out to the corridor, biting my lip, pretending to look for John and Mark. So many cardigans, bodysuits, dresses for her, but where was Layla? What did she look like? Was she dead or alive?

The rosewood wardrobe, pine display cabinet, two mahogany chests of drawers, two antique side tables, Indian mirror, bedside cabinets and dark domed travel chest full of Elizabeth's clothes and personal belongings were lined up on the pavement, waiting to be picked up by Natasha's boyfriend.

I went back to the kitchen and looked at the unpacked and ruffled baby clothes covering the kitchen table and laughed. Gwen and Parvin joined in.

'She is mental,' said Parvin.

Gwen holding Imran's hand began rolling her eyes and babbling.

'*Salaam jiddu*: hello, Granddad,' I said to the old man in the kebab van on the high street. John was holding Imran, who looked great in the blue cardigan and matching hat Gwen had netted for Layla, a king with a jasmine garland.

'*Ahlan wa sahlan binti*: welcome, Daughter,' he said.

'Remember me? I am the woman who used to sit behind your van sniffing the air,' I said.

'Yes, yes. We thought you were a tramp or MI5.' He smiled. He was tall, spindly, with large eyes whitening with age, grey stubble, thinning hair covered by a crochet white skull cap, wide embroidered black trousers tight around the ankles, brown leather pointed mules and an embroidered North African shirt.

'This is my husband John and my son Imran,' I said.

'*Ahlan wa sahlan*. By Allah, you must have some falafel,' he said.

My Geordie husband scoffed the falafel and said, '*Shukran*: thank you!'

'*La shukr ala wajib*: don't thank me for upholding my duty,' he answered.

Clapping his hand on the shoulder of a dark young man in blue jeans and black T-shirt with 'Bon Jovi No Pain No Gain' printed in large red letters on the front, his thick dark hair spiked up with gel, his eyes large and hidden behind thick black curled-up eyelashes, his eyebrows plucked, his face smooth and glistening in the dim light of the van and his full chapped red lips parting with a smile, he said, 'Meet my son Rashid, he a little effeminate like English people, but is OK.'

'*Marhba*: hello! That's it really. I cannot speak much Arabic,' he said and smiled.

We shook hands, talked and ate on the pavement by the kebab van. If you did not know me you would have thought that we were an ordinary family on a day out enjoying the brief winter sunshine. I should have been happy, but something was holding my heart back. I imagine you, Noura, soaring above our heads, dark, dignified, with arched eyebrows, seductive eyes, crimson lips, your pearl-shaped teeth masticating chewing gum then blowing pink bubbles, Rima and Rami, cured of his diabetes, holding your hands. You look at the square roof of the white van, the black-circle dots of our heads, at Imran taking his first steps towards his father, a frilly blue flower, at the cars skidding behind the van, at my face searching for your light and laugh, an irreverent, resilient, timeless laugh that reverberates in your ribcage.

Black Iris

IT WAS A DARK MOONLESS NIGHT AND I COULD NOT GO TO sleep. Whenever I closed my eyes I heard distant but amplified wheezing as if it were coming from the bottom of a well. I ran in the dark following footpaths all the way down the hill from the Long Well to the farm. Then I stood still, panting, sniffing the air, listening for rustling leaves, watching for movement. Rhythmic squeals came from the other end of the farm. I followed the stench of sour baby milk and rotting limbs. It was the smell that took me to her. Layla was swinging from the fig tree naked, her hands and legs tied together in an obscene way and shackled to the trunk, her neck slashed, face cut up and her private parts rotting. A black cloud of flies buzzed frenziedly around her. She was burning. I got up drenched with sweat, a helpless moth.

'They will kill you,' said Parvin.

I held her face and said, 'I have to go. Look for her. She is calling me. She needs my help.'

'I've not spoken to my family since I left. They don't know my whereabouts. Do you think my heart is made of flint? I miss them too, *yaar*,' she said and blew up at her straight fringe. She was annoyed.

'It my daughter, Parvin,' I said and pushed my hair off my face.

'This is madness. What's wrong with you? Since you've given birth you've gone downhill. You don't eat. You cry all the time. You look like a tramp. Have you started seeing men with rifles again?'

'I depressed. I dream of Layla almost every night. Something must have happened to her. Mother's heart know,' I said.

'I don't know what to say,' Gwen said. 'If Salma feels she should go, then we cannot stop her, I'm afraid.'

'I won't let you, Salma. What about our son? What about me?' John choked.

'We can notify the police. Interpol can contact your friend, can look for her,' said Mark.

'I am a British citizen now and the British will protect me,' I said.

'Oh! Yeah! Look at the colour of your skin. You are a second-class citizen. They will not protect you,' said Parvin.

'No one would recognize me now. Especially if I have my hair cut and dyed.'

'They will recognize your smell. So many Asian girls were killed when they went back,' said Parvin.

'She wouldn't stop crying. Her sobs echo in my head,' I said.

Parvin stood up with difficulty and held me tight. 'Please, please don't go!'

'Cannot you see?' I screamed. 'I've got no names. I haven't even got Noura's or Madam Lamaa's family name. I have to go. My daughter is in danger.'

'What about your son?' asked Gwen.

'Sons are treated better. They can fend for themselves. Daughters are helpless,' I said.

'You're wrong. He needs you,' she said.

'He has a good father. He will take care of him if anything happens to me.'

John hid his wet face and walked out of the kitchen holding Imran against his ribcage the way my father used to hold me.

I had the same dream again, but this time Layla's muffled cries intensified. My heart knew that I had to go and find her before it was too late. I got the red silk Chinese box, which Parvin had given me for my birthday, out of the wardrobe, opened it and began tidying up its contents: a return rail ticket to Exeter now yellow around the edges, my mother's letter, a lock of Layla's hair, Noura's mother-of-pearl hair combs, the bottle of perfume, the Mary Quant lipstick from Madam Lamaa and Françoise's turquoise silver necklace. When I pulled the lock of hair out of the leather pocket I had made especially for it and my mother's letter an electric current ran all the way up the fingers of my right hand, my arm, my shoulder then the back of my neck. The fine hairs at the back of my neck stood up and my scalp twitched. I put everything back in the box, shut the lid, and secured the loop around the button made of twisted silk fabric sewed together.

I began writing a letter in my head: *To whom it may concern: My name is Salma Ibrahim El-Musa; I have been in Islah prison. During the first year I gave birth to a baby girl and she was instantly taken away to a home for illegitimate children.*

I wonder if you can help me locate her. My postal address is . . . then I tore the imagined letter up. How could I reveal my true identity and address? I would risk being traced and killed. How could I ignore Layla's cries, her calls, her constant pleading? I stood in the kitchen, a woman with a twisted neck looking both ways: backwards and forwards. The tea I made at four o'clock in the morning was tepid, tasteless; the floor tiles were so cold against my bare feet. The hills, which were covered with green grass, weeds and shrubs, were suddenly erased – puff – and turned into dry brown mountains covered with silver-green olive trees, plum, almond and fig trees and grapevines. What was better: to live with half a lung, kidney, liver, heart or to go back to the old country and risk being killed? If my son, who was sleeping peacefully in his cot in the bedroom, began crying I would run upstairs without thinking and hold him close against my jugular vein until he felt safe again and stopped crying. Over the years things must have changed in the old country, people change, I changed. I might not get killed even if I were recognized. I had my hair cut, straightened, dyed blonde and bought some crimson-red lipstick. If I wear a sleeveless low-cut top, a short skirt and sunglasses they would never think I belonged to their tribe, they would see only a shameless foreign woman, whose body, treasures, were on offer for nothing. Why would you give her family twenty camels if you could get her for free? When I finally looked up the hills were covered with Hima's black iris, which swayed in the wind in unison and whispered her name. A feeble sound echoed in my head, 'Mama? Mama?' then it suddenly stopped. I covered my face with both hands pressing hard on my forehead, just above my eyebrows and eyes. How precious was your eyesight? How precious was your daughter? I must not go, I should not go, I would not go.

Imran was nine months old and it was time to wean him. I wrapped my nipple with cotton wool and offered it to him. He spat it out and began crying. I held the bottle full of brewed camomile and aniseed up and placed the plastic teat in his mouth. He spat it out, spilling the tea around his chubby neck and began crying again. His soft bib had 'I love whoever feeds me' printed on it. I wiped his tears with it and pulled him out of his cot. When I held him close he stopped crying, but when I kissed his fine dark hair he began crying again. This time it was a heart-rending cry as if he had just lost a limb.

Weaning was three days of intermittent crying, sleepless nights, dribbling, trying to feed him with a spoon, bribing him with sugar, and holding him and pacing around the house until he finally went to sleep. My mother did not wean my brother Mahmoud until he was three and his long legs were dangling and almost touching the floor. He used to go and play with the dog and come back ruffled and say, 'Give me your *ziza*: teat!'

But I had to stop breastfeeding Imran and to teach him how to eat normal food. I had to go to look for Layla. I began seeing her swollen face everywhere, on window panes, in my breakfast bowl swimming in the milk, in the water whirling down the drain of the kitchen sink, in all the mirrors. I began hearing her muffled cries whenever a breeze hit my face.

One early morning I held the cold washbasin and looked at my bloodshot eyes in the mirror. Imran was finally used to eating from a spoon whatever I blended for him and drinking from a cup. He was sound asleep next to his dad. I was the one who was neither eating nor sleeping. I also began talking to myself, 'Oh, how I love you, Imran! Oh, how I love you, Layla! He will be all right. I will cook him enough food for a month and put it in the freezer, a bag for every day I am away. Marked clearly,' I said to my reflection. 'Hug him as much as you can, and don't leave him at the nursery for more than three hours. Hold his hand when he walks towards you because his feet are still weak. Cup his head and hold it close against your chest, he is used to that. When he cries make a sash bundle of aniseed and crystal sugar and put it gently in his mouth, behind his tiny white tooth. Cover him with his blue velvet blanket and hold it close to his tiny hand. Love him treble: one for you, one for me and one for his Arab grandmother. I command him to your protection, John,' I said and wiped the tears with the back of my cold hand.

The taxi ride to my village took about two hours from the airport. With my dyed short hair, straw hat, sunglasses and short sleeves the Bedouin taxi driver, with the red-and-white-chequered kufiyya fixed into place by a black rope, assumed that I was a *khawajayya*: a foreigner. He mumbled his disapproval under his breath. He thought that I had come to their country to study their way of life and get them some money to encourage them to continue living in squalor, sleeping with their camels and sheep. '*Cigara?*' he said, pointing an unlit cigarette at me, leaving the car to steer itself down the narrow run-down road.

'No, thank you,' I said.

He lit the cigarette, turned down the window to release

his tea glass, secured between the roof and glass panel of his car window, and had a swig then a puff. He swung the car left and right without spilling one drop; the sticky liquid swirled in the cup, a mini storm in a tea glass.

'Smoking bad.' I pointed at his cigarette.

'Wife bad. Smoke good,' he said, tilting his headdress to one side and raising his eyebrows.

It reminded me of Hamdan's secret mating call, which I answered by rushing to the vineyard and taking off my pantaloons. Hamdan would propose, I thought, but he left me in the valley and took to the mountains.

Looking at the almost bare brown mountains, the olive groves, the relentless sun and hazy blue sky, I felt my mother's rough hands run over my face. I sniffed my father's musk and snuggled against his ribcage.

When I saw olive trees in the distance I felt like running back. I wanted so much to be sipping tea with John in our kitchen in Exeter, but the driver was singing along with some new pop singer, 'Bahibak ahhh: I love, yeah' and pressing on the accelerator. The street sped towards me and the village was approaching with its makeshift concrete houses and mud storage rooms. The sun was sitting behind the thorn-covered hills and the sound of shepherd dogs and the call to prayer filled the air. I wiped the cold sweat on my forehead and was about to ask the driver to turn round and drive me back to the airport. Then I saw a group of young men walking up to the mosque, slapping each other's backs, fixing their headgear, twisting their moustaches, and suddenly changed my mind. Layla was out here somewhere and I must find her. Olive, apple, plum trees sped across the car window. I would help her settle in the new country, teach her English, register her in a college. If my eyes would ever meet hers we would both be fine.

When I saw the two storage rooms that used to be our house I asked the driver to stop and handed him forty dinars.

He spat on the ground and said, '*Adjnabiyyeh wa bakhileh*: foreign and mean.'

A woman in black was sitting on the raised platform in front of the two badly built new rooms. I waved. She did not wave back.

My son, my heart, was teething. He was drooling, irritable, endlessly chewing on things. He began crying again so I took him to the guest room, which used to be my bedroom when Elizabeth was alive, placed him on the bed, wiped his face with a wet cloth and ran my finger gently over his sour gums. He chewed at it then began crying again. I held him tight against me and began rocking him and singing:

> 'Go to sleep, *habibi*, go to sleep.
> May the eyes of your enemy never sleep!
> Please, doves do not cry.
> Imran wants to go to sleep.'

Finally he closed his eyes and sighed. I covered him with a blanket, got a pair of scissors out, cut a tuft of his shiny, soft hair and hid it quickly in my pocket. I sniffed his neck, filling my heart with his baby scent; I ran my hand over his tender head, placed the palm of my hand over his heart. Would he be all right if I left him for two weeks? John was a good father whispering poems in

271

English and endearments in pidgin Arabic in his ear all the time.

I looked through the window at the dark silhouette of trees bordering the fields on the hillside. They were all swaying in the wind, now this way and now that. When I pushed the window up a gust of wind rushed into the room. I stuck my head out and looked at the outline of the hills, the sheen of the river and the steel rail track. The rustling sound of leaves was followed by a swish.

There he was. His dagger tied to his side, his ammunition belt wrapped across his chest, his leather sandals worn out, his feet covered with desert dust, his yellow toenails long, chipped and lined with grime and his rifle slung on his right shoulder.

Listen for the galloping of horses, for the clank of daggers being pulled out of scabbards, for flat-faced owls hooting in the dark, for bats clapping their wings, for light footsteps, for the abaya robe fluttering in the wind, for the swishing sound of his sharp dagger. Sniff the air for the sweat of assassins. Listen to his arm grabbing Layla's neck and pulling it right back, to his dagger slashing through flesh and breaking bones to reach the heart. Listen to your daughter's warm red blood bubbling out and drip dripping on the dry sand. Listen to her body convulsing on the ground. A ululation. A scream. Rending of black madraqas. Rhythmic banging of chests. A last gasp.

'Kill me instead,' I screamed at Mahmoud's shadow by the steel railway.

Everything seemed smaller, the well in the yard, the storage rooms, the horse tied up to the fig tree, the dog, my father's riding saddle, the pots and pans, even the plum and apple trees. 'Hajjeh, are you all right?' I said to the woman sitting on the raised platform and hiding her face with the black mask. Her head was covered with a black veil tied into place by a black head band, the sign of mourning. Her protruding green veins ran down her dry and wrinkled leathery hands.

'Who is it?' She cocked up her covered head towards the sound.

There she was, hajjeh Amina, my mother, whose letter had kept me alive all these years, fine tunnels of wrinkles running down her cheeks, yellow discharge oozing out of her sticky eyes. She looked as if she were smiling, the red cracks on the corner of her pale lips tilting upwards.

'A visitor to your dwelling,' I said in Arabic, holding my heart tight.

'*Ya hala bi il-daif*: welcome to our guest,' she said and got up leaning on the metal door frame. 'I will brew you some tea,' she said and ran her fingers over the mouldy wall. She stood in the middle of the room lost, not knowing which direction to go. 'Where is the damn Thermos cooker?' It was in front of her, but she could not see it.

I held her hand and asked her to sit down. She pulled it back as if it were smouldering iron bars ready to cauterize. 'Who are you?' she asked.

'Shahla sent me,' I said.

'She is dead,' she said and sat on the uneven cement floor, wiped her eyes with the end of her veil and added as if she were addressing the whole tribe, 'All our guests are welcome.'

I put seven spoons of sugar in the brass teapot and a spoonful of tea then boiled the water. I carefully handed

her a slim cup. When she sipped the tea she began crying.
'Are we alone?' she asked.

'Yes, Mother,' I said.

I spent hours sitting on the kitchen floor leaning on the
cabinet. When John found me I was unable to speak,
the muscle on the right side of my face, under my eye, had
seized up. I opened my mouth, but no sound came out.

'You are letting this nightmare destroy our life. You have
a chance of happiness and what do you do? You throw it
away,' he said, pulled me up and hugged me. 'You are so
thin and cold. You must stop this madness, sweetheart.' He
sat me down and made me a cup of sweet tea.

When I'd had a few sips my face muscles began moving.
'I will. I promise,' I said. My voice was hoarse as if not my
own.

'Please hold on to Imran and let go of Layla,' he said.

When I heard her name coming out of his lips my
ribcage collapsed as if I was punched. I breathed in, but no
air whatsoever entered my lungs. I began coughing hard
to be able to breathe.

John hugged me and said, 'There, there. Everything is
going to be all right. You'll see.'

But a cup of tea and 'there, there' were not enough.

I said goodbye to them while they were asleep. My
packed bag was hidden in the wardrobe among my winter
clothes and my British passport and ticket were in my
handbag waiting for the right moment to leave. Imran was
asleep in the wooden cot bed by the radiator next to the
window. He sucked his lips and whimpered, his eyes reel-
ing under his closed eyelids. I sniffed his head, kissed his
forehead, tucked the blanket with Snoopy riding among

the stars under him, kissed his tiny hand and stood up. John was asleep on his side. I ran my fingers through his receding hair, kissed the top of his head, kissed the beauty spot on his back, kissed the back of his hairy legs and when he sighed, turned and settled on the other side, facing Imran, I tiptoed out of the room.

I repeated, 'Forgive me, Imran, forgive me,' with every step I took in her direction. I had to go to find her. I had to go to find me.

Sadiq's shop was already open and he was performing his morning prayers. He did the *tasleem* then looked up. When he saw me he came out and said, 'You look like a ghost. Are you going somewhere also?'

'Yes, Sadiq. There is something I have to do,' I said.

'Going on a mission?'

'Going back home,' I said.

'Handle with care. You not only coconut. Your son cabbage. They will not be on the moon,' he said.

'I know. Will you ask John to forgive me?'

'Wait, wait. You haven't asked for permission?'

'No. Don't tell me. Angels will soar above my head cursing me day and night.'

'You said it,' he said.

'They have been cursing me since I was born,' I said.

'Turning into Indian movie this,' he said.

'Please listen! Ask John to forgive me and tell him that I love him and Imran so much. I love them so much.'

'Love them? Stay then,' he said.

'I cannot. My daughter is calling,' I said.

'You have a daughter back there? You must go and save. I have two sons and a daughter. Mother says an old man want marry her. She is only seventeen,' he said and ran his hand through his oiled hair. 'I think about going back every day.'

'Will you take care of them for me?' I said hurriedly and kissed each cheek.

'Cabbage or no cabbage, I will,' he said.

'Ask them to forgive me,' I said.

'My eyes will wait for your sight, Salma. Be safe!' he said, jerked his chin then pressed his fine, dark forefingers at the corners of his eyes.

One foot then another I walked on towards the railway station as if in a trance. I thought I heard some muffled sobs, snuffles, a man calling my name, the whistle of departure, a feeble call. *Ya Allah!* Would I get there in time?

'Shut the door and windows quickly. Don't worry about your brother Mahmoud. He is often in the capital "seeking solace",' she said, sobbing.

It was difficult to shut the door, which had probably never been shut before. I went round shutting and securing the two windows, listening for voices, watched for movement. When I was sure we were alone I sat next to her, held her hand and ran it over my face. She kissed my forehead and said, 'The last words on your father's lips before he died were your name and her name. Grief sucked him dry. Look, he left me here blind, alone.'

'I brought you some glasses, Mother,' I said.

'What use will they be?' she said, wiping her tears.

I kissed her rough hands, the top of her head and said, 'Your tears are pearls, diamond, don't let anyone see them,' which was what she used to say to me when I was young.

'The day they took you he suddenly turned into an old man walking with difficulty and leaning on a stick. From the horseman of the tribe to the butt of their jokes and gibes. His daughter had tarnished the honour of the tribe and got away with it.'

'And Hamdan?'

'He is a changed man. A mere shadow, creeping around.'

His touch was tender, my love was kicking and shoving in my heart like a mule, his betrayal was final. She was meant to be born, beautiful and perfect like the red flower of a pomegranate tree.

Heart held tight, chin quivering I asked, 'What about my daughter, Mother?'

'The little one? I took her from the Socials. I said to your brother she was innocent. She filled our hearts with joy, so fresh, so beautiful,' she said and wiped the cracked corners of her mouth with her index and forefingers.

'Thank God I am blind. If only my heart could be blind too,' she said and covered her face with both hands.

A chill ran through me all the way from the ends of my hair to my toes. I pressed my hand on my chest to stop my heart from jolting out.

'Two months ago her good-for-nothing uncle threw her in the Long Well. "Like mother, like daughter," he said. Your father and his friend Jadaan fished her out and buried her remains in the cemetery against the wishes of the men of the tribe.'

She pulled the mask against her face and said, 'Then, grief-stricken, your father died too.'

'*Yubba!* My father! *Yumma!* My mother!' I howled blowing my cover to the tribe then collapsed on the floor and began chanting my grandmother's keen for the dead one, 'My precious eyesight, I could not save you from him. Smear soot on my face! Wrap me with her sash shroud! Bury me instead! *Ya Allah*, where is she? I want to see her face. Bring me a lock of her hair!'

Face blackened with ashes, T-shirt sticky with spilt tea, sweat and tears, I sat on the ground sprinkling sand over my dishevelled hair. My right arm flopped down in my lap paralysed. Her grave was almost indistinguishable from other graves. The ground was slightly raised and my father had stuck on it a makeshift rotting wooden box with 'Died 1990' carved into it. With my left hand I began pulling the weeds and thorns covering the mound and clearing the space around it.

The black iris at the end of the graveyard looked taller and more menacing in the twilight. Standing there covered with sand, arms cut and bruised stretched towards the sky, Layla tingled her way back to my heart. I knew that breeze. A sudden chill ran from the roots to the ends of each hair on my body and my chest collapsed as if I were drowning. She was tired, whimpering, hungry, looking for a foothold for her tiny feet. I knelt down and embraced her grave. My familiar smell, tender breasts and warm ribcage might reassure her, make her feel safe and protected. One day she, 'the buried one', might stop crying.

Layla was standing there, where the white clouds met the shredded blue sky, a thoroughbred mare, her taut body dark, coffee with milk, her eyes bright amber, Hamdan's mouth, ripe pomegranate seeds, her hair cascading on her shoulders. She smiled, a pearl in her grave, and walked away among the vines, glittering through the soft young leaves, a column of diamond dust. I tried to hold on to her, but the column whirled towards the black iris then disappeared where John, holding our baby, our son, against his ribcage, was standing between the black iris and the overcast sky.

Suddenly I heard voices behind me. A woman was pleading with a man not to do something. A young man saying, 'It's his duty. He has to hold his head high. *Il 'aar ma yimhiyeh ila il dam*: dishonour can only be wiped off with blood.'

'Let go of me, you old senile woman!' a man cried.

I thought I heard my mother say, 'You can have the farm, everything I own, she has a suckling now, I beg you . . .'

When I turned my head I felt a cold pain pierce through my forehead, there between my eyes, and then like blood in water it spread out.

Acknowledgements

I started writing *The Cry of the Dove* in 1990, but a winter of despair had set in. I finally emerged from under the yew tree and picked it up again in January 2005. While writing, and not writing, *The Cry of the Dove*, I had guiding spirits of my own: Angela Carter, Malcolm Bradbury and Lorna Sage, now dead but their souls will always soar above my head.

The story of King Shahriyar's visit to his brother Shahzaman is adapted from *Tales from the Thousand and One Nights* translated by N. J. Dawood. Gwen's father is based on factual accounts by my dear friend Gwyneth Cole. They were adapted with her permission.

I am also grateful to Mike Daley, Sue Rylance, Sue Frenk, Anne Woodhead, Carol Seikaly, Carmen Boulton and Ronak Husni for their friendship, which sustains me in the grey towers of Durham. I am also indebted to my Welsh friend Roger Fenwick.

I am grateful to my nucleolus and extended family for their continual support, especially my fine mother, my youngest sister Eman, *malikat ruhi*: the queen/holder of my soul, my brother Salah, and my cousin Samir Makanay. *Shukran jazilan habayib!*

I am indebted to Xinran and Toby Eady, my agent, whose friendship and limitless kindness have brought me so far.

This novel would not have been possible without the numerous cups of tea and the attentive heart of my Magyar/Irish/English husband, Dean Torok. *Koszonom szepen!*

THE CRY OF
THE DOVE

Fadia Faqir

A BLACK CAT READING GUIDE
PREPARED BY SUSAN AVERY

ABOUT THIS GUIDE

We hope that these discussion questions
will enhance your reading group's exploration
of Fadia Faqir's *The Cry of the Dove*. They are
meant to stimulate discussion, offer new viewpoints,
and enrich your enjoyment of the book.

More reading group guides and additional information,
including summaries, author tours, and author sites,
for other fine Black Cat titles, may be found on
our Web site, www.groveatlantic.com.

THE CRY OF
THE DOVE

Fadia Faqir

A BLACK CAT READING GUIDE

QUESTIONS FOR DISCUSSION

1. At the end of Chapter 1, the narrator, Salma, describes herself as "a rootless windblown desert weed" (p. 26). What does she mean by this? What are Salma's impressions of her new home in England? What do the vibrant memories of her native soil and the way of life of her Bedouin tribe explain about her?

2. Salma's narrative alternates between her present existence in England and her past as a shepherdess in Hima. Salma relates her past and why she had to leave her country. She seems to be trying to fit in, but is full of self-hatred. How does she express this? Does this feeling spring from her transgressions against the traditions of her people or her feelings of isolation and alienation in Exeter? Explain.

3. "He would tug at my hair and say, 'You are my courtesan, my slave.' 'Yes, master,' I would say" (p. 39). How did you feel about Salma's sexual initiation with Hamdan? What did her mother's reaction reveal about their relationship in particular and their tribal family in general?

4. Salma has important relationships with a number of women, including her English landlady, Liz; her Pakistani friend, Parvin; and her Welsh friend, Gwen. Each of these women sees a different Salma. Describe their different views of Salma. Do Salma and Sally have different personalities? In what ways do Parvin, Liz, and Gwen affect Salma/Sally?

5. Both Liz and Parvin are straddling two cultures just as Salma is. Liz in her drunkenness often cannot distinguish between her present life in England and her life as a privileged girl in the bygone India of the Raj. Parvin has left her hometown to escape an arranged marriage and is trying to make her way away from her family. How do the circumstances of these two women help to shed light on Salma's story?

6. "Religion was as weak as the tea in this country. What was left of it was, 'Is this your maiden or Christian name?' which the immigration officer had asked me and I did not know how to answer. 'Muslim no Christian.'" (p. 34). While the story is a tragic one there are numerous instances of humor produced by cross-cultural misunderstandings like this one. What are some other instances of humor in the book?

7. "If I kept stitching and fasting; if I keep silent, I would slip slowly out of my body like a snake shedding her old skin. I might stop being Salma and become someone else, who never had a bite of the forbidden apple. Time might pass quickly so I would slide gently from prison to grave. No pain, resistance or even boredom" (p. 46). Give some examples throughout the story where Salma attempts to be someone she isn't. Does she take comfort from these attempts?

8. Salma has a black shawl that once belonged to her mother. How does she use this memento of her past life? Talk about other mementoes.

9. Salma is haunted by her past and especially by the baby girl that was wrenched from her at birth. "Suddenly the fine hairs on the back of my neck stood up. I knew that breeze. She was out there crying, looking for a foothold. I knew that wind. A sudden chill ran through me so I bent forward as if winded and hugged my erect nipples" (p. 209). What emotions do you think are directing Salma here? Would you say that she is in a permanent postpartum depression?

10. Why do you think Salma marries John? Why after all the years that have passed, a new baby, and the beginning of better prospects for Salma does she decide to go home? What choices would you have liked to see her make after all her years in exile? Explain how you think she could have made these choices.

11. Did you feel the ending was inevitable?

12. What other cultures condone "honor" killings?

SUGGESTIONS FOR FURTHER READING:

Brick Lane by Monica Ali; *The Saffron Kitchen* by Yasmin Crowther; *Small Island* by Andrea Levy; *The God of Small Things* by Arundhati Roy; *The Namesake* by Jhumpa Lahiri; *The Kite Runner* by Khaled Hosseini; *Reading Lolita in Tehran* by Azar Nafisi; *The Almond* by Nedima; *The Inheritance of Loss* by Kiran Desai; *The Girl in the Tangerine Scarf* by Mohja Kahf; *The Attack* by Yasmina Khadra

FILM:

Water directed by Deepa Mehta; *Heat and Dust* directed by James Ivory; *Mississippi Masala* directed by Mira Nair; *My Beautiful Laundrette* and *Dirty Pretty Things* directed by Stephen Frears; *East Is East* directed by Damien O'Donnell; *Bhaji on the Beach* directed by Gurinder Chadha